CHAPTER 1

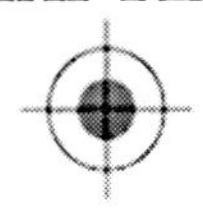

Thursday, October 16th
Maddsen, Florida

The grocery bag slipped.

Mandy pivoted on the sidewalk to keep from dropping it and, at the curve, spotted a flood of police cars in the street in front of her mother's house. Her heart rate shot up. Her pulse throbbing in her throat, in her temple, she ran toward them, cut across the lawn, veered onto the walkway to the wide front porch, and then climbed up the bottom step.

A uniformed police officer in his fifties raised his hand, blocked her path. "Stop. You can't go in there, ma'am."

Mandy shook her shoulder, trying to shoot past him, letting the grocery bag bump against his chest. "Of course, I can go in."

"Detective Walton." He called out then motioned for a man in a gray suit to join him. "Over here."

"Yeah, Hank." The detective said to the officer.

Out of patience and fighting panic, Mandy interrupted. "What are you people doing here?" She let her gaze slide between the two men, hoping one of them would answer her. The detective was a good ten years younger than the uniformed officer but looked far more rumpled, worn and weary.

A guard slid down over the detective's eyes. "Do you know Olivia Dixon?"

"Yes, I know her. She's my mother." Mandy frowned at him. "What's going on? Why are you here—and *where* is my mother?"

"I'm Detective Walton. Maddsen P.D." He reached for the two grocery bags she'd forgotten she held. "Let me take those for you. Why don't you sit down, Miss . . .?"

She instinctively passed the bags. "Madeline Dixon—Mandy," she said, a sinking feeling dragging at her stomach, broadening the growing fissure of fear inside her. All around them, officers went in and out of the house. One rushing past brushed against her back, mumbled an apology, but didn't slow his steps. "No more questions. I want you to take me to my mother. Are you going to do it or not?"

"I can't take you to her right now, Miss Dixon." Regret flashed through Walton's eyes and his tone softened. "Won't you sit down here on the step? Please."

If she didn't, he'd tell her nothing. Clear on that much, Mandy sat down on the rough, top concrete step. "Is something wrong with her?" *No. Please, no. Not her. Please, not her.* "Is she sick?" She couldn't let herself think anything worse. This many cops didn't show up for someone sick, but she couldn't wrap her mind around more.

"We didn't know who to call." Walton passed the bags to the uniformed officer, then sat down beside Mandy on the top step. "None of the neighbors knew her or your name, though some had seen a woman fitting your description come and go from here."

Of course, she wasn't sick. Something bad had happened.

Cops swarmed like bees all around her, and one was stretching yellow crime-scene tape between the trees separating her yard from the next-door neighbor's. Something wickedly bad. "She's lived here a relatively short time—maybe a year."

"A year, and none of her neighbors know her?" He clearly found that odd.

"Mom has always kept to herself." *She's a recluse for good reason.* Mandy shunned the thought, vowing she wouldn't whisper another word until he told her what had happened. She stared at him, and then waited . . . and waited.

Realizing she would stay clammed up, he shifted on his concrete seat, resigned. "I'm sorry, Miss Dixon. There's no easy way to say this. I wish there were." Regret flashed through his eyes, genuine and sincere. "Your mother is dead."

The bottom dropped out of her stomach. "Dead?" He had to be mistaken. Wrong. *Dead? Impossible.* "No. No, you've made some kind of mistake. She can't be dead." Mandy disputed him and shunned the shock pumping through her body. "We just talked a few hours ago. We're having dinner together here tonight. I'm cooking. I—I brought the groceries."

"There's no mistake." Walton spoke slowly, distinctly, giving Mandy time to absorb his words. "Your mother is dead. I'm so sorry for your loss, Miss Dixon."

"No," she insisted. "I talked to her. We're having lasagna and a Caesar salad—"

Walton didn't dispute her, just continued on. "The neighbor across the street called." He pointed to the white house trimmed in yellow, one house over and opposite her mother's. The neighbor who'd had an insane amount of flowers in her front yard last summer. "She was out winterizing her flowerbeds, heard shots fired, and phoned us. We responded right away, but we arrived too late. We found your mother inside the house. The coroner is with her now."

Her mother? Dead? Dead. Oh God, dead! No. No . . . No! Spots formed before her eyes and her stomach pitched. Hot and cold at once, she broke into a clammy sweat and her trembling intensified to shaking. Her world tilted and fighting to clear her head, she screamed inside.

Outwardly, she took a moment and then forced cold-steel calm into her voice. "If you're telling me she killed herself, you're wrong. My mother would never do that." She might want to; heaven knew she'd threatened to often enough over the years, but she wouldn't do it for the same reason she never had: she wouldn't deliberately leave Mandy alone in the world.

"No." Walton let his gaze slide away. "She didn't . . . hurt . . . herself." He dragged his gaze to Mandy's. "It's clear to us," he said, and then paused as if seeking the right words. Apparently deciding he wouldn't find any, he leveled his tone and went on. "Your mother was murdered."

More shock. More pain. A full-out assault. *Murdered.* Mandy hissed in a sharp breath, and then another. And then yet another. Her mother was dead. *Murdered?* "By who? She didn't associate with anyone but me."

"That's what we have to try to figure out." Walton looked past his shoulder to the uniformed officer he'd called Hank. "Time the grocery receipt."

"Yes, sir."

Walton returned his focus to her. "I really am sorry, Miss Dixon." He blinked hard and fast. "You shouldn't be alone. Is there anyone I can call for you?"

Tim's image filled her mind and her heart shattered yet again. She wanted and needed him, but she couldn't call him. "Give me a minute to think. Just a minute to think." Scanning her mind, she thought of her father. She *definitely* couldn't call him. He'd never forgive her.

She had learned young that she could never contact him under any circumstances. That no matter how hard she wished or prayed he might be like other fathers, he wasn't and he never would be, and he certainly would never be a dad to her—not like other dads. Every single day in each of her twenty-eight years, she'd had no choice but to accept those facts and to live with them. Neither he, nor her mother, had ever permitted her to harbor any fantasies. No, she couldn't call him. But when he heard about her mother, he would be devastated.

At least, Mandy thought he would. *Please, let him be devastated. Please.*

The idea of her mother sacrificing all she had and him not being devastated inflicted more pain than Mandy could bear.

"Any other family?" Detective Walton asked. "A grandmother or cousin?"

Biting her lip, she nodded that there wasn't any. Bitterness settled in her stomach. Her father had always kept them isolated.

"What about a friend?" Walton asked, lacing his fingers and draping his arms between his knees.

Again, she nodded negatively. Friends were for families not keeping secrets.

"Detective, excuse me. I need to see you inside."

He lifted a finger at the man, then looked at Mandy. "I'll be right back. If you need anything, just tell Hank."

Mandy nodded and watched the detective ease inside. He must have signaled Hank. He kept his distance at the edge of the porch, but stood watching her.

They were suspicious of her. She couldn't blame them, but that too, was her father's fault. Dirty secrets required distance, silence, staying apart.

She sought solace. Her father would be devastated at losing her mother. He had loved her. Even as a child, on his Tuesday visits, Mandy had picked up enough evidence of that to never doubt it. He'd always been a part of their lives, but they never really had been a part of his life. He'd never lived with them, or been the husband her mother deserved, or the father that her mother claimed Mandy deserved, but he'd loved her mother, and for reasons clear only to her, she had loved him.

And how that grated at Mandy.

Charles Travest might be a high-powered attorney and he might have every single material trapping that went with it, but all he had ever shared with her mother had been money and leftover crumbs of affection. With Mandy, he had shared even less.

Not once in her whole life had he ever said he loved her. Sometimes when he looked at her, she thought he might. But then he'd say, "You remind me so much of your mother" or "You look more like your mother every day," and Mandy had known. It wasn't her he saw or loved. His feelings for her were, in his own strange way, an extension of his love for her mother. Nothing more. Mandy surmised long ago she had been, was, and would never be anything more to him than an inconvenient complication.

At seventeen, when the truth revealed itself in all its sordid ugliness, her theory proved fact. Until then, she'd tried to win his affection by being clever and witty. She hadn't succeeded, though now and then, he had found her amusing. Starved for anything, his amusement had seemed like a lot to her hungry heart. At least it had, until the event. That day, everything had changed forever.

She'd seen him in St. Augustine. He'd passed her on the street and looked right through her as if he'd never before in his life seen her. He hadn't been alone . . . and Mandy had discovered the truth about him.

Later, her mother had confirmed Mandy's deductions, and that was that . . . until Mandy had met Tim Branson three years ago.

The conversations going on around her faded to a dull drone of voices, and she let herself find comfort in her memories.

Tim Branson. From the very beginning, Tim *saw* her. Outside and inside. He'd walked into her jewelry store, charming and sophisticated, approachable and emotionally wide open. He spoke his mind, and his honesty arrowed right into her heart.

When he had invited her to dinner, no one had been more surprised. Lured by his openness, his straight talk, Tim fascinated her. So much so that she ignored her better judgment warning her that, while he was nothing like her father, men like Tim were never seriously interested in women like her and she had to keep everyone distant, and she accepted the invitation.

One dinner turned into another and then another. He listened to her dreams. Looked at her with tenderness and truth. He trusted and cherished her, sought her opinions, and respected her ideas. When he told her he loved her the first time on a walk through town square, he became the one man in her life that she knew with total and complete certainty did love her.

That was far more precious to her than all the diamonds and jewels in her well-stocked store.

Detective Walton returned to her, still sitting quietly on the step. He looked concerned and even more weary. "You didn't call anyone?"

"No."

A nodding Hank confirmed that, and Walton looked back at her, almost desperate. "Surely there's someone I can call for you, Mandy."

Tim.

Memories flooded her, stacked and tumbled and shattered. Her heart squeezed her chest tight. Her eyes filled with tears that blurred her vision. His proposal had stunned her—still stunned her. At the time, she'd been beyond stunned. Awed. Awed and, in her eyes, witnessing a miracle. *He* wanted to spend his life with *her*? She challenged him. *Men like you don't marry women like me. You marry women who have it all.*

You have it all.

I don't. I—I She'd looked away. *There are things about me you don't know.*

There are things about me you don't know, too. We'll learn together.

It took him a while, but he'd convinced her. She was *the one* for him.

And heaven knew he had been the one for her. No one touched her heart, captivated her like Tim. No one else ever had, or would again.

An ache hollowed her heart. They would have been married—*should have been married*—now. But she'd been warned off. Persuasively. Permanently. Irrevocably. And so she'd done the hardest thing she'd been asked to do in her life. She'd walked away from Tim and closed the door on his love.

She had regretted that decision since the moment she'd made it.

Now, she regretted it even more.

She looked directly into the detective's eyes. "No. There is no one to call." Her throat went tight and her chest felt squeezed. "Not anymore."

Tim was a former Shadow Watcher—one of the secrets about himself he revealed after she had accepted his proposal. A spy who spied on spies. He was part of a team of them and, after an incident, the details of which he had not shared, his entire team had left active-duty and had started their own private-security consultant firm. They—Tim—could find out who had murdered her mother.

She considered reaching into her purse for the secure phone they always had used to talk. It never rang anymore; it hadn't since she'd broken their engagement. But she couldn't make herself put the phone away or get rid of it and break their final physical connection. She'd tried—many times—but she just couldn't do it anymore than she could stop loving him.

Temptation escalated to an urge to phone him and it fired through her with the force of a physical blow. She absorbed that, too, and then the successive series of urges that followed, denying them all. She couldn't call Tim any more than she could call her father. After what she'd done to him? Knowing what could happen? No. No, she had no right . . .

Resignation slid onto her like a heavy coat. With a sigh, she faced Detective Walton, who sat patiently, giving her time to fight her way through the first wave of emotional turmoil his news had triggered. "No, but thank you for your kindnesses. There's no one to call. It's always been just my mother and me."

"What about co-workers?" Walton pushed. "Employees?"

That stung. "Yes, I have employees, but they are not involved in my personal life."

"What about neighbors from an old neighborhood?" He frowned, either not believing her or surprised. "Surely you and your mother interacted with someone."

Charles Travest. The idea of disclosing him flitted through her mind, but the potential consequences halted her. It would only cause more pain. She'd been on the receiving end of that pain in St. Augustine. No way would she willingly inflict the nightmare on another. He might have sacrificed her, but responsibility for that rested on his head. She wouldn't sacrifice him or destroy his life. "Afraid not. There's no one."

Her chest ached with shame and embarrassment. In Walton's line of work, he'd seen and heard it all, and clearly he thought their isolation was odd. She agreed with him, but she couldn't admit it.

"I'm sorry." Walton said and meant that, too. Pity burned in his eyes.

When seeing it stopped putting spasms into her throat, she swallowed hard. "I want to see my mother."

"Soon. But I can't allow that right now." He glanced down at Mandy's feet, avoiding her eyes. "We're still gathering evidence."

She'd contaminate the crime scene. "I understand." Protecting the scene, she could grasp. Her mother being dead just didn't make sense. "You, personally, are certain it's her?"

"I am. I found her driver's license in her handbag. There's no doubt."

Dead. Her mother was dead. Why?

Immediately, Mandy's mind went to the threats against Tim. But surely not. She'd done exactly what she'd had to do and hadn't heard a word about it since then. There had been no contact. None. No, this couldn't be about him. It had to be unrelated.

"I know it is terrible to bother you with questions, but time isn't on our side. If we're going to stand a chance of catching whoever did this . . ."

Get it together, Mandy. Clear your mind. Focus. "I understand. Go ahead."

"You say there was no one else, so I have to ask." His voice softened. "Did you kill your mother?"

"What?"

"I have to ask," he repeated. "It's my job, Mandy."

"I told you. It's been her and me my whole life." Mandy looked him right in the eye, let him see her pain. *Alone. Vulnerable. Lost. Empty.* "She was all I have." Her broken heart shattered again. "No, Detective. I didn't kill her."

His expression didn't alter. "Where were you at about six tonight?"

Routine questions? Or he suspected her, anyway? Could that be possible? Seriously? That it might, strained at her fragile composure and the fissure of fear she'd been fighting internally cracked wider, stretched and yawned like a canyon. "Buying the groceries I needed. I told you, I came over to make her dinner."

"Sir?" the uniformed officer interrupted. "Timed receipt. She was at the store at 6:10."

"So Miss Dixon is clear?" Walton pointedly asked.

"Yes, sir."

"Thanks." Walton looked back at her. "Sorry, Miss Dixon. I want to find who did this to your mother. I can't take anything for granted."

A part of her felt deeply offended, but the more practical side she used to run her jewelry store appreciated his thorough approach. "No problem." A hard lump settled in her chest. Who could have done this? What was done? "How did she . . .?" Mandy couldn't say the word out loud. Her voice failed. She ordered herself to be strong, to suck it up, and tried again. "How was my mother murdered?"

"She was shot, Miss Dixon."

"Shot?" That stunned Mandy.

"We received a shots fired call—from the neighbor. Remember?"

A shadowed memory returned. Walton telling her that the flower-lady neighbor had heard gunfire and called the police. "Yes, I remember now."

"Your mother was shot," he repeated slowly, as if realizing Mandy needed still more time to absorb and process.

She did need more time. None of this fit. It just didn't. "But my mother hated guns and forbid them in the house." Mandy looked from the crime-scene tape, twisting and crackling in the wind, back to Walton. "She must have known the person."

"Or he or she entered the house without your mother knowing it."

That was possible, and a little less terrifying. A stranger was bad, but someone you knew turning on you like that had to be worse.

"Excuse me, sir." Hank again interrupted. "May I speak to you a second?"

The detective stood up and stepped away, down to the end of the wide front porch, beyond the tall fichus, near the two white rockers. "What is it, Hank?" Walton asked, his voice carrying clearly to Mandy, still seated on the step.

"We found the point of entry in her bedroom—a window close to the corner of the house."

"Get forensics on it. Maybe we'll get lucky and pick up some prints." The detective looked over the slope of his shoulder at Mandy and elevated his voice. "Do you live here, Miss Dixon? With your mom, I mean?"

"No. I have a house on the water near my jewelry store."

"And so far as you know, no one else has been here. Just you, when you visit, and your mom."

Guilt stabbed at her. "I haven't seen anyone else here, and she hasn't mentioned anyone else being here." True, but not the whole truth. They didn't talk about her father, so she honestly didn't know if he had been here. Did he still come over every Tuesday? Mandy had no idea but, if she were a betting woman, she would bet he did. Today, however, was Thursday. From the time she was born until she had left and built her own home, she knew of no time when Charles Travest ever deviated from his scheduled Tuesday visits.

Had he deviated today?

Could he have killed her mother?

Honestly, she didn't know. Uncertainty had her again clammy and breaking into a cold sweat. He had been decent and kind to her mother and to her, and Mandy had never seen a hint of violence in him. But he'd been always been clear. If either of them crossed his lines . . .

Lines like the one her mother had set against her marrying Tim. *It isn't just your life you're putting at risk . . .*

Oh, yes. The warning had been clear and irrevocable.

Mandy's chest grew heavy, her heart tattered and weary. She could, and probably should mention that. But she didn't dare.

Tim.

Oh, you've no idea how badly I wish I could talk to you. You'd know what to do. Tears threatened. She swallowed hard three times, trying to avoid them. *I—I don't know what to do…*

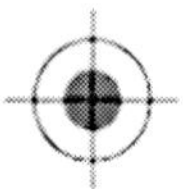

Tuesday, October 21st

Five days later, the coroner released the body. Mandy had made arrangements with a local funeral home and withstood, without withering, the director's surprise that there'd be no service other than graveside.

The world spun on, seemingly unchanged and without notice—as arrogant as can be to someone heartbroken and mourning—and the sun shone and laughter flowed, grating at her eyes and ears and every frayed nerve in her body. For everyone else, it was a normal, largely unremarkable day.

For Mandy it was terrifying.

Little memories of her mother ran like film loops through her mind. Last week, last month, her childhood. Regardless of what she did, they wouldn't turn off. She considered going to the jewelry store to work, but she couldn't think; she'd only be in the way. Her assistant manager, Erin, had things well in hand there, so Mandy stayed home.

She'd spent years dreaming of her business and more years building it, but today she honestly couldn't care less about it. It, or anything else. Grief ruled, and ravaged and tormented her. Too weakened to fight it, she curled up on the sofa in her bathrobe with a box of tissues and let herself grieve. She had no one now. No one who cared if she lived or died. No one for her to care about or to share triumphs or troubles. No one to comfort her and assure her that no matter how dark things were now, they wouldn't always be dark.

This too shall pass. She tried comforting herself.

It rang hollow, like tin to her ears. Would it pass? Logically, she believed it would. But her heart doubted it, bombarding her with questions she didn't want to hear much less try to answer. *Is this all there really is to life? If so, why bother?*

Aching, lost, Mandy cried until she had no more tears, then cried some more. And long after the arrogant sun set for the day and the pink streaks in the sky faded to deep blue, she lay curled on her sofa, hugging the box of tissues, half of which lay wadded on the coffee table. *Help me find my way. Can you just please help me find my way?*

The following Friday, Mandy stood on the outskirts of Maddsen Cemetery at her mother's graveside. She'd always said that's where she wanted to be buried.

It was a picturesque small cemetery, very peaceful and shaded by huge, old oaks. Fresh flowers always sprinkled the graves; Mandy had seen them many times when driving by.

Thunder rumbled overhead.

It wasn't supposed to rain today so no tent stood stretched above the coffin to protect it or mourners from the weather. It sat in the open above the gaping hole prepared to receive it once the service was done.

In the distance, lightning flashed. The faint scent of it carried on the wind. The minister she'd hired reacted accordingly and spoke faster, but not fast enough. Mid-service, the sky split open and rain poured down, pinging against the top and sides of the coffin, spitting droplets that pounded the flowers placed on its top. Water gathered among the leaves and spilled over, running in rivulets down the coffin's coppery sides and dripping off into the gaping hole.

God was mourning with her.

The thought oddly comforted Mandy, and she opened her umbrella, held it over herself and the minister. Between intermittent claps of thunder and jagged streaks and flashes of lightning, she listened to him lay her mother's body to rest.

When he was done, she couldn't recall a word he'd said. Over and again in her mind, she'd remembered herself as a child playing wedding with her mother. Her mother at the piano, playing the Wedding March, while Mandy walked down a makeshift aisle of throw-rugs with a scarf-draped lampshade on her head. Her mother always added an extra note at the end of the chorus. They'd giggled about it so many times. *It's my signature note, darling . . .*

The minister claimed her attention. "I'm so sorry for your loss, Miss Dixon. Is there anything I can do for you?"

Pity burned in his eyes. Pity and curiosity that she'd stood alone to bury her mother.

She'd covertly notified Charles Travest of her mother's passing, and until she had stood through the service with only her and the minister present, she had believed her father would be here. Not that he'd said he would, but because he loved her mother. She'd even held out a glimmer of hope that, while he wouldn't live his life with his daughter, he would at least mourn her mother's passing with her. Yet, he had failed them again. One more time in a long list of times.

Oh, Mandy had sensed him nearby. Somewhere in the distant shadows watching the service. But he hadn't risked actually coming to the service or showing his face. *Coward.*

Cowardly, yes, and unfortunately typical for him. He hadn't phoned, emailed, or even sent her mother flowers with an impersonal note. No one had. The lone bouquet on top of the casket, Mandy had ordered. A white rose in her hand was the only other flower for her mother.

A tidal wave of new resentment washed over Mandy, partnered with the old. She steeled herself against its weight, lifted her chin, and then answered the minister. "No, there's nothing to be done, but thank you. I'm fine on my own."

She placed the rose onto her mother's coffin with a loving stroke, and then turned and walked away.

Safely in her car, she blotted the rain from her face and arms with a tissue, then drove off . . . and cried all the way home, shedding the tears she hadn't permitted herself to shed at the service.

Why couldn't she cry? Would that be so awful—to cry at your own mother's funeral?

Maybe not for ordinary people. But they were not ordinary.

Her mother wouldn't approve the absence of emotional control; she never had. But even if she didn't disapprove this time, under these circumstances, she would need to know Mandy would be all right without her as much as Mandy needed to know her mother was all right now that she'd passed. Tears would rock her mother's confidence. Mandy couldn't do that. She wanted to imagine her mother resting in peace, not worried sick her daughter was a basket case.

That night, alone on her backyard deck, Mandy sat staring at the phone used only for secure conversations between Tim and her. Since dusk, she'd picked it up and put it back down on the little wooden side table a thousand times. Once, she'd even dialed him. Well, all but the last number. Then her mother's warning came rushing back, kicking in, and Mandy had set the phone down and had not touched it again.

Now, she fell to temptation and reached for it. She wouldn't call Tim, but she would send him a text message. He was free to respond or not without a direct confrontation. She could live with that—and if she didn't talk to someone, she was surely going to lose what was left of her mind. No one was safer or more trustworthy than Tim Branson.

Still, her heart beat hard and fast. She keyed in the text then stared at it a long moment. Her hands shook, her pulse throbbed in her throat, her head. *Please, don't let this be a mistake. Please . . .*

Before she could second-guess herself yet again or let fear back her down and force her to change her mind, she quickly pushed Send.

CHAPTER 2

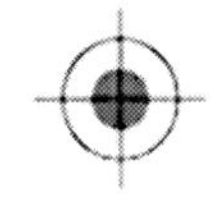

24th
Seagrove Village, Florida

The former five-member team of Shadow Watchers entered Mark Taylor's Seagrove Village home single-file.

Tim Branson, wearing perfectly creased khaki slacks and a butter-yellow golf shirt, led the way, stepping past Mark, their former team leader and current head of their private security consulting firm. Tim, second in command, narrowed his eyes. "You're wearing an apron, Mark?"

"Hurry and get in here, and shut the door." Mark headed back toward the kitchen. "If I burn this . . . stuff, Lisa will have my head on a platter."

"We've seen your head in worse places." Sam sauntered in, bearing a strong resemblance to a younger Larry the Cable Guy down to his ripped out sleeves, jean shorts and flip-flops—*Florida formal.* "But I gotta tell you, buddy, that red apron don't do a thing for ya. Maybe next time try a deeper red."

"Spoken like a true Alabama redneck." Mark hustled back to the stove. "Remind me again why we consider you an invaluable member of our team."

"Because he's a genius," Tim said. "With the best nose in the South for sniffing out gaps in security, terrorist activity, and dirt no one wants anyone to find much less expose."

Mark cast Sam a half-sneer. "Why a deeper red apron?"

Sam harrumphed. "That you gotta ask says more than enough about why you need me to cover your backside, buddy."

"He's alluding to Crimson Tide." Joe lifted his sunglasses from his eyes and parked them atop his head, then slid onto a stool at the breakfast bar across from the stove.

Tim nodded his agreement. Joe was naturally cool, insightful, and one of the most well-connected investigators or special operators Tim had ever known. His go-to contacts were impressive by anyone's standards, and his reach extended beyond known borders.

"Dang straight, I'm talking Crimson Tide." Sam smiled, his ball cap resting low on his forehead. "Roll Tide Roll."

Tim half-smiled. Sam loved football and had been an ardent Crimson Tide fan for as long as Tim had known him. None of the other guys were that attached to their alma mater teams, but they indulged Sam in his, and in his Civil War reenactments, and in his penchant for monster truck rallies. Those, Tim admitted, were intriguing. Dusty but intriguing.

"See the emblem on it?" Mark pointed to his apron. "Seminoles."

"Whatever." Sam grunted.

"What's the problem in there, bro?" Joe asked Mark. "I thought Lisa was cooking dinner."

Lisa and Mark were a couple and had been for a good while now. Why Mark didn't get off the dime and marry the woman, only he knew. He'd been in love with her a couple years before he'd made a move. She'd been in med school and under a lot familial pressure and he hadn't wanted to complicate her already complicated life.

"Smells like she did cook." Nick opened the fridge, reached in, and then and tossed the guys cans of soda. "Sorry, Sam. No canned tea."

The barb hit its mark and others laughed, including Tim. Sam had a cursing problem and the people at Crossroads Crisis Center—namely, its director Peggy Crane, and the village's mother-in-chief, Nora, were bent on breaking him of it. Sam never went anywhere without a glass of iced-tea in his hand. Whenever he cursed, one of them—or one of the guys—spiked his tea with jalapeno pepper juice. He was getting the point, but he still had a way to go. Bad habits are hardest to break.

"So where's Lisa?" Tim asked, agreeing with Nick that the house did have a distinctive scent Tim also connected to Lisa's cooking: *Burned to a crisp*. But, credit due, she tried hard, and growing up with Nora as a surrogate mom, it was hard to believe she hadn't picked up some tips. But the evidence that she hadn't spoke for itself. If she cooked it, she burned it.

Maybe she didn't want to cook, or to learn how to cook from Nora.

Tim hadn't considered that possibility before, but it seemed more likely than she just couldn't cook. Lisa was a woman of many skills—a medical doctor, a self-defense instructor to at-risk women. A survivor. If she wanted to cook, she would cook. It had to be that she didn't want to, and he sure couldn't fault her for that. Her days were plenty full without it. *Interesting.*

Mark pulled the lid off a pot and dunked in a huge spoon. "She went home to change clothes. She's so excited about all of you coming to dinner. We have a little announcement to make."

"Why's she excited about us being here? We're here all the time." Tim registered the other half of Mark's statement. "Wait. An announcement. She's nervous." She wouldn't say that, she'd say excited, but nervous fit.

"Beside herself. She wants your approval." Mark glanced his way. "You'll be giving it to her."

Message sent and received. "Got it."

"Biting the dust, eh?" Sam popped the question on everyone's tongue. "So when's the wedding?"

Mark frowned at him, swept them all with a warning gaze. "At least fake being surprised and happy for us."

"Of course, we will—fake being surprised, I mean." Joe rifled through the pantry and pulled out some chips. "We are happy for you."

"Dang straight. I ain't much on marriage, but Lisa's special. I'd consider biting the dust for her myself."

"She's taken, Sam." Mark's tone came across extremely territorial.

"I know, bud. I meant if she wasn't. Like if you dumped her or something."

Tim and Nick grunted their disagreement. "That's not happening."

"No way, bro." Joe agreed with them.

Nick glared at Sam. "Even if it did, Lisa isn't your type. A redneck man needs a redneck woman. Know what I mean?"

"Yeah. But she's awesome—for a non-redneck woman." Sam stole the chip bowl. "Uh, exactly what's in your caldron over there?"

"Honestly, I don't know." Mark dropped the spoon onto its rest. "If I did, then maybe I could do something to salvage it."

Joe found a veggie tray in the fridge and put it on the island bar. "Add cayenne pepper." He removed the clear film and then crunched down on a carrot. "It'll fix anything."

"Or hurt you so bad you forget it ain't fixed." Sam groaned and rubbed his stomach. "Mark, don't do it, bud. I can't handle cayenne right now."

"Let me guess." Tim bit back a smile. "You got here

yesterday, which means you spent the day at the center today, which means Peggy and Nora have already juiced you because you're too hardheaded to remember not to curse around them."

"At least three times—so far." Nick hiked a thumb toward Sam. "He either loves jalapeno tea or he's a really slow learner."

"He's not slow, he's pigheaded." Mark corrected Nick, looked at Tim. "Should I put cayenne in it? It might cover the, um . . ."

"Too-well-done smell?" Tim suggested, stretching for diplomacy while walking around the bar. He peeked into the pot at the lump of black sunk in a swirl of dark brown gravy that resembled a decent mud puddle. *Oh, boy.*

"It's charred, pure and simple." Mark looked desolate.

"It is that." Was there a word for beyond charred? *Oh yeah, Lisa, you definitely hate cooking.* "Why don't you just tell her it's burned?" he asked Mark. "She's a doctor, she knows burned when she sees it." Tim hiked a shoulder. "We'll order a pizza or something."

Nick shoved his glasses up on the bridge of his nose and growled in Tim's direction. "Are you crazy?"

"Crazy?" Tim glared at Nick. He'd ditched his tie but had worn a deep blue suit. Blue, black, gray—that was the extent of Nick's color palette, and for style it was suit, tux, or camo. He rarely had been spotted in anything else. "What's crazy about ordering a pizza?"

Nick grumbled out his frustration, then spoke up so everyone could hear. "She's a black belt, genius. Think." Nick thumped at his temple. "You've seen her take down bigger men, and you want to tell her her food isn't fit to eat?"

"I ain't telling her spit," Sam said. "Upset Lisa, and Peggy and Nora will burn out my gut-lining for the rest of my life." He cast an apologetic look toward Mark. "Sorry, buddy. I'd die for you, but getting on the wrong side of those two? I ain't that brave."

Sam was one of the bravest, and most underestimated men Tim had ever met. They all were. Spies who spy on spies and fight terrorists off the grid had to be. But like Sam, Tim wasn't eager to take on Peggy or Nora. Either of the senior women in Seagrove Village was formidable standing alone, not that they ever were. Cross them, and you had to fight everyone else in the village—and the other Shadow Watchers. Nora had claimed them as "her boys" along with the rest of Mark's personal security staff. No one messed with Nora's boys and went unchallenged by everyone in the village.

Mark dropped the top back onto the bubbling pot. "I don't know what this is. I do know it's burned to a crisp, and I know we're going to eat it anyway—no pizza." Mark cut to the chase. "I don't know how we'll eat it, but we will. Nobody upsets Lisa."

The men groaned like they were dying. Tim couldn't blame them. They all loved Lisa. She was an admirable woman who had gone toe-to-toe with NINA—Nihilists in Anarchy—the team's archenemy and one of the worst terrorist groups and criminal activists in the nation. They'd come after her with an arsenal. She'd survived interception and abduction, being kidnapped, and an attempt to sell her in a human-trafficking scheme. She could have walked away on the trafficking—the Shadow Watchers had advised her to walk away—but the doc had stayed to help the other women captured and the team to take down the operation. Lisa Harper had guts, and that all the team admired. But they loved her because she loved Mark. He'd never been loved, and he needed it badly.

Lisa loved Mark like Mandy once had loved Tim.

At least, the way Mandy had loved Tim *before* she'd met Mr. Wonderful and had broken their engagement to marry the man.

Tim's heart clenched. He stiffened, pushed off the bar and grabbed a carrot, then dragged it through a creamy dip. "We understand, Mark. Upset her and die."

"I wouldn't have put it exactly like that, but, yeah, that'll do."

Mark would put it *exactly* like that. He always cut to the chase. Fortunately, he loved Lisa *and* the team.

While their team had been active-duty, they'd been through hell together more times than any one of them could recall—and even more times since then in their work as off-the-grid security consultants. They relied on each other for everything, including survival, and when someone messed with one of them, they'd better be ready to fight them all. "Don't worry," Tim told Mark. "Whatever it is, we'll choke it down and nobody will hurt Lisa's feelings. Right, guys?"

"Not me." Sam repeated, no doubt still visualizing a pepper-charred gut.

"Of course not," Joe said. "We all adore Lisa."

In truth, Joe adored all women and they knew it, which made him a virtual woman-magnet. It was as if they sensed that he genuinely respected and appreciated everything about them. That deep sincerity came in handy sometimes and was a nuisance at others. The team put up with it because it was honest. Joe couldn't deny that part of himself anymore than he could not be cool. Both were in his genes, encoded in his DNA.

"Right." Nick nodded. "We like Lisa, Mark. There isn't a man in this room who wouldn't die for her."

Like was a strong, positive word from Nick, who was the best man in the world on computers but he always bent to the dark side in everything. And he was right. There wasn't a man in the room who wouldn't die for Lisa—or one who hadn't almost died for her, when her nut of a NINA-connected stepfather had paid a fortune to have her abducted and shipped down to Mexico for resale.

Joe gave Nick a subtle thumb's up for a constructive effort. "What's not to like? The doc's a remarkable woman. Gorgeous, talented, good hearted, and—"

"A black belt." Mark finished for him and raised an oven-mitted hand. "First man makes her cry is going to wish he were facing her black belt instead of me."

"Quit threatening us, bro. Didn't we tell you we've got this covered?"

"Listen to Joe, Mark. It'll be fine." Tim joined Mark at the stove. "Move over."

"Why?"

"Recon." Tim did a little pot-snooping and then set out to brief the team. "Okay, the meat is pot roast. That's broccoli with something in it that resembles water chestnuts." He snagged one and crunched down on it. "Definitely, water chestnuts." *Scorched* water chestnuts. *She didn't just not like to cook. She hated it.*

"Nice work, bud." Sam slapped a hand to his knee. "Nick, Tim's taking you down on the investigative identification front. Better watch your back, bud."

"You're safe, Nick." Tim interjected. "I have zero certainty on that one." Tim pointed to a white open-cover dish with brown-crusted something on top. "Can't even comfortably speculate."

Sam studied it, then his face wrinkled in confusion. "Beats me, bud. Maybe it's potatoes?" He backed off and checked it out from a different angle. "Sort of looks like it might be."

"With your legendary nose, you can't tell?" Joe asked, seemingly surprised.

"No way." Sam shook his head. "The burn smell in here is overpowering everything—even Nick's gallon of cologne. My sniffer's all out-of-whack."

Joe looked closer. "I'd say the big lumps are definitely potatoes. But I'm not making a call on the brown stuff. Not a clue."

"Morons." Nick groused. "I can't believe I put my life in your hands. You're all dead from the neck up." He swept the air with a broad hand. "Step aside and let me see it." Nick rounded the bar to peer into the dish atop the stove. He dragged a tentative fingertip at its outer edge. "Some kind of cheese—or it was."

"Ah, I got it." Tim nailed it. "Potatoes au-gratin."

"Or scalloped potatoes." Nick returned to his seat at the end of the bar, his back rigid. "Close enough. Mystery solved."

Half an hour later, the men sat at the table with Lisa. Over small talk, they choked down every single bite.

Then Mark noticed Lisa wasn't eating. "You okay?"

"I'm fine." She dipped her blond head, avoiding his gaze. "Is everyone finished?"

"Oh, yeah."

"Stuffed to the rafters."

"Thanks, Lisa." Tim shot a warning look at the others to drop the enthusiasm about the meal being over. "You worked hard, and we appreciate it." That was sincere, and the best he could offer.

"Great." She stood and then gathered dishes.

Sam started to leave the table. She stopped him with a gentle hand to his shoulder. "Don't get up yet. We have dessert."

Sheer panic filled their eyes. Lisa didn't seem to notice; she stepped out of the dining room and headed to the kitchen.

Sam glared at Tim, his voice a stage whisper. "You didn't tag dessert. Nobody said spit about dessert. How're we supposed to know what it is?"

Mark shot him a warning look. "Upset her and die."

Sam frowned but settled back in his seat. "All I got to say about this is somebody better identify it fast and cue the rest of us."

Tim and Joe shot each other amused glances.

Lisa returned with plates and a white-frosted cake topped with fresh strawberries. She set them down on the table then went around and pressed a butterfly kiss to each of the men's cheeks. "Thank you." She smacked Sam, then moved on to peck Nick, Joe and finally Tim. "How you swallowed that stuff is beyond me. And not one complaint." She dazzled them with a smile. "You're my heroes—again."

Mark frowned at her. "Is that why you didn't eat?"

"It was awful, Mark. I couldn't swallow it." She cut the cake. "Sam, stop freaking out down there." She glanced to him at the other end of the table. "The strawberry cake is beyond good. I promise."

His Adam's apple bobbed like a rock in his throat. "I'm, uh, sure it's great, Lisa."

She laughed. "Bet on it." She cut an extra-large piece and passed him the plate. "Nora baked it."

Relief flooded his face. "Awesome."

The village mom-in-chief, who adopted all strays, made great food, including cakes and pies.

Ted, Joe and Mark cleared their throats, signaling Sam not to sound so happy.

Nick, being Nick, kicked Sam under the table.

"Umph." Sam laid a you're-a-dead-man look on Nick, then swerved a soft gaze on Lisa. "Um, Nora makes good cakes," he said, his face flushing. "But I'm sure you do, too, Lisa."

"You're a terrible liar, Sam, but you're a wonderful man." She kissed his cheek a second time avoiding his backward baseball cap, and then served the rest of the cake. "Congratulations on your Civil War Reenactment. Mark tells me you were the general this year."

"Sure was." He laughed. "We still lost, of course, but the kids like it. Brings history to life for 'em."

"That's important," she said.

Sam sat a little straighter.

"Now," Lisa went on. "I have a pleasant surprise for you guys."

Here it came. The engagement announcement. Tim shut out thoughts of Mandy. Memories of how happy for them the team had been when they'd announced their plans. This was Mark and Lisa's night.

"What kind of surprise?" Nick asked. "You know I'm not fond of surprises, Lisa."

An understatement if ever Tim had heard one.

"You'll like this one." She smiled. "As a reward for your bravery in choking down that mess, I promise not to cook for you anymore."

"Lisa," Joe said. "Anything you do is fine with us. We're here for the company."

"And I bless you for it. But for the sake of your stomachs and mine, in the future, I'll stick to sandwiches or we'll order in." She shot Mark a *sorry* look. "I tried. I just can't seem to grasp cooking."

"You have many other talents, doc," Joe reminded her. "Besides, Mark's a decent cook so it's no problem."

Nick added, "We can't all be good at everything—myself excluded, of course."

"Arrogance doesn't become you." Mark slid him a frown.

"It's nasty," Sam said, a twinkle in his eye. "Better keep an eye on your tea, bud."

That created a stir of laughter. The idea of Nick getting spiked tea struck everyone as hilarious—and likely.

Ah, sweet balance. Tim breathed a sigh of relief. They *would* get through the meal without Mark killing anyone.

Tim's phone vibrated at his hip, signaling an incoming text. He removed it from its belt-clip and checked the message.

In trouble. I need you now. M.

His heart dropped to his stomach.

"What's wrong, Tim?"

"I'm not sure." He stood up. "Oh, wait. Mark, you have an announcement to make?"

"After dinner, yeah. Are you leaving now?"

"I have to go." Fear roiled in Tim's stomach. "The text just in is from Mandy—her secure phone." He let them see his worry. "She's in trouble."

"Oh, no." Lisa's fork stilled mid-air. "Our announcement

can wait. You do what you need to do, Tim."

"He doesn't *need* to do anything," Sam told Lisa, then glared at Tim. "She's not your problem anymore, bud." Sam sniffed then took a bite of cake. "She dumped you and married Mr. Wonderful. Let her call him to help her out."

"Here, here." Nick emphatically agreed, clearly still miffed at Mandy.

"I don't know if she married him or not," Tim admitted. "I haven't seen or talked to her since she broke our engagement."

"To marry him," Nick added. He grumbled something under his breath about her having set a wedding date.

"Yes, to marry him and, yes, I heard the date." Tim's voice sounded starched enough to compete with Lisa's potatoes. Joe had spent that day on the phone with Tim, and helped him get through it.

"So, married or not, why's she calling you and not him?" Mark asked, then sent a questioning look at Lisa. "Wouldn't you call me?"

"When I was in trouble, I did call you."

Tim cocked his head, perplexed. "I don't know why Mandy's calling me, but she is."

Sam opened his mouth to say something, but Joe lifted a staying hand. "I have to say, bro, this doesn't sound like Mandy. She pretty much deals with whatever comes to her on her own. You sure the message is from her?"

"It's from the secure phone I gave her. She's only used it to contact me." *In the past. What about now?* Tim had no idea.

Joe nodded. "So what kind of trouble is she in? Did she say?" He put down his fork. "Regardless, you need backup. I'm going with you."

"She didn't say, so I don't know what this is about." Tim rubbed at his neck. "But, you stay here. This could be nothing." Tim's mind whirled. Joe was right. Mandy did handle things herself, yet she wouldn't text him for nothing. She'd never, not once, called him for nothing. "I'll check it out and, if I need you guys, I'll let you know." Tim headed toward the door.

Lisa joined him and gave his forearm a gentle squeeze. "Be careful, Tim."

"Secure phones to us, just in case," Mark reminded him.

"Right. Look, don't worry, okay? Like I said. This could be nothing." It didn't feel like nothing. It felt . . . desperate. The Mandy he knew would have to be in lethal jeopardy to contact him after skating out on him—especially after all this time.

Mark sobered. "Ordinarily, I'd agree, but this is Mandy, Tim. It could be nothing, or a whole lot of something."

He too knew her habits.

"I figured she'd come running back to you long before now, buddy." Sam helped himself to more cake.

Nick shot Sam a gloomy look. "It's been eight months. If that's running, she must have started her return in Siberia."

"Nine months," Joe corrected him automatically. "What?" Joe shot Nick a sharp look. "Facts are facts. Keep them straight."

"Facts are facts," Nick countered. "And, apparently, Mr. Wonderful isn't so wonderful after all."

"Nick, ease up. You don't even know what's wrong yet." Mark called for a fair assessment. "She might be married."

He lifted a hand. "Then surely she would call her husband and not Tim for help."

"She might call Tim," Lisa said. "If she knows how good you guys are when someone's in a jam." Lisa nodded for added emphasis. "Me? I wouldn't even think about calling anyone else."

Nick digested that and then grunted. "But Mandy's not you. She's got secrets, Lisa. Quit snarling at me, Mark. She's always had secrets. Every one of us knows that's true."

"Forgive Nick, Lisa," Tim said without rancor. "He's still ticked off at Mandy for breaking our engagement and dumping me."

"Bet on it." Nick growled. "She broke your heart."

Fiercely protective. They all were, including Tim. "She did." No sense in denying the obvious.

"So why are you running off to help her, buddy?"

Tim paused at the door. "We were engaged, Sam. I loved the woman enough to ask her to be my wife. She calls me saying she's in trouble and, of course, I'm going to help her."

"Understood." Mark said, closing the door on challenges to the discussion.

"Report in ASAP." Joe shouted to Tim's disappearing back. "She at home?"

"Yes." Tim stepped out.

Lisa stroked his shoulder, gently squeezed. "Let us know."

"I will." Tim nodded and shut the door.

"He's terrified for her." Lisa's heart felt stuck in her throat. Tim was a great guy. Sophisticated, wealthy, charming, an all-around good man who looked as wickedly handsome in a tux as he did in fatigues. "Shouldn't someone go with him, Mark?"

"He said if he needs us, he'll let us know."

"But he shouldn't do this alone." She turned a beseeching gaze on him. "Can't you see that his heart is still breaking?"

"Oh, yeah, I see it," Mark agreed.

"Has to be breaking," Sam rocked back in his seat. "One text and he transforms into the proverbial white knight and rushes off to save her." Sam clicked his tongue against his teeth. "I don't care what she's done. He's still in love with her."

"Definitely." Nick sighed. "Poor fool."

"Loving is always a mistake worth making, Nick. But this has to be something . . . more." Joe looked around the table. "Mandy is indisputably capable of saving herself. She wouldn't call Tim unless she had no choice."

"Could mean she ain't in trouble, but she's got trouble. Or maybe she's finally come to her senses and is just missing him."

"It's possible," Mark said.

"I'm with Joe. Tim said *in* trouble." Lisa rubbed her hands together. "It's more, all right." She hiked in a shuddered breath.

"Oh, I've got a bad feeling about this."

"Lisa's right. He did say *in trouble*, bro."

Mark shot Joe a look heavy with reprimand. "Not you, too. Don't encourage her. She'll worry herself right off the deep end."

Lisa swatted at Mark's shoulder.

He slid her a *really?* look that should wither her knees.

"Okay, I might worry myself off the deep end. I probably will," she admitted. "But if you don't hear from Tim within an hour, you go after him, Mark Taylor. I can't stand the thought of him facing whatever this is by himself. If nothing else, he needs moral support, and he's your friend. So be a friend."

"Mandy lives two hours away in Maddsen. But quit worrying. Tim's not facing anything by himself. We're all with him, all the way."

She looked to Joe for confirmation. "Anywhere. Anything. Any time," he said.

"Promise." Nick held up his right hand. "We're just waiting for him to make the call."

"Oh, I see." She crossed her arms. "If he wants help, he has to ask you guys for it?" She didn't much care for that and let them all hear it in her tone. "That's just wrong. When there's trouble, friends show up. No invitation required. They just show up. Period."

"We're respecting his boundaries, Lisa," Joe explained. "It's a guy thing. We don't want him to think we believe he can't handle this on his own."

There for him, but not emasculating him. Yet another *guy-thing*. But at least it sounded a lot better than them waiting for an invitation. She drew in a long breath, hoping some patience came with it. "Okay, then. Respect anything you want, but first sign of him facing trouble . . ."

"We're there, hon," Mark reassured her.

"Absolutely," Joe agreed.

Nick held his *promise* hand up again.

"You bet, Lisa." Sam sniffed. "Well, one good thing. Whatever this is, at least odds are good it ain't got nothing to do with NINA."

Lisa shivered. She and the Crossroads Crisis Center family had tangled with NINA operatives twice in the last year, and the team had been involved in resolving the issues then, too. Everyone in the community knew the notorious Raven, a high-ranking NINA official, had infiltrated their ranks. They'd stopped her by the skin of their teeth and now she was cooling her heels in Leavenworth. But only a fool wouldn't recognize that no matter how many NINA operatives Mark and his team took down, there would always be more in line, eager to replace them. Chessman led to Raven who led to Jackal—they still hadn't identified Jackal—and nobody doubted there was a string of NINA honchos above Jackal.

NINA was involved in all kinds of criminal activity. It used its criminal proceeds to fund furthering its political ideologies. A worldwide, well-funded organization, NINA ran a ruthless operation and it had global interests at every level. Lisa had learned all that firsthand, and nearly had died in the process. "I pray you're right, Sam." Looking around the table, she saw her fears confirmed in their eyes. "But honestly, not one of us would bet a nickel on it."

"Considering what they've pulled in Seagrove Village twice already . . ." Sam shrugged and conceded. "Yeah, I guess you're right. It'd be a sucker bet."

CHAPTER 3

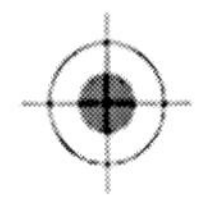

Friday, October 24th

Tim hit Interstate 10 and merged into traffic. The soft, rhythmic purr of the Rolls Phantom had Joe's question replaying over and again in his mind. *Had it really been Mandy who'd texted him?* Maybe she'd ditched the phone. Surely if she'd married Mr. Wonderful, she had ditched it. Which meant, anyone who had found it could have called him. This could be a trap.

You're acting like a rank amateur. Trust but verify—then verify again.

He really should know just what he was walking into here. Why hadn't he called already? Typically, he would have thought to call right back and he would have done so.

Admit it. There's a part of you that wants to believe she called. That she'll say she'd made a mistake. There's a part of you that wants her to say she's still in love with you.

"Okay. Yeah. Yeah, I want all that. I want her," he admitted aloud. "But if this is a trap, I don't *want* to know it. I *need* to know it."

Swallow your pride—that's what this is really all about—and call her.

He fought the battle between his battered heart and clear logic and pride, and pride sank in undisputed defeat. It would have to fend for itself. If he walked into a field of landmines on this, he would need help to get out of it. He wouldn't bring the team in and humiliate himself further by admitting that he lacked the courage to verify it had really been her seeking help from him *before* he ran into the zone. Endangering himself for a glimpse of her was one thing. Endangering the team was another.

Reaching through the dark to the console, he snagged their special phone, hoping he wasn't going to regret this. He hesitated on dialing her, thinking this through. There were three possibilities. She could not answer. She could answer or…

What if her husband answers? What do you do then?

His heart rebelled. Mandy would not give Mr. Wonderful their special phone. But even if she did, Tim would be the last person on earth the man would text for help. No, she wouldn't do it.

Yeah, well, she wouldn't walk out on you either, except she did.

Tired of the mental battle, Tim muttered, "This is nuts." He dialed the phone, returned the call. Whatever the truth turned out to be, he'd deal with it. The last nine months had taught him one thing. If he could handle losing her, he could handle anything.

She answered on the third ring. "Tim." She sounded breathless. "Thank you so much."

Relief and gratitude, he hadn't expected. "For what?"

"You called me back." Her voice sounded thick. She'd been crying. "I—I didn't know if you would—not that I'd blame you, if you didn't."

Tim resisted the urge to stare at the phone. He'd give an eyetooth to be able to see her face right now. This was Mandy and yet it wasn't her. She never skated on anything like this, torn and uncertain, floundering. Mandy knew her mind. Often, she knew her mind *and* his before he did. "You didn't doubt I'd answer your text, Mandy."

"I—I hoped you would answer it."

She really hadn't been sure. And she'd definitely been crying. "So what's this all about?"

"My mother." Mandy's voice cracked. "She's dead, Tim."

"Dead?" He'd liked Liv Dixon. She was quiet, calm, soothing, with a ready laugh and a gentle temperament. "I'm so sorry." Mandy and she were close. Very close. And all they had was each other. "Had she been sick long?" Guilt rammed through his chest. He should have checked on her. Why hadn't he done that?

"She hadn't been sick at all." A hitched sob caused Mandy to stutter. "She didn't just die, Tim. She was murdered."

"Murdered?" His skin crawled. "By who?" The woman was a recluse.

"The police have no leads. It doesn't look promising that they'll ever have any." She let out a sigh, and then went on. "The detective—Walton is his name—says it appears to be the result of a random break in. No one saw or heard anything until a neighbor heard shots fired. She watched but didn't see anyone. The detective says they've exhausted every lead."

"They've got nothing?"

"Nothing."

That explained that. "So you called me to see if I can find anything," he guessed. His fantasies of her wanting him back popped like bubbles and faded away.

"Actually, I didn't. Detective Walton and his team have been through everything with a fine-toothed comb. I'm convinced there's nothing to find or they would have found it."

She wouldn't be easy on them. Not about this. "When did

this happen?"

"Last Thursday—the 16th. We were going to have dinner. I got the groceries and when I got to her house, the police were everywhere. They hadn't known who to call."

From the 16th to the 24th and Walton was already giving up? The first forty-eight hours after a homicide were golden, but come on. Surely there were still things to check out. "If they're pretty much done and you're satisfied they've done a good job, why did you text me tonight that you're in trouble?"

"The funeral was today. I was the only one there." She hissed in a breath. "It really hit me that I—I'm so lost, Tim. And I hurt so deep I can't tell where it even starts. It's like I'm stuck in this dark hallway and there is nothing there. Nothing bad or good—nothing at all. Have you ever felt the total absence of everything? Oh, I hope you haven't. It's horrible. It's . . . desolate and more empty than anything I've ever felt in my life. I try and try, but I can't find my way out of it." She paused, sniffled, then added, "I didn't know a body could hold this much hurt. I—I don't know how to handle this."

All her life, it'd been just Mandy and Liv against the world. Now Liv was gone and Mandy was lost. "I'm sorry. I know grief is hard and mean."

"It's merciless, Tim."

"That, too." He'd grieved when she'd left him. He still grieved losing her. "I wish I could tell you it gets easier, but the truth is, it doesn't. You just get better at coping with it."

"I don't want to cope. I'm angry." The phone crackled from a sharp stifled sob. "I'm so angry I can barely breathe and . . ." Her voice trailed.

He waited, but she didn't go on. "And what?" He nudged her, passed a green pickup, and then eased back into the right lane.

"I'm . . . scared."

That surprised him. She was alone and being alone was scary, but Mandy wouldn't ordinarily admit it. In fact, she'd deny it. Cover fear with belligerence, if needed. It'd take dire circumstances to get her to ever admit fear, and that she had, worried him most of all. That prompted him to dig deeper. "Why are you afraid?"

"He went after Mom and got her. Am I next?"

He? An alarm went off inside Tim. Hers was not a generic fear. She lived alone. Not in the same house as Liv. So why did Mandy fear *he* would come after her in her own house? Only one reason. She didn't directly connect what happened to her mother to a random break-in. She connected Liv's murder to something else. Something specific. "Does he have a reason to come after you?"

Mandy hesitated a long minute. "I—I don't know."

She might not know, but she suspected something. *Gentle. Don't push too hard and scare her off.* "Do you think there might be a reason?"

"Maybe. My mother warned me . . ." She stopped suddenly. "No, this is wrong. I can't tell you this on the phone. I just can't. I know it's asking a lot but could you meet me somewhere?"

If she thought he was letting her hang up, she had another think coming.

Maybe she feared someone was listening . . .

He kept her on the phone and talking all the way to Maddsen, though neither of them said another word about her mother or what might be going on. They talked about her new jewelry designs, her business, a buying trip she'd taken to Italy last spring. About any and everything except what was happening and whether or not she had married Mr. Wonderful.

Tim left the Interstate and ten minutes later found himself parked at her house. "I'm in the driveway, Mandy, at your old house. I drove there automatically. Is that where you live now?"

"Yes, I still live there."

So her husband, if she had one, had moved in with her. A part of Tim deeply resented that. He looked at the pale brick two-story house. The upstairs shuttered windows they'd washed together stood dark, but lights were on in several rooms downstairs. *Bury it. Think steel.* "Is it okay for me to come in?"

"Of course. I'm hanging up now to get the door."

So either Mr. Wonderful didn't care if she'd called Tim, or he wasn't there. Or he was there and he also would be waiting inside.

None of those possibilities appealed.

Tim shut off the engine. *Give me the strength to do this. To live without her and help her. Take away my bitterness. Replace it with compassion.*

Fortified, he opened then shut the Phantom's door, locked it, then headed up the driveway to the sidewalk.

Mandy came running out of the house, wearing gray sweats, her long brown hair flying. She lost one of her fuzzy slippers on the sidewalk and kept running to him.

"Thank you for coming." She slammed against him, wrapped him in a bear hug and held on tight, as if trying to crawl into him. "Thank you, Tim."

The gratitude in her voice ran so deep that it triggered every protective instinct he'd ever had and a few he hadn't known existed inside him. She sounded so fragile and vulnerable; not at all like herself. Mandy was in trouble, all right—and whatever that trouble was, it was really bad. "Of course, I came. I'll always come when you need me."

She burst into tears and uttered between staggered sobs. "You're such a good man."

Tim closed his arms around her and for long minutes, he just stood there and held her while she cried.

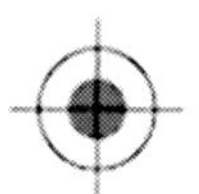

When Mandy had soaked Tim's shoulder and cried herself out, she pulled back, seeming sheepish and surprised by her own emotional outpouring. "Sorry about that," she said, choosing not to ignore it.

"It's been a hard day."

"It has." She lifted a hand toward the front door. "Let's go inside."

He followed her to the landing outside the door, then lightly clasped her arm. "Wait."

She looked back at him and stilled.

He glanced beyond her, at the glass inserted in her front door. "When I walk in with you, is your husband going to be friendly or hostile?" It was a fair question, and reasonably asked.

Mandy swallowed hard. *Truth time.* "Neither reasonable nor hostile," she admitted. This revelation could have him reacting in several ways and she had no idea which way to expect. "I don't have a husband, Tim."

He lowered his lids to shield his reaction to that news. "What happened to Mr. Wonderful? You didn't marry him?"

"I haven't married anyone." Her throat hurt, speaking those words. But if she expected Tim's help, she owed him the truth. She could only hope and pray he wouldn't hate her for it. "Listen, I owe you an explanation, and I promise to give you one, and to answer all your questions that I can answer. But let's do it inside, okay?"

He paused a long moment and studied her. Finally, he said, "All right."

Grateful he'd trust her that much, she turned and walked in, held the door for him to enter behind her, then when he had, she closed and locked it. "Living room or kitchen?"

"Kitchen," he answered, not surprising her.

He'd once told her that in his home growing up, all of the important discussions had taken place in the kitchen. All the important conversations between the two of them had, too. "I can't believe you came. I hope I didn't cause you or the team any trouble."

"You knew I'd come, Mandy. Let's talk straight. We owe each other that."

"I owe you far more." She let him see her regret and the truth in her eyes. "But you owe me nothing. Not after what I did to you."

"Exactly what did you do to me?" he asked, sliding onto a chair in her oversized kitchen. The chair he'd always favored, facing the window. "Other than the obvious."

Breaking his heart. "Tea? I have Earl Grey." His favorite. When he nodded, she filled the kettle then put it on the stove. Water sizzled on the hot burner.

"Are you going to answer me?"

"I am." She stretched and got two cups down out of the cabinet. "But I need to start at the beginning so you understand all I'm saying."

"Do I need backup?" he asked bluntly, borrowing a Mark Taylor method and cutting to the chase.

"No, you don't." She worried her lip. "Not for this."

"Then let me make a call. We can talk afterward."

Mark and the guys were worried and waiting. Mandy nodded.

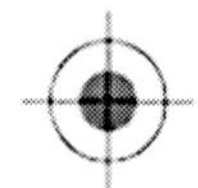

Tim stepped out the back door onto the patio and called Mark. When he answered, he said, "It's me."

"What's going on?"

"I'm not totally sure yet but Mandy's mother's been murdered. A detective named Walton is handling the case, and get this—he's already claiming he's bone-dry and out of leads. Apparently, he's giving up."

"When did it happen?"

"The 16th. The funeral was today." And Mandy had endured it alone. He shook those ravaged images from his mind.

"So is she married, or what?"

"Or what." Tim stared across the lawn to the sandy beach at the water's edge. "Apparently, Mr. Wonderful fared about like me. Dumped before making it to the altar."

"Interesting. Did she say why she dumped him?"

"Not yet."

"Something doesn't pass the smell test here, Tim."

"I know." It didn't with him, either.

"Any clue what it is?"

"Not yet." He frowned on the moonlight. It looked so benign, but light shined in dark places often sent rats scurrying, and he feared that's what their discussion would reveal. Rats. "She says she'll explain. I just wanted to get you guys off the waiting hook before we get into it. It could take a while. She's rattled and upset."

"Not liking the sound of this. I'll get everyone busy on this end, and we'll see what we can find out."

He'd hoped that would be Mark's reaction. It mirrored his own. Every instinct in his body hummed. "Call me—" Tim started.

"Anything we uncover, you'll know it."

"Thanks." Tim ended the call confident that within minutes Mark's media room would look like an operations center. Joe would be working the phones, reaching out to every contact he ever had, a considerable and impressive list. Nick would be at his tricked-out computer, running deep background. Sam at his computer, equally tricked-out but in his areas of expertise, digging deep into everything untouchable through conventional means, and Mark would be setting up the organizational command. Even Lisa would be in action. On the phone with Peggy Crane at Crossroads Crisis Center, activating the Prayer Warriors to put out their own brand of inquiries.

Within half an hour, it'd be all hands on all decks.

Hopefully, nothing Mandy would reveal to Tim in their talks would reveal or create serious complications. Either way, he couldn't stumble in the dark, and whatever this trouble was, one thing was clear: It terrified Mandy.

That worried him. She didn't scare easily and knowing it, he feared what he didn't yet know could be more important than what he did.

He went back inside and, on closing the door, his instincts alerted. The teakettle whined, shrill and full-throated, and there was no sign of Mandy.

Reaching to his back at his waist, he pulled his gun, and methodically began searching the house. Living room. Dining room. *Both clear.* All the downstairs rooms—*clear.* His heart rate kicking up, he took the stairs and began searching the upstairs, sliding, back to wall, from room to room. All three bedrooms, the two baths, the master bedroom—*all clear.*

Confused, he stilled. Was this a trap? Had she departed the fix as soon as he'd stepped outside? Could she do that to him? Would she?

He took the stairs back down to the lower level two at a time, paused, but didn't pick up on a sense of anything malevolent. Relieved by the absence, he headed for the garage to see if her car was inside. If she'd brought him here and then run out on him—he swung open the laundry room door—there was going to be—

She sat huddled in the corner next to the dryer, her arms covering her head, her mobile phone in her hand. Her skin had drained of color. If she'd looked terrified before, it was nothing compared to the way she looked now.

He softly called out to her. "Mandy?"

She looked up at him, wild-eyed and haunted. "You have to go. Now, Tim. Right now."

"Go where?"

"Away!" She clutched at her knees, her voice shrill and urgent. "Run as far as you can run, and don't come back.

Never come back."

"Why?" Obviously, while he'd been outside, she'd received a phone call. But from whom? What would provoke this kind of reaction? He reached for her hand.

She slapped it away. "Will you just listen to me? You have to go now." She let out a keening wail. "Hurry, Tim. Run!"

He stayed put. "Tell me why."

Tears leaked from her eyes, washed down her face. "Because if you don't, he'll kill you."

She feared for him. This upset was for him. He, not she, had been threatened. "Who will kill me?"

"Jackal."

CHAPTER 4

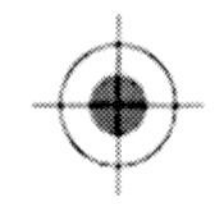

"Jackal?"

"Yes!" Mandy screamed at him. "Run, Tim."

His mind tumbled into dark places. There was a connection between Mandy and Jackal? How? Why? Since when? What did she know about Jackal and NINA?

Tim didn't wait for explanations or bother to ask questions. The threat had come here, to her home. They had to get out of here. Get someplace safe. Then he would find out what this was all about and how she fit into it. "Get up." He hauled Mandy to her feet. "Jackal called you?"

She nodded, and Tim added, "Pack. Fast. Move it, Mandy." He urged her to the stairs and then into her bedroom.

"Where am I going?" She walked in a little circle between the bed and her closet, seeming confused and lost.

He found a purple suitcase in the closet. Dumped it on the bed, and then unsnapped and opened it. "Just pack. Hurry, Mandy." He checked the window through the narrow blinds. The street was ink-dark. Still. Silent. Glancing back at her, he saw she just stood there. "Will you please move it? We can talk after we're away from here."

She didn't move, stared at him as if he'd lost his mind. "We can't outrun him. You need to leave me here and go. It's the only way you'll be safe."

Him. Jackal was a guy. "I'm never safe," Tim admitted. "And I'm not leaving without you."

"You're scared." She tilted her head. "You're never scared. Well, until now." She sounded more shocked by that than anything else. "I've never seen you scared."

"I'm always scared. You don't know the difference," he said, not mincing words. "In my line of work, staying scared is essential to staying alive." He frowned at her. "Will you please move? I'm not asking again. You pack now, or go with nothing." He held up two fingers. "Either way, we depart the fix in two minutes."

She rushed into motion, slinging belongings and cramming her case full. Her nose down, he couldn't read her expression, but he didn't need to see her face or to read anything. Terror didn't begin to describe where she was mentally.

And it infuriated him, seeing her going through it. *Jackal. Even away from her, this was his fault.* Tim snagged his phone from its case at his belt then dialed Mark. "We've got a problem."

"What kind of problem?"

She rushed into the adjoining bath then returned with her arms full of toiletries and a straight metal rod . . . curling iron? It was a curling iron. "While I was talking to you, Mandy got a call threatening my life."

"Mr. Wonderful?" Mark guessed.

"Close." At the window, Tim parted the blinds, checked the street again. *Still empty.* "Jackal."

"You've got to be kidding me." Mark didn't bother trying to hide his shock.

"Do I sound like I'm kidding?" Tim forced a steadiness he didn't feel into his voice.

"Bug out."

"One minute. Mandy's packing." Mark would get that Tim couldn't leave her here. First, they needed information from her. And secondly, Jackal would snatch her then use her to draw out Tim and the team. They didn't know Jackal's identity, but threatening Tim through Mandy made it clear that Jackal knew theirs. Tim's, anyway. But for safety's sake, he and the team had to plan as if the NINA honcho knew them all.

"Mach one, Tim." Mark suggested they move in high gear. "How does she know Jackal?"

"To be determined, but she referenced him as male."

"Report with her ASAP. We need answers."

As soon as possible. He automatically translated the familiar acronym. "My thoughts exactly." There, they had top-notch security and resources—the team—none of which should or could be underestimated, and their community beyond it. Professional and personal.

Tim ended the call. "Let's move," he told Mandy.

She grabbed her purple case. A wad of several somethings hung out between the lid and bottom.

He snatched the case from her, his weapon in his free hand. "Stay close to me. From the time we leave the front door, focus. Run straight to the car. Don't look around, don't slow down. Get to the car as fast as you can, get in, and buckle up."

"Tim, this is a bad idea. I'm poison for you."

Nothing generic in that statement. "Save that to explain later, too." He clasped her arm, took the point position to exit the room, then moved down the steps. Studying the hallway with his senses wide open, he picked up on nothing and went on, cutting through the kitchen, pausing to shut off the stove and moving the whistling kettle off the burner. He visually scanned the locks then made sure everything was turned off, spotting her handbag on the seat of a stool at the bar. "Get your purse."

She reached for the phone and her purse in one swoop.

"Leave your regular mobile here."

"Why?"

"They can locate you through it."

"But the location is turned off."

"Doesn't matter." He slid her a flat look. "Leave it."

She dropped her mobile onto the granite counter. It bounced into the sink.

Just inside the front door, he paused. "Stay here." When she nodded, he slipped out of the house and ran reconnaissance. The night remained as silent as it had appeared from the upstairs window. The wind still, the streetlight casting wide pools of light on the asphalt street. No one was out on the sidewalk. Lights burned inside some of the windows, looking like a typical neighborhood settling in for the night. No strange noises or smells caught his attention, and nothing struck him as alien or out of place.

Satisfied, he moved to his car, parked in her driveway, double-checked the Phantom's frame, found no devices or signs of tampering, then went back to the house's front door and collected Mandy. "Everything seems fine, but remember what I said. Focus. Don't mess around. Get to the car, get in, and shut the door just as fast as you can."

"Understood."

"Ready?" She nodded yes, and he whipped open the front door. Mandy shot past him. He slammed the door shut behind him, and long seconds later they were seated in the locked Phantom. Another half-minute, and they were racing out of the neighborhood and toward the Interstate.

Mandy stared out the windshield, then the side mirror, checking behind them. Her gaze darted non-stop from one to the other.

Until she got out of hyper-alert mode, he'd be wasting his breath seeking answers. So he waited, biding his time. Even though her color was coming back, instead of her usual stoic silence when upset, turning it all inward, she sat curled as small as she could make herself, her teeth chattering. Intermittently, she mumbled something, but he couldn't make out a word of it, and frankly he needed to focus on the road to be sure they weren't being followed. When he did hear her explanations, he innately knew his full attention would be required to catch not only what she said but also what she didn't say.

Jackal? Jackal!

Calling Mandy.

Questions burned in Tim's mind. He started to ask them a half-dozen times but held himself in-check. When they arrived at Mark's would be soon enough. Considering Tim couldn't be objective, one of the other guys should handle questioning her anyway, and it should be first-time questions and answers. Before she started second-guessing every word that came out of her own mouth. They couldn't afford for those filters to kick in, and they always did. Not with Jackal involved.

"Are we safe?" she finally asked, her skin cast in amber from the dash lights.

How did he respond to that? She'd stopped scrunching down in her seat and he couldn't hear her teeth chattering anymore, but he didn't dare do anything to get her started up again. This reaction from her was bizarre. For Mandy? It was beyond bizarre.

She had a low tolerance level for nonsense, and an even lower one for any kind of force being exerted against her. He'd seen that in her shop when she'd encountered an assertive customer. There'd been no need for Tim to step in. She given as good as she gotten.

"Do you think we're safe now?" she persisted, glancing over at him.

"For the moment." It was as honest as he could be at the time. "We aren't being followed." At least, not from the ground. By satellite? Who knew? NINA had the capability.

Seeming a little reassured, Mandy stayed quiet and didn't visibly relax much. It took a few dozen more miles for her to stop darting her gaze. Eventually, she let out a deep shuddery breath. "I know you're eager for answers, but I think we should wait until we get where we're going to talk about all this."

Even if he'd reached the same conclusions, her suggestion had to be for different reasons, and it fired off an alarm in his mind. "Why?"

She worried her lip with her teeth. "Because you're not going to like what I have to say. I'd prefer you not be barreling down the Interstate at ninety miles per hour when you react. Someone could get hurt."

Ominous or practical? "Fine." He passed a red minivan and pulled back into the right lane. "I'll trust your judgment on that." Agreeing came easily. They were on the same page, just in different books. "Just answer one question for me now."

She clasped the door's armrest and squeezed, raising her knuckles. "If I can."

He gave her a second. She could answer. He didn't doubt that. He wasn't so sure if she would. That was his question. "I've pretty much gathered you didn't break our engagement because you met Mr. Wonderful and wanted to marry him."

Mandy didn't react, or utter a word. When he glanced over at her, she lifted her left hand. "I'm listening. I haven't yet heard a question."

He frowned and held it so she wouldn't miss it. "There isn't and never was a Mr. Wonderful, was there?"

Silence.

"That was a question, Mandy."

"I heard it."

"Well are you going to answer it?"

"I am." She took in a steadying breath, exhaled it slowly. "No." She looked him right in the eye. "There isn't and never was a Mr. Wonderful."

She'd lied. She'd broken their engagement and his heart, and she'd lied to him. He expected that had been the case, but hearing it confirmed had an explosion of warring emotions detonating inside him. *Relief. Anger. Frustration. Resentment.*

Disbelief. All that and more flamed and singed the walls of his mind, burned through the chambers of his heart. *Betrayed.*

He grappled with the flood of feelings, isolated them, and one by one tamped them down. *Think steel. Think steel. Think steel.* He repeated the phrase the team used in dire and impossible situations, when the risks were astronomical or the pain so intense it threatened to prohibit them from doing what had to be done for mission success. "Why?"

She swept her hair behind her ear. "I will explain . . . when you're not behind the wheel."

He was a seasoned operative and she knew it. Entrusted with high-level security matters for an entire nation, charged with missions that at times carried one to three-percent survival odds, and vested with enormous powers to make things happen or not happen, and she won't talk because he's driving a car on a half-empty road in the middle of the night? Anger simmered in his stomach. "Are you *that* afraid I'll risk your life?"

"No, Tim, I'm not," she said softly. "I'm that afraid of risking yours."

CHAPTER 5

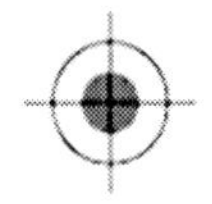

Of course, Tim had no idea what Mandy had meant—she hadn't given him enough information to figure it out. And, of course, that he couldn't figure it out rankled him enough that he seethed for the rest of the ride.

The problem was that he no longer trusted her, and she couldn't blame him for that, so his simmering was uncomfortable for them both but it was also for the best, even though tension pounded off him in waves that rippled through her stomach, leaving it sour and a bitter taste in her mouth. She'd earned it, and she'd endure it.

She had no idea exactly where they were going but accepted that, too. He didn't look receptive to questions or discussions, so she just let the silence between them settle in and hoped he calmed down a little before they got wherever there was.

Half an hour later, when she spotted an exit sign with a familiar name and he signaled he'd be leaving the Interstate, she wasn't surprised. His old military team, now his partners in the security consulting firm, had to be in Seagrove Village, and he was taking her to them.

Comfort and dread warred inside her. They would be best able to help him protect himself, but after breaking her engagement to Tim, she would get anything but a warm reception from any of them—or any of their friends in the village.

The whole bunch would definitely close ranks against her. She couldn't blame them for that. They loved Tim and the fault was solely hers. Yet, angry with her or not, they would do everything humanly possible to keep Tim alive, and that's what most mattered. Of course, she'd have to explain.

That fact had the deepest dread imaginable threatening to smother her. *Humiliation. Degradation. Shame* . . . Revealing secrets she had concealed her entire life. Sweat beaded on her brow and she went clammy all over.

Clasping her hands in her lap, she squeezed them into fists. *Suck it up and endure, Mandy. There's no help for it. Not now. Jackal is back* . . .

A silent fifteen minutes later, she sat in a kitchen chair placed in the center of Mark Taylor's media room, the large screen behind her, and all members of the team—Tim, Joe, Nick, Sam, and Mark—seated in front of her.

She glanced at them from under her lashes. The only non-stone expression was on the face of Lisa Harper, who from all signs was involved in a serious relationship with Mark—not that she was friendly. But at least she stood aside and she wasn't snarling at Mandy.

Nick was. Sam had his baseball cap pulled low on his forehead, its brim shielding his eyes, and his mouth flat, a grim slash above his chin. Joe, who had always been kind and charming, looked like his expression was carved out of rock and, ever since Tim's hushed huddle with Mark near the door, Mark's face looked even harder. If his tone got any colder, the sounds coming from his mouth would frost and freeze before reaching her. Already, his words traveled to her on the Polar Express.

Inwardly, she stiffened and talked herself out of being angry or feeling isolated and alone. *It's not their fault. They're protecting their own. You hurt Tim, and they hate you for it. It's that simple.*

It was. *That simple, and that complex.*

The downside was they were justified. The upside was, if they knew how much more than all of them combined she hated herself, they'd consider their own dispensation of hatred toward her an unnecessary duplication. Wasted emotion.

You can take it, Mandy. Their disdain is cubic zirconia. Yours is diamond. Harder. Deeper and more dense. Far stronger.

She kept talking to herself, preparing for the onslaught. Truthfully, she despised having to talk to herself like this, and she really resented feeling so negatively about herself, but she'd been backed into a corner now and, while she'd tried, she couldn't fight her way out of it alone.

Jackal had to have been watching her all this time. Or had he come back after her mother's death? Her instincts hadn't warned her of a thing out of the ordinary. Not once had she suspected she was being followed or monitored in any way.

Except . . . She had sensed her father at the funeral. Could it have been Jackal she'd sensed there instead? Had there been other signs of her being followed and she'd just missed them? Or maybe Jackal had somehow tapped her secure phone and he'd just waited for her to get weak enough to call Tim so he could locate him?

She had no clue, but oh how she hoped she hadn't led Jackal to Tim and now to the entire team!

Rattled by that most of all, she tugged at the hem of her gray sweat top, refusing to squirm outwardly where they could see it, and just waited. This inquisition was going to be bad. But it wasn't as if she hadn't known that before getting here. Under the circumstances, it couldn't be anything else.

Tim moved to the kitchen bar, filled a glass with water and then gulped it down. When he'd drained it dry, he set the glass on the bar and took a seat next to Joe.

As if waiting for Tim, Mark stood up, moved to her left, then signaled to Nick. He pushed a button on his electronic equipment to start video recording. Her heart sank. So her humiliation would be on record for the duration, and only heaven knew who all would end up seeing it. *Great.*

"Mandy," Mark said. "Would you please state your name, the date and time, and that we have your permission to record your statement."

She shot Tim a hard glance. This would have been difficult enough with him questioning her, but . . . "Madeline Nicole Dixon. You have my permission to record this statement." She'd forgotten the date and time. Before she could add them, Mark did.

"Saturday, October 25th." He paused and checked his watch. "Four twelve A.M." He took two steps toward her. "Last night at your home in Maddsen, you received a phone call. Would you tell us about it?"

"Actually, I received two calls." She had to strive for accuracy. Her credibility was already in trouble and it'd soon be worse. That made it all the more critical her responses were as explicit and as precise as possible. "Tim phoned me first, and then later, while Tim was on his phone with you, Mark, I received a second call from a man who identified himself as Jackal."

"It's the call from Jackal that's of interest to us," Mark said. "What did Jackal say?"

"He threatened me. Said if I told Tim anything, he—meaning Jackal, not Tim—would kill us both." The memory sent an icy chill up her spine.

"Jackal threatened you and Tim, then. Not just Tim."

"Yes."

"How are you connected to Jackal?"

"I don't know that I am connected to him at all."

"But you knew who he was, and you obviously considered

his threat viable." Mark lifted a hand. "If you don't know him, then why do you fear him?"

She could hedge. She glanced at Tim and decided against it. There had been too many secrets between them already, and keeping them buried hadn't spared anyone from anything. Her mother was dead. She'd lost Tim. Now Jackal had made it clear that Tim, she, and all the Shadow Watchers were still at risk. "Because of his exact words."

"Do you recall them?"

She would remember them even in her grave. "If you tell Tim anything, I'll kill you both—just like I killed . . . your mother." Her voice faded. She swallowed trying to force the fear out and some strength back into her tone. "Until that moment, I believed the police--that my mom's murder had happened in a random break-in. That's what they felt certain happened." She risked glancing up at Mark. "Discovering it wasn't . . . shocked me."

"I can see that it would." Mark's expression softened slightly.

Or it seemed to her that it shocked her. She started to add that to her statement but, right now, she couldn't even be sure it was accurate. She did know one thing, and she didn't hesitate to disclose it. "Until that call, I'd never before heard Jackal's voice."

Mark glanced at Tim then back at Mandy. "But you have met him."

How did she answer that? How could she *honestly* answer it? "I don't know. Not to my knowledge." But if not, why would what she did matter so much to him? It didn't make sense. None of it made any sense.

"So you'd never before heard the name Jackal." Mark sounded a little confused. "Yet the man identified himself as Jackal to you? Why would he do that and believe you'd know him?"

"I didn't say that I had never heard his name. I said I'd

never heard his voice. I'm not sure why he'd do anything since I'm not sure who he is, and even if I did know his identity, I still couldn't crawl inside his mind and explain his motives or actions, Mark."

Jackal had expected her to know his name; she recognized that much in his tone. Looking down at her sneakered feet, she swiveled her gaze back to Mark, avoiding Tim for fear of seeing skepticism in his face. She didn't think she could bear being honest about everything and seeing doubt in him. Not in him. She could and would admit the truth, but she couldn't look at him while she did it. That much courage was beyond her; out of reach. "I'd heard his name one time before. Nine months ago."

Tim stiffened.

"Tell me about that."

She cleared her throat, took a drink from the glass of water Lisa passed to her. Mandy's hand shook, nearly sloshing it. "It was the morning I broke my engagement to Tim." *Think steel.* Tim had told her that phrase a thousand times. It worked for him. Maybe it would work for her. *Think steel.* "My mother called me early—it wasn't even dawn yet. She said I needed to come over to her house right away. It was an emergency."

The images from that morning flooded her mind. The fear. The rushing. She'd spilled half a cup of scalding hot coffee on her favorite charcoal skirt. It was heavy enough to keep the scalding liquid from burning her skin, but the skirt was history. So were Mandy's nerves.

Her mother never threw around words like *emergency* and Mandy would have had to be unconscious not to hear the fear in her mother's voice. *Raw. Stark.* Fear in her had been even more rare than the emergency word.

"So you went straight over to your mom's to see what was wrong."

"Yes."

"And what did you find?"

Mandy exhaled a slow, heavy breath. "She was beyond afraid and crying." Wadded tissues had littered the floor near the wastebasket. "She and my father had been in an awful argument."

"I thought your mother lived alone."

"She does—did. My father . . . is Charles Travest." She wished for the thousandth time she'd told Tim about her father long ago. "My mother was his mistress for nearly thirty years. He's an attorney in Jacksonville."

Intercepting a subtle nod from Mark to Nick, she saw Nick out of the corner of her eye take to a computer. Already running a check on her dad, she supposed. "He didn't live with us; he never has. He came to see my mother on Tuesdays. Only on Tuesdays." Her voice cracked. She gave herself a second, and then went on. "He's not something I choose to talk about for obvious reasons. I'm his dirty little secret. Well, me and my mother." Mandy didn't look at any of them. She feared she'd see their condemnation or, worse, their pity. "He acknowledges that he's my father to me and my mother, but his name isn't on my birth certificate or anything else. He's always taken care of us but I've never had a real father-daughter relationship with him. I'm tolerated," she said without heat. "Fondly most of the time, because he truly loves my mother—" At least, Mandy had believed that he did. Now, with him not even showing his face for her mother's funeral, well, Mandy just didn't know much of anything anymore.

Joe interrupted, his voice soft, his tone gentle. "Fondly tolerated, but not loved."

"Yes," she said, hoping they moved on to something else quickly. Before she had too much time to think and be sad and remember just how alone in the world she was now. She'd always felt it was the two of them, her mom and her against the world and they could face anything together. Now she had to accept that her mother hadn't completely stood with her, either. She'd lied to Mandy for years, and obviously lied by omission to her for her whole life. That was a hard, bitter pill to swallow. Resentment welled inside her, made her stomach tumble.

She worked to settle the upset. To be reluctant to judge, which was admittedly harder. There had to be much more she didn't know than the little she did.

"I'm sorry, Mandy," Mark said.

His regret sounded genuine. Stiffening against it—she couldn't afford any more weakness—she sniffed. "Thanks. But we don't choose our family, do we? It is what it is, and what it is must be accepted."

"I hear that," Joe interjected, adding a heartfelt headshake.

A memory of Joe flashed through Mandy's mind. Him once warning Sam to back off in commenting on Joe's family. *Yeah, they're all thugs, thieves and outlaws, but they're my thugs, thieves and outlaws. Remember that, bro.* She shifted on her seat. With his family, Joe surely understood her uncomfortable predicament.

She didn't look at Tim to see how he'd taken her revelation.

"So what you're saying is you think your father is Jackal?" Sam asked, tired of waiting for her to get around to voicing her suspicions straight out.

"No, actually I don't." Mandy swiveled to look at Sam, feeling tight and wound up and a shade shy of panic. While she'd prefer to avoid the subject of her father altogether, she wasn't foolish enough to believe she could do it here. Not with Tim's team, and not now. Yet, the last thing she needed was for anyone to ask questions that upset her father's nice little life. These men could definitely create havoc for him.

Be honest, at least with yourself, Mandy.

Okay. I don't think he's Jackal, but I don't know if he is or isn't. Mom had him and me. I'm not Jackal. Who else is there? And—oh, this sounded lame even to her-- *what I have with him isn't much, but he is all the family I've got left. I don't want to lose him, too.*

Logical. Reasonable. But honestly, she'd never really had him so she couldn't lose him. Still her mother would be devastated if after all this time Mandy created problems for him in his other life.

"Mandy?" Tim nudged her, wanting more of an explanation.

"Sorry." Because she owed him one, she took in a steadying breath, then answered. "There wasn't what I considered a viable alternative, so I did wonder if my father could be Jackal, but it just didn't fit." She sat forward, braced her arms on her knees. "Mom was so upset that morning because she'd been paid a visit by *Jackal*. That's what she called him. If he and my father were one and the same, she'd have said, *your dad*, but she didn't. She said Jackal. So he has to be someone else."

"Your mother and Jackal met?" Tim flattened his feet on the floor. "She knew him?"

"Apparently, she did. Though I never saw him, and she'd never before spoken of him. I've wracked my brain trying to figure out how she'd known him or who he could be, but you know how she was, Tim. She didn't go much of anywhere or interact with anyone else." She glanced at Lisa. "Mom was one step shy of being a recluse. I think maybe she suffered from that fear of leaving her house."

"Agoraphobia?" Lisa asked.

Mandy nodded.

"Sounds possible if she lived as isolated as you believe."

Looking back to Mark, Mandy added, "Frankly, I don't know what I can believe anymore, and I have no idea who Jackal could be."

Clearly disappointed by that disclosure, Mark asked, "What did he want from her?"

"She said he was livid about my engagement to a spy—his words, not hers or mine—and he gave me until noon to break the engagement. If I refused . . . " Mandy couldn't say it. The words *would not* come out of her mouth.

"He'd kill you or your mother?" Mark suggested.

Mandy stared down at her hands, laced in her lap, and gave

him a negative nod.

"He'd kill me?" Tim speculated.

Mandy shot her gaze to him. "Not just you." Her chin quivered. "All of you."

"The whole team?" Mark asked, his voice incredulous.

She nodded. "And your families. He named you all, one by one."

That caused a stir.

Mark lifted his hand, silenced everyone. "So you concocted the story about meeting another man and falling in love with him and broke your engagement to Tim to protect us."

Again, she nodded. "I was afraid you'd go after Jackal and he'd kill all of you." She licked at her parched lips. "If by some miracle either Tim or I lived, that would destroy us. You. Your families." She shook. "I didn't want to lie, but what else could I do? I couldn't endanger you like that."

"Why not?" Nick asked, his disbelief evident in his deep, dark tone.

"Excuse me?" She didn't track his line of thought or his skepticism.

"Tim, I get. But why would you care if Jackal killed us?" Nick's shoulders lifted and fell. "You don't know us that well, so why would you care?"

He had to be kidding. He didn't look like he was, but he had to be . . . didn't he? She looked to Tim, who shielded his thoughts. So did all the others.

They all wanted to hear her reasons. What was the matter with them? Humanity 101 covered it sufficiently, but evidently not for them. Infuriated enough to not bother to try to hide it, she glared at them. "Right now I'm half-wondering myself. But at the time, I had two reasons." Lisa gave her a supportive nod and, encouraged, Mandy went on. "One, you're human beings and I think you're more than capable of getting yourselves killed without any added help from me."

That stunned them silent, and she half-wished she'd kept

her temper in check.

"She's got a point on that one." Finally, Joe backed her up, an amused twinkle lighting his eyes. "What's the second reason, Mandy?"

She looked directly at Joe and let him see her sincerity. "Tim loves you—all of you and your families."

The men looked at Tim. "Don't get big heads," he told them. "I love puppies, and chocolate chip cookies, too."

"Yeah." Sam whacked Tim on the shoulder. "You help old ladies cross streets, too. You're just a boy scout with a big heart, bud."

"Careful, Sam. I know where your skeletons are buried."

"We all know where all our skeletons are buried." Sam grunted. "I gotta say, Tim, that's one weak and pitiful attempt at a threat, buddy. You need some lessons from Nick."

"Don't drag me into this—and, for the record, I keep all my skeletons in tombs where nice bare bones belong."

"Not all of 'em." When Nick glared at Sam, he snorted, then looked back to Mandy. "Okay, enough. Let's get back to business. We need to look at this a little differently now."

"Now that you don't hate me anymore?" She dared to hope but doubted anyone would be that forgiving.

"We didn't hate you," Sam said, not missing a beat. "We just didn't like you anymore. You can't spit out Tim and expect us to like you, Mandy. It ain't natural."

"True," she said. Did that mean they did like her now that they knew she'd forfeited her future partly for them and wholly for Tim? "That's fair."

Lisa passed her a small bowl of nuts and whispered. "They like you again or they wouldn't be needling each other. Now they've got to figure out if they can trust you."

Mandy glanced up. Lisa was speaking in earnest, helping her. "Thanks."

Mark dragged a hand through his hair. "Can we get back to the matter at hand?"

"I was going there, bud." Sam lifted an impatient hand. "So, Mandy, you'd never met Jackal or even ever heard of him, but through your mom, he tells you that unless you ditch Tim, he's going to kill all of us *and* you and your mom, so you made up a lie and ditched Tim. You bailed to protect us all. Is that right?"

"That's pretty much it," she admitted.

Sam shoved his cap back, his tone decidedly skeptical. "So why did you believe him? I mean, these were threats coming from a stranger? Why didn't you tell Tim and see what he said? Or even run it by us?"

"I suggested doing exactly that—to my mother," Mandy told Sam, remembering her mother's reaction. She'd been in a full-fledged revolt about that. A cold shiver crept up Mandy's spine. "She said if I did, we'd both be dead within minutes of talking to him or any of you. Then, you'd never know anything about Jackal, much less what he knew about you."

"Was that her fear talking, or did she really believe it."

"No doubt, Sam. She believed it." Mandy paused to sip at her water. Her mouth felt dust-dry. "After seeing her reaction, I believed it, too. I've never seen my mother like that. She was scared to death." Placing the glass back on a little table Lisa had positioned near her elbow, Mandy added, "She came up with the *other man* story. It seemed like the right thing to do for everyone's sake." It'd devastated Tim and her, but at least they'd stayed alive to be devastated. Her mother had too until now. "Mom felt strongly 'another man' was the one story that would keep Tim from asking a lot of questions. I agreed." Losing out to another man. Men found that hard to stomach and discussed it as little as possible.

"In a situation like this, the fewer questions, the better," Mark said. "Logical."

Mark seemed to totally grasp their situation. Could he really understand? "Under the circumstances, I considered being asked no questions vitally important. I wanted Tim distant from me."

"No, you didn't. You wanted him safe," Lisa corrected her.

"Yes." Mandy wouldn't apologize for that. She'd done nothing any of them in a similar situation wouldn't do. Protect loved ones. Of course, they would. Well, maybe not in the same way, but they'd protect them.

"I have a couple questions." Joe rubbed at his neck. "The call last night. The voice. Did you sense even a hint of recognition?"

"None. I don't think I've ever before heard it, which is another reason I don't think Charles Travest is Jackal. I'd know my own father's voice."

"Maybe. Maybe not, especially if he didn't want you to. Mechanical alterations are easily assessable and commonly used." Tim looked at her down the slope of his nose, his eyes shielding his thoughts. "Let's go back to the conversation at your mother's nine months ago. Was your father in on the Jackal discussion with your mother and you?"

A little baffled, Mandy admitted the truth. "No."

"Why not?" Nick pushed. "Surely your mother told him about it."

"I—I don't know if she told him or not." Mandy thought about it, then added, "I doubt she did. It would have been reasonable to go to him, of course. He's a very successful criminal attorney. But my mother never bothered him with anything, so I doubt she told him."

"Bothered him?" Joe sounded perplexed. "But you're his daughter."

Heat rose to Mandy's face. "He didn't get involved in minutiae."

"Minutiae? A man's daughter's life being threatened isn't minutiae, Mandy."

She spared Tim a glance, kept the heat out of her voice. "When it's *this* daughter, it is to him."

Nick tapped his black-framed glasses on his nose. "Was he

like that with your mother, too?"

"I think not," she admitted, fighting against falling to the old fear that something was wrong with her. That he didn't love her because he couldn't. He'd measured her worth and she'd somehow fallen short. "He seemed very loving with her. At times, even doting." Mandy let the pain of admitting that out loud subside. "At least, that's the way it always seemed to me. But who knows what really goes on between two people? Especially considering their special circumstances."

"Loving. Doting. But he couldn't be bothered when his daughter's life was threatened?" Until that moment, Tim had seemed more surprised than angry. Now, he looked outraged. Suddenly, he stilled and his expression turned dark and dangerous. "Wait. I understand now."

"What?" Sam asked.

"He's married." Tim frowned. "Charles Travest is married to someone else."

Shame flooded her. Mandy nodded, unable to meet his eyes. "Yes."

"Oh, no. How long have you known?" Lisa asked, her voice gentle.

"I wondered most of my life, but I didn't dare ask," Mandy said. "Then, when I was seventeen, I didn't have to ask."

"What happened?" Joe asked, his voice tender.

"I went to St. Augustine. I like to visit the fort—the Castillo de San Marcos—down in the historical district. It inspires me. You know, in my jewelry designs."

"You designed even then?" Mark asked.

"I don't remember a time when I didn't design." The memory of that day had her eyes stinging. "I came out of the fort, stepped onto the street, and there he was."

"What did he say?" Tim asked, clearly trying to get a grip on this.

"Nothing." Her breath hitched. "He passed right by me." She forced herself to go on, to speak aloud words she'd only allowed herself to speak once, later that same day when she had asked her mother for the truth about him.

"He didn't say anything at all?" Nick asked.

"No." And how that had hurt. "He stared through me as if I were a total stranger."

Mandy paused, took in a deep breath, hoping when she exhaled, the pain of that day would be expelled with the spent air. "His wife was with him." Mandy squeezed her eyes closed. "So were their children." Her half-brother and sister—people she didn't know who certainly didn't know she existed. "I didn't know for fact who they were then."

A knot lodged squarely in Mandy's throat. She swallowed it down, forced herself to express what she'd buried deep inside herself a long time ago. "I went home and did some research. Their son and daughter are close to my age. He's a year older. She's a year younger." And on the street, her father had looked at them the way she'd hoped and prayed that just once he'd look at her, but he never had: with love.

"Whoa. That had to be rough, and you were just a kid." Nick let out an exaggerated sigh. "I bet he'd want to know if they'd been threatened."

"Nick." Tim shot him a warning.

"What? Facts are facts, and I do bet it," Nick said. "Mandy deserved better than she got from him."

"Dang straight, bud." Sam snorted. "Sorry sack of . . . peppers."

Odd saying, but the others found it amusing, not that they'd laughed out loud or anything. But their defending her, being outraged on her behalf touched Mandy's heart. It felt squeezed. "Thanks. I wish I could say I never considered what his response would be if it had been one of them threatened, but it'd be a lie. I have."

"That's cold, looking right through you like that." Sam swept off his cap and shook his head, sent his riot of red curls swinging. "Jackal or not, I vote we give the man an attitude adjustment." He jammed the cap back onto his head and tugged the brim low, shading his eyes.

"No!" Mandy forced herself to calm down. "No, but thank you. Don't waste your time. He's not worth it."

"He's your father." Mark slid a look at Lisa. "He should man up, right?"

"He should," Tim said. "But if he didn't man up for Liv and attend her funeral, he's not going to man up on anything."

Nick frowned. "A little gentle persuasion could show him the error of his ways."

The Alabama redneck stood ready to rock and roll. "Works for me," Sam said.

Lisa stroked Mark's face. "He should man up, but let's all leave it to Mandy to decide how she wants to deal with Charles Travest or to not deal with him. He is her father. She knows what she wants or needs or expects from him, and what he's capable of giving her. We should trust her and accept whatever decisions she makes."

"I still want to smack him around, but all right." Sam gave in. "Anytime you want his clock cleaned, Mandy, you just say the word."

Moved, Mandy nodded. "Thank you, Sam."

"Fine. But count me in on the clock cleaning." Nick closed the laptop. "Accountability is warranted."

Tim's jaw tightened. "I don't like it. Sorry," he said sliding a glance at Lisa. "It's reasonable, but you can't deal rationally with irrational people. It won't work. Men like him understand one thing. Power through strength. We need to take him down." Tim glanced at the guys, clearly avoiding Mandy, then back at Lisa. "Yet, there's merit in respecting Mandy's decisions. I agree with that. So I'll bow to her wishes. Reluctantly." He shifted his gaze to Mandy. "But if he makes one more step toward you, we do this my way. I won't have him treating you like this, Mandy. It's unacceptable."

After all they'd been through, and all she'd done, that Tim

stood ready to defend her awakened strange, new emotions in her. It was so far outside her realm of experience. She'd never had a man as her protector. None had considered she needed one or that she might want one. And she had. Desperately, because it proved she was worthy of protection. She'd adjusted, true, and lived without it, but also without feeling worthy.

Now she had not only Tim but his team, which spoke to their feelings for her but even more about their feelings for Tim. "Thank you, Tim. All of you. I—I'm grateful." More at ease now that the tone of this interrogation had shifted, she continued. "Back then, I decided to let him live. I'll stick with that now—unless we find out he's Jackal, which I really don't think he is." She sipped from her water, then returned it to the table. "It hurt then. But I've adjusted. I don't need him."

"No, you don't. But you wanted him," Joe said. "He's your father. He was supposed to be your first hero."

Tender, she smiled. "Tim was my first hero."

He met her gaze, held it.

Nick sniffed. "So Travest didn't say anything to you, but did you say anything to him? On the street in St. Augustine or afterward, I mean."

"Not then, no." The shock and pain had been too intense. It'd overtaken everything else. The crowd, the noise, the traffic—it all had faded away. Nothing she could say now could begin to explain how she'd felt then. *Betrayed. Hurt. Heartbroken. Abandoned. Rejected. And guilty. So very guilty.*

"What about later?" Nick persisted.

"I rarely spoke to him after that. Never, if I could avoid it without being rude."

"How'd he take that?" Sam asked.

She shrugged. "To tell you the truth, I'm not sure he noticed."

"How the spit could he not notice?"

"Getting loud there, Sam." Tim shot him a warning.

Joe stepped in. "So you went home, did some research on

him and his family, then asked your mother about him, and she told you the truth."

Mandy nodded, blinked hard but couldn't stop the fall of silent tears spilling down her face. "She said that, until I was born, she hadn't known he was married or that he had children. They had often talked of marriage. Then I was born and . . . she realized . . . She thought he'd marry her, but of course he didn't. He couldn't. She told him to get out and stay away from us. But over time, he somehow convinced her he would marry her if he could, but he was stuck."

"Stuck." Lisa grunted. "I hear that a lot—at the crisis center."

"Yeah, well. He didn't look stuck on the street that day."

"How did he look?" Nick asked.

She looked him right in the eye. "Happy."

"His kids, too, I'll bet."

"The two that he parents, yes. They looked very happy. I was a wreck."

Sam swiveled his hat around so the brim rested on his neck. "Man, we have got to do something about this. It ain't right."

"We don't, but thanks, Sam. It's never been right." Mandy shook off the weight of the whole sordid mess. "The bottom line is it doesn't matter. My mother knew the truth and she didn't leave him." Mandy had so many issues with that. It had remained a bone of contention between them and especially one between her and her father. How could he do that to either woman? Especially women he supposedly loved? Well, he had loved her mother, and he must have loved his wife or he never would have married her. Mandy tried but she just didn't understand it. She didn't understand him, and she'd stopped wanting to understand him a long time ago.

"I'm sorry, Mandy."

She looked at Tim and saw the pain she felt reflected in his eyes. "I am, too. I should have told you, but all this is such a hard thing to admit." Not honest. She tried again. "I was ashamed."

"Ashamed?" Sam elevated his voice. "Why? You didn't do anything."

"Take it down a notch, bro." Joe frowned at Sam. "The situation embarrassed her. What her father was doing. Her mom staying. Both of them lying to her." Joe glanced at her. "I totally get it, Mandy."

She was developing a real appreciation for Joe. Tim said he had a special way with women, and he certainly seemed to, she had to admit. "Who wouldn't be ashamed?"

"We all get it, except for the lump." Nick told her, hooking a thumb toward Sam. "It's a bad situation, and you were the one stuck." He set the laptop aside and dipped his chin to his chest. "They made the choices. You got the consequences."

"If Jackal did kill my mother, then I'd say she suffered consequences, too, Nick."

"But Charles Travest didn't." Nick said.

Tim and Mark exchanged a look Mandy didn't understand so she ignored it. "He never suffers consequences," she said, and then told them what little else she knew of him. Hearing herself, she realized it was pitifully little. Why hadn't she noticed that before now? Had her anger at him since St. Augustine blinded her to everything involving him? She had attempted to blot him out of her life in every possible way. Civil when unavoidable, but always distant. Different planets would have been close enough for her liking. If not for her mother, Mandy would never have spoken to him again. She had avoided him, except for command appearances. Had he noticed the difference in before and after St. Augustine? If so, he'd given her no sign of it. And that might hurt most of all.

The questioning continued, back and forth and on and on, until everyone felt they had a firm grip on the whole situation and Mandy had laid her soul bare for them to pick over her proverbial bones. Yet, as strange as it seemed, emptying the skeletons from her closet hadn't been as awful as she'd feared it would be or imagined it could be. And now that it was done, the absence of the secrets she'd harbored for so long about her father . . . That heavy burden finally had been lifted. She felt more relieved than violated.

Sam claimed the floor and looked at Mark. "So what now, bud?"

"You and Nick run deep background on Charles Travest and on his wife and kids. If they're grown and found out about Mandy and Olivia . . ."

"Got it." Nick's dark expression turned even grimmer. "Any are possible suspects."

"Yeah, they are. And them aside, there's Jackal and his threat." Sam tugged at his cap, focusing on Mark. "You know they're going to come after us."

They? Who did he mean? Mandy couldn't imagine. "I doubt the Travest family has a clue about me or my mother, Sam. But Jackal . . . I have no idea. If he hasn't bothered you in the last nine months, maybe if I disappear, he will leave you all alone again," Mandy said, praying she hadn't put them all in greater danger by telling them what she knew. "I don't know who he is or why the idea of Tim and I as a couple freaks him out." If Tim knew, he would have said something by now.

"He won't leave us alone," Tim told her.

"He's right," Nick added. "That isn't going to happen."

Before he could add more, Mark looked at Tim. "You thinking what I'm thinking?"

Tim nodded that he was. "We need to force him to come to us."

"My thoughts, exactly," Joe added. "The question is how?"

Tim held up a wait-a-second finger then looked at Mandy. "I'd prefer to talk to you privately about this, but with the situation being what it is, there isn't a snowball's chance of that happening."

"Say whatever you like." After everything she'd disclosed, what could he possibly ask that would hold a candle to that humiliation? Anything else had to be uphill from where she'd been with this group.

He worried his lip a long second, then forced himself to meet her gaze. "Do you love me, Mandy? I mean, still. Right now." He stammered and sputtered, his expression changing to show his disgust with himself, then he asked her again. "Do you love me now?"

Nothing but honesty. Not ever again. "More than anything."

Pent up tension melted from his face. "And you're still in love with me, too, right?"

"Definitely," she confessed. "Since the first time I saw you."

He smiled and pivoted his gaze to Mark. "Then we've got a plan."

"What plan?" Sam asked. "I didn't hear a plan."

She hadn't heard a plan either.

Joe rolled his gaze. "Are you dead from the neck up, or what?"

Baffled, Sam lifted his hands, palms up. "What?"

Mandy was just as confused.

"And we put our lives in your hands." Joe squeezed his eyes shut, as if praying for patience.

Sam took offense. "Yeah, you do—and I've saved 'em more than once. And I still ain't heard no plan."

"Come on, Sam. She's still in love with him." Joe lifted a hand, swung it between her and Tim. "Jackal doesn't want them married. We want Jackal here, so . . ."

Sam's face flushed. "I know you ain't saying—"

"I am," Tim interjected. "A wedding."

Tim wanted to *marry* her? Mandy's heart started a hard, skidding beat. Skipped like a well thrown rock on water.

"That should get Jackal here." Joe mulled over the possibility.

Nick agreed. "And probably an army of his cohorts with him."

"Jackal has an army?" Mandy asked. Who was this guy? That, her mother hadn't told her. Mandy had tried everything, but her mother had flatly refused to discuss it, and she'd stuck to her silence. "What army?"

"NINA," Tim said.

Another man with another woman? "Who is Nina?"

"NINA isn't a she. It's an organization." Tim lifted a hand. "I'll explain later. For now, it's enough to say they're terrorists, really bad and powerful, and they want us all dead."

Her mother knew people like that? *Terrorists?* Mandy couldn't believe it. But Tim did, and he wouldn't lie to her. He must have good reasons for thinking Jackal belonged to this NINA group.

Mandy forced herself to still, to let the shock wear thin, knowing it'd be with her a long time, then asked Tim, "If they're so powerful and they want you dead, then why haven't they killed you?" She shrugged. "Not wishing it on you, but if they threatened me to get to you, then clearly they know where you are. So why drag my mother and me into it. Why not just kill all of you?"

"They've tried twice in the last year," Tim told her.

Sam and Nick nodded, backing Tim up on that, and Lisa added, "That's right. They came close both times, too."

"Lisa, don't."

"Well, it's the truth, Mark. Don't what? I was there. I saw it."

"You were neck-deep in it not a bystander, and almost losing you still knocks me to my knees," he corrected her. "We need to be on our toes—all of us. So let's focus on now, okay?"

Mandy heard a cease and desist order in that statement. "Well, obviously they failed. You are all still here." She pulled at her memory, recalling what she knew of Lisa's abduction and that whole human-trafficking mess. She focused on Mark. "You think Jackal went after my mother to get to you? You think he killed her because he figured out she had insisted on the breakup between Tim and me. But why would he do that? He wanted us apart."

"Did he? We can't prove that. I hope he didn't kill your mother."

Joe lifted a finger. "He said he did, in the phone call."

Nick agreed. "Historically, when NINA claims responsibility, it's responsible."

"But historically, that's on mass cases involving innocent civilians," Tim reminded Nick. "This case is personal to us. We don't have a history to guide us. So did Jackal really do what he said? Did he kill Liv?" Tim lifted his hands. "We don't know."

"Tim's right," Mark interjected. "Jackal could have been manipulating her to get to us. Whether he wanted Tim and Mandy together or apart is debatable." Mark looked at Mandy. "People often say or do the opposite of what they mean. It is possible Jackal wanted you two apart, or he didn't like what your mother did to bring about the split."

"You think he might have objected to the way she did it, even though he got what he wanted?" Mandy tried to wrap her mind around this. When Mark nodded, Mandy asked, "Why would he wait nine months to come after her, then?"

"Astute question." Mark nodded.

"Simple answer," Tim told her. "NINA is notorious for its regimented actions. It demands obedience. If you're with them or against them, you do what it says, when it says, the way it says or you pay the consequences—and they're always steep."

So Jackal had interjected himself into her mother's life to get to Tim and Mandy. He took exception to how she and her mother had handled the breakup. "Okay, but if Jackal is NINA—"

"It is," Tim told her.

No doubt there. "Accepted. If NINA tried and failed twice recently to get you guys, would they really try again so soon through Jackal?"

"They would." Mark answered her.

"Dang straight."

Nick frowned at Sam. "Think pepper tea."

"They definitely would," Sam quickly amended.

Tim explained. "The failed attempts cost them a fortune in business. Their criminal activity funds their political objectives, so they've been off licking their wounds, waiting for things to cool off a little before their next strike. We all knew there would be a next strike. With NINA, there's always a next strike. They might be patient for a couple months before striking again, but they never give up or forget people who've disrupted their business and cost them money."

"I see." Her worst fears confirmed. "They've got you in a holding pattern, then I call Tim and they turn on the attack spigot again." Boy, did she see. With that one phone call, she'd put all of them in lethal jeopardy—again. Guilt slammed through her, and her heart sank. "I'm so sorry. If I hadn't called—"

"No, Mandy," Tim said. "It's not your fault. NINA would attack us again anyway."

"Not if they couldn't find you. My phone call could have been just the break they needed to pinpoint your location." She'd be shivering in her bed for a month. *Mom, what were you thinking? Getting involved with people like that and trying to face them on your own? How were you involved with them? Was it because of Tim and me? Or was it because of Charles Travest?*

Oh, how Mandy wished she could answer those questions. But she couldn't; she had no idea. Not the first clue.

"So what do you consider our odds?" Tim asked Mark. "They wanted our wedding stopped enough to threaten. Does it follow that they'll try to stop our wedding from taking place?"

That was what he'd meant? Mandy's heart nose-dived. "You want to use a wedding between us as bait for terrorists?"

Joe sighed and sent Tim a flat look. "Bad delivery, bro."

"I see that it is." Tim agreed.

Lisa touched Mark's shirtsleeve. "Shall I call Nora and Annie to plan the wedding?"

"Not just yet. It's barely six in the morning."

"Of course."

Mandy just stared at them, all engaged in different conversations.

"We'll only do this if you agree, Mandy." Tim assured her, speaking over the rest.

The others fell silent.

Tim continued. "Before you decide, you should be aware that we know nothing about Jackal except his name. Until you told us, we weren't certain if he was male or female. We still can't identify him. But he can identify us, so he has a huge advantage. If we know when and where to expect him, then we increase our chances of getting him before he gets us. It's safest for us all."

Safety for the team and their families was a masterful touch. True, and a masterful touch, and from Joe's easing expression, he agreed.

"I see the wisdom of it," Mandy told Tim. Give Jackal what he doesn't want to flush him out. "The wedding plan has merit."

Of course, it had merit. But what did a wedding mean to them on a personal level? Would it be real or fake? It could be real. Tim had asked if she still loved him, though he hadn't said if he still loved her.

Still, he didn't need for her to love him or to be in love with him for a fake wedding. Well, not unless he thought it was essential to the success of the mission. Then, he might. Bottom line, she didn't know what to make of this for them.

Mark lifted the phone, and Lisa stopped him. "Who are you calling at six in the morning?"

"Crossroads. We need a meeting with Jeff Meyers and Peggy, Nora and Annie."

Mandy looked at Tim. "Who are all these people?" More and more being called into this circle. That made her nervous.

"Jeff's law enforcement. Successful working with us against NINA in the past. Peggy runs the crisis center. Annie is Lisa's mom, and Nora mothers everyone in the village. The two—Annie and Nora—are the local wedding planners."

Tim's slotting them jarred Mandy's memory. He had talked about Annie being attacked during Lisa's ordeal. And Nora was elderly and nearly blind. "They work together now?" A wedding. Mandy was going to marry Tim. Real or faked, it'd be a memory she'd treasure the rest of her life—for however long she had a life.

A wedding. *Her* wedding. And no one who knew her would attend. Not her mother, her father, not a friend, not even an employee from the store.

You've lived your life nearly alone. You can do this alone.

She could. But she didn't want to do it. She wanted someone . . . There was no one, and she had to just accept it. She and Tim would be there. That most mattered.

He'd be present, but would he really be there? What about after the real or fake wedding? What about the marriage? Would he really be there then?

A real or fake wedding followed by a real or fake marriage that could be just an essential pretense required for their pursuit of NINA and Jackal.

This was *not* the kind of wedding and marriage women dream about all their lives.

The questions about her life and future ran through her mind and made her uneasy, but those thoughts tumbled and churned and raised another question, and it haunted her. If, as Tim and his team hoped, Jackal showed up at the wedding, would either of them—*any of them*—survive long enough for the wedding or the marriage to be either real or faked?

That she didn't know the answer worried her most of all.

CHAPTER 6

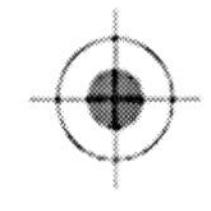

Henry, the actor known to NINA as Jackal, sat on a park bench facing the ocean and tossed bits of bread to the seagulls. "You called this meeting, Johnson." The real Jackal was no doubt close by and, while not wired to communicate, Henry had no doubt the bench upon which he sat was bugged so that he wouldn't miss a word. Jackal would never admit to bugging him, of course, but Henry knew the man's ways, having taken on this role for him multiple times before. Jackal left as little as possible to chance, and went to extreme lengths to protect his true identity. Dealing with NINA required it, if one wanted to live. "What do you want?"

That Paul Johnson was in Jacksonville at all irritated. It was an unnecessary risk. Why had NINA taken it? True, few would recognize the ex-convict who once had been the personal assistant to Gregory Chessman, a senior-level NINA operative now in prison, and Johnson had been highly trusted in the upper echelon of the NINA chain of command. But why chance using him now? Since his release, Homeland

Security and half a dozen other agencies had to be tracking his every move.

Henry needed to relax. Anyone who might recognize Johnson wouldn't recognize the man on the bench beside him, though the two meeting could arouse curiosity and result in a probe of his own identity. He didn't much like that, but precautions to protect himself had been taken. Any investigation would lead to nothing but dead-ends. Good money was being paid to others to see to it, and to take on those risks for him. Still, at least from what he'd been told about operations, the breach of protocol wasn't warranted.

NINA never breached protocol unwarranted.

That concerned him.

"Actually, Phoenix called for the meeting. I'm working for him now." On the other end of the bench, Johnson let his gaze sweep the water.

"Doing what? I'd think for any of his activities he'd need more anonymity than you can provide."

He swept his gaze. "Whatever he asks." Johnson shrugged. "You know how it is."

Actually, he didn't. Not firsthand, and Henry intended to keep it that way. Keeping his thoughts to himself, he waited for Johnson to get on with the reason for the meeting. He didn't seem in any hurry, though only a fool wouldn't realize he was monitoring everything going on around him.

Fortunately, this early in the morning, that wasn't much. Dawn was just breaking. The beach stood deserted, aside from a few early-bird walkers out strolling. The seaside park remained still and quiet; not yet fully awake, which made it perfect for his purposes. Later today, thanks to unseasonably high temperatures for October, it'd been teeming with children and adults in swimsuits, crossing the path to and from the ocean. "You haven't yet explained why Phoenix sent you here. What's so important it couldn't be covered in a phone call?"

"Phoenix does things the way he wants to do them."

"I know that, and I'm not questioning his judgment." He didn't dare. That was a sure-fire way to wake up dead. "Has something happened?"

Johnson nodded. "Tim Branson took Mandy to Seagrove Village last night." The left side of Johnson's face twitched. "Phoenix wants to know if you plan to interdict."

Grateful that topic had been anticipated, Henry inhaled deeply, relishing the salty tang heavy in the air. He'd been warned long ago by his NINA recruiter that, regardless of how high-level one happened to be, being caught unaware was a red flag rewarded with a death sentence. The organization tolerated no errors, accepted no excuses, granted no second chances, and left no loose ends. "Not at this time. I'm just observing." He spared Johnson a look laced with condescension. "Since you were directly involved, you know the Shadow Watchers have interfaced with NINA three times in the past year—I know, they consider only two clashes but we know it has been three—and three times, they have destroyed lucrative operations that will take NINA years to rebuild."

"I'm aware of that, yes." Johnson's jaw snapped tight. "As you pointed out, I was directly involved in segments of all three failed missions. My segments were successful or I wouldn't be sitting here."

"True, but segments of success is not success. Three expensive failures are more than enough. I don't want the Shadow Watchers interfacing on future operations, causing more failures. For that reason, observation alone seems prudent . . . for now."

"Additional complications were Phoenix's concern as well. Since Mandy is involved, he wanted your personal assurance."

"He has it." That woman had been a thorn in his side since her first breath. "For now, we're staying away from their forsaken village. Let them congregate. Our organization and its current operations should be insulated." This all could have been discussed on the phone. That it hadn't been and Phoenix had flown Johnson in from Europe to ask these questions personally, warned that he had not yet revealed the real reason for this personal visit. "Is there anything else?" The sun was getting brighter now—dawn quickly fading to morning. He glanced up and squinted. Only traces of pink left in the sky.

"Just one thing." Johnson retrieved his sunglasses, put them on, and then tapped them higher on the bridge of his nose. "How much does Mandy Dixon know?"

"About?"

"Us."

Ah, there it was, the real reason for the visit. "Next to nothing, we think. We intercepted the phone call between her and her mother. Olivia intended to disclose everything to Mandy during dinner. Of course, we took swift action and prevented that meal and any disclosure from ever taking place."

"How did you do that? Exactly?" Johnson probed, clearly already knowing the answer.

Phoenix had been closely monitoring. If he knew Mandy was in Seagrove Village with the Shadow Watchers, then he knew Olivia was dead. "We silenced her," he said, noting Johnson didn't flinch. He showed no emotion. Oh, yeah. He and Phoenix knew exactly what had happened. Still, Henry continued so that the real Jackal couldn't be accused of withholding information. "By the time Mandy showed up at Olivia's house, the police were on-scene and the investigation was underway. They have no leads, of course. For practical purposes, the investigation has already wound down. Her funeral was yesterday."

"Did you attend?"

"With the authorities looking for her murderer? Of course not." He and others had witnessed it from a distance, naturally. The images had burned into his mind. Mandy, standing alone at her mother's grave, holding the umbrella over herself and the minister, placing a rose atop Olivia's casket and then walking away. She hadn't looked back. Oh, grief had ravaged her. No denying that. But she'd done a respectable job of doing what she had to do. She'd always been strong and self-reliant like her mother.

"So you're confident Mandy knows nothing of NINA."

"Next to nothing, I said," he corrected Johnson. "She knows nothing of NINA and only the name Jackal. That's it." Precision and full disclosure was essential to his own well-being. One didn't withhold anything from Phoenix and live to tell it. And anything but certainty about Mandy would leave Phoenix no choice. He'd obtain an authorization code and order that she be executed immediately. Honestly, if Phoenix had to issue a death warrant on her, he'd issue two: One on Mandy, and one on Jackal.

Johnson dabbed at his throat and the back of his neck with a pristine white handkerchief. It remained precisely folded. "Nothing else to report?"

"No," he said. "Nothing else."

"Very well." Johnson stood up. "I'll brief Phoenix. He'll take it from there."

"Take what from there?" While accustomed to being told only the portions of overall plans that fell under Jackal's responsibility to execute, he currently had no portions of any plans to execute. Was there an ongoing operation from which he'd been excluded? If so, that was the worst possible news—for him and for Henry.

"Whatever he chooses."

"Is there an active mission?" Henry asked Johnson. "Have I been cut out?"

"If you had been black-listed from the organization, we wouldn't be talking, Jackal. You'd be dead." Paul Johnson stood up and then walked away.

Like Mandy, he didn't look back.

Still seated on the bench, Henry watched Johnson cross the small park and keep walking until he reached the parking lot and then his black Lexus. He got inside and then leisurely drove away.

When the car disappeared from sight, Henry breathed his first easy breath, knowing Jackal hoped but remained uncertain he had stopped Olivia Dixon in time to spare Mandy's life and his own. If she had shared anything with the Shadow Watchers, Jackal would have no choice but to kill her.

For his own protection and Henry's, Jackal should order her hit now. As much as Henry would like to deny it, the woman was problematic; headstrong and bitter. She had been a potential powder keg for years. Now, with her mother gone and nothing to coerce her into keeping her mouth shut, she'd be even more dangerous.

Still, Jackal hadn't killed her, and Henry suspected he wouldn't unless she gave him no choice. Why? Henry had his suspicions—and they had nothing to do with protecting Henry—but no proof, and he didn't dare to rely on speculation. That would surely get him and Mandy killed.

He remained silently relieved she was still alive and breathing. Jackal didn't know it, but Henry had ties of his own to the girl, and he didn't want them exposed. His life, and hers, depended on it.

Jackal approached and stopped at the bench. Henry squinted and looked up at him. Lean face; masked, of course; expensive shoes and a quality gray suit that cost more than most earned in a year. His age was anyone's guess. Henry had never seen him without the mask, and he hoped he never did or he too could become a statistic. Neither NINA nor Jackal left witnesses.

"Yes, sir." Henry focused on the face of the masked man. The glare all but obliterated his face.

Jackal didn't sit down. "Everything go all right? Johnson have any surprises?"

"No surprises. Everything went fine." Considering the circumstances, Henry understood being questioned. "I'm a professional, Jackal. It never occurred to the man that I wasn't you. It's never occurred to any of them."

"What did he want?" Jackal already knew, of course. He'd planted a listening device on the bench and had overheard the entire conversation. But Henry had proven to be astute, an excellent observer, in the past and, this time, those skills could prevent nasty consequences from striking close to home.

"Phoenix sent him for personal assurance Mandy Dixon knows nothing about NINA or you and to find out if you planned to interdict her or the Shadow Watchers in Seagrove Village." Henry then accurately relayed the exact conversation between them.

He'd missed nothing. Satisfied with the verification, Jackal nodded. "Went fine, then."

"Just as it always does." Henry banked on that.

So did Jackal. He passed over a sealed envelope. "That's why you make the big bucks."

Henry took the envelope then tucked it out of sight in his pocket. "Yes, sir."

Satisfied that everything was under control, Jackal let the tension holding him rigid ease. Posing as Jackal on the rare occasion was the easiest fifty thousand a pop Henry had earned in his life. Risky? Yes. But knowing that if he crossed Jackal he was a dead man kept Henry practical and discreet. Any risks, this side of his death, were acceptable. Only he knew why. And only he cared why. "Stay ten minutes after I've gone," Jackal told Henry.

"Yes, sir." Henry settled back on the bench, hooked a bent knee over his other one.

Jackal took the path to the parking lot, mentally reviewing everything even remotely attached to him to be sure all bases had been covered and Henry's services wouldn't be required for anything else, including taking any unforeseen fall.

By the time he reached his car, he'd finished his mental review. With careful deliberation, he checked his watch then hitched a hip against the rear fender of his car and surreptitiously watched the bench.

Henry sat as instructed with his back to Jackal, looking out at the water. Exactly thirty seconds after the watch check, the received signal was executed. Henry's body jerked, and he slumped over the bench's armrest.

Henry was dead before his head hit the wooden slats.

Regrettable, but necessary. Jackal didn't dare risk using Henry again to pose as him. Not after a face-to-face with Paul Johnson. Any link between the two of them had to be permanently severed—and now it had been.

A lean runner made his way up the beach to the bench, snatched the envelope from Henry's corpse with barely a missed step, and then ran on down the beach. Minutes later, he veered around and wound into the parking lot, passed off the envelope to Jackal, and then returned to the water's edge and his run. When he neared the strip of beach near the bench, he jerked, stumbled, and fell to the sand.

Dead.

Loose ends all tied up. Jackal slid into his car. The shooter was efficient, a good hire. One who had never seen Jackal and one Jackal had never seen. The tie to the runner also had been severed. He was a low-level NINA operative. Minimal skills but willing to do anything. Men like him were a dime a dozen. Totally disposable. The important thing was no link remained between Jackal and Henry or the runner and the shooter.

None of them, including the NINA shooter, could identify Jackal. He was clear to go.

Mission accomplished.

He cranked his engine and drove out of the park, bent on putting a great deal of distance between it and him as quickly as possible. He hated killing men just for doing their jobs. Particularly when they did them efficiently. But with what he was about to do, he'd have to be a fool to leave anyone standing in his wake, and it'd take a fool to allow Henry or the runner to live, even with neither of them knowing Jackal's real identity. Only a fool would underestimate NINA's ability to get information where it seemed there was none and there should be none. Jackal was not a fool.

Three miles away, he pulled into a tourist trap and spotted a trashcan out front. He parked, pulled on a pair of gloves, removed his life-like mask, cranked open the car door and then doused the mask with bleach. It began melting, the features distorting into something horrific and grotesque. He dumped it into the trashcan, and then returned to his car.

Another five miles down the road, he spotted a second can outside a diner. He bleached then ditched the gloves, and then went inside and washed his hands. At the counter, he ordered a large black coffee to go. When the woman placed it on the counter, he paid her, and then returned to his car.

Jackal hadn't survived and climbed the ranks of NINA while remaining anonymous by being foolish. Only one person ever had known of his connection to NINA and his true identity. Only one, and though he hated her for it, he'd married her to buy and keep her silence.

The dead tell no secrets.

They didn't. He should have seen to her years ago. But she was the mother of his children. They hated him as much as she did, but they were his, nonetheless. Not that it much mattered anymore. After today, he wouldn't see any of them again. Not in their lifetimes.

Not after Olivia's death.

How long had his wife known about Liv? How long had his son and daughter known?

He'd been so careful that even NINA couldn't identify him. All this time, and not one hint that they'd discovered the truth. Then they learn Olivia's dead and Mandy exists and they lash out, threaten to blow his whole world apart.

That infuriated him. Almost beyond rational thought.

Memories of the merciless confrontation rammed through

his mind, left his pulse pounding and his chest tight. They'd all turned on him. His princess, the son he'd given every opportunity anyone could hope to have, and they'd sided against him. The sting of their betrayal would be with him the rest of his life. *Ungrateful spoiled brats.* Everything. He'd given them everything, and they'd cursed him. Screamed in his face as if he were nothing. Nothing!

They had no idea how far he'd come. He'd had nothing and no one. He'd made his own way, created a dynasty for them, but did they appreciate anything? No. Not a thing. They acted as if the world was theirs by right. *Idiots.* They had no idea how to struggle or fight for what they wanted. He'd handed it to them, and they'd betrayed him. Well, they'd soon regret it. He was done. No more running interference for them with their mother. No more smoothing their paths, cleaning up their messes. A quick trip to the office to clean out his safe, and then he would retake control of his life.

Finally.

He wished Olivia could be with him to enjoy it. His regrets, if he had any, were about her.

His son had called Liv awful names. His wife had shouted worse ones, labeling her with vile monikers that were not true.

Don't think about it. It's futile. It's over now. Let it go.

He pushed the ugly thoughts and images away. Everything was going to be fine. Jackal had prepared. He'd planned. And he was ready, willing and able to do now what no other NINA operative had ever done: retire.

Alone.

With the last links to NINA eliminated, it was time for Jackal to fall off the face of the planet and never resurface.

His blackmailing widow and ungrateful orphans would object that he wouldn't be around to torment anymore, but once they settled into their new circumstances, they'd rejoice. At least, until the first time they landed in trouble. When he wasn't there to bail them out, they'd be sorry. Then, he'd rejoice.

What about Mandy?

A spear of guilt shot through him. He shunned it. Once, Mandy would have done anything for his approval. But then she'd seen him on the street in St. Augustine and everything had changed.

Whether or not she hated him, he couldn't be sure. But she'd never again hung on his every word or sought his approval on anything. Not once since then had she looked him straight in the face or said a single unnecessary word to him. Oh, she'd been polite, yes. No doubt Olivia demanded it. But since that day on the street when she'd seen him with his wife and their children, Mandy had remained distant. She'd never forgiven him.

Being the fallen hero had been inevitable with her, he supposed. Would it have made any difference if she'd known that even after his fall, she'd treated him better than his family?

Probably not. More likely, she'd be happy that he'd be as alone as she had been, or as she'd felt she'd been, her whole life.

Of course, she didn't know the truth. Now, with her mother dead and buried, she never would. Maybe it was better that way. So far as she could ever know, he had two ungrateful children that wanted nothing to do with him, and one who wanted him until she didn't.

Yeah, it was better that the truth stay buried and she continued to believe the fantasy they'd spun for her in lieu of the truth. So she'd wallow in a little self-pity at being alone. At some point in her life, she'd probably realize worse things could happen to a person. She could be stuck in a situation similar to the one he'd been in most of his adult life.

She hated feeling alone.

He couldn't wait. *Alone?* He harrumphed. *No, not alone. Free!*

Smiling to himself, he cranked up the air-conditioner and then pulled out into traffic.

CHAPTER 7

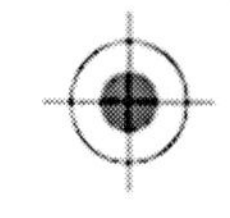

Saturday, October 25 th

"Mandy?"

Half sitting on Mark Taylor's sofa, Mandy awakened to the sound of Tim's voice. She unfolded her elbow and cranked open an eye. "Sorry. I didn't realize I'd dropped off."

He smiled, looking gorgeous in dove-gray slacks and a teal golf shirt, and he smelled freshly showered. "About three hours ago." He sat down beside her, sinking into the soft-brown leather. "Sorry to wake you, but we're all due at the center for the meeting in about half an hour."

"Thanks." She shook sleep from her foggy mind.

"I brought you coffee." He offered her a mug. "Shower's available, if you'd like one."

She took a steamy sip. Swallowed it. "I'd like one very much."

"I wanted a minute to talk with you before we join the

others." Worry flickered through his eyes. "We don't have time to tiptoe around anything, so I'm just going to talk straight—to be sure we're on the same page."

"I'd appreciate that," Mandy said. Having more questions than answers about her own life already had worn thin. "And I'll be just as direct."

"I'm counting on that," Tim told her. "Last night, I didn't really ask you if you wanted to marry me, so I'm asking you now." Red stained his neck and crept up his face. "Since you still love me, I assumed marrying me would be okay with you, but Joe pointed out that I came across as not giving you a choice, and you should have a choice. You *do* have a choice."

How like Joe. "So you intend for this to be a real wedding?" Did she dare? Wanting something didn't mean it was right or wise. It didn't mean Jackal wouldn't make good on his threat. The bride he'd marked for death could take all the rest of them with her.

"Totally legal, yes."

Legal. Were *legal* and *real* the same thing in Tim's eyes? "What about Jackal?"

"He'll come for us either way, Mandy. The big question is you. Do you want to marry me knowing it?"

Either way. "Life's full of risks," she said, looking at him through the cup's rising steam. "I tried, but I don't work without you."

His relief was immediate. It shone in every feature in his face. "I don't work without you, either, and I'm really tired of pretending I do."

"I am so sorry I hurt you." She cupped his jaw.

Joe appeared at the edge of the living room. "Tim? Hate to interrupt, but our sources picked up a transmission you're going to want to hear."

Tim stood up, looked at Mandy. "So you're okay with this, right?"

She didn't know much more now than she had before their

brief conversation. Not really. A man not working without you didn't mean he loved you or that he wanted a real marriage with you. Her mother's life stood as proof of that. Mandy hesitated a second, then followed her heart. Jackal was coming for them either way. Together, they improved their odds against him. "Yes, I'm okay with this."

That pleased Tim; he smiled. "Oh, with Nora and Annie, you tell them exactly what you want and who you want there. It'll be short notice, but they'll do all they can to make the wedding just right."

"What do you want?"

Moving toward Joe, Tim paused and looked back at her over the slope of his shoulder. "I want you happy."

"Are you happy?" The words were out of her mouth before she could check them.

"I am." He paused. "Worried, but happy."

She was getting there. It'd be easier to get closer to happy if she knew Jackal would fade away, but all of the guys insisted that he wouldn't. They would know better than she, and yet she wondered. Since she had no idea who he was, why wouldn't he disappear from their lives?

The answer immediately came to her. He wouldn't fade away because he couldn't. Jackal was NINA, and the team had cost NINA resources. Serious money and their reputation had taken serious hits. Terrorists relied on their reputation for recruiting and funding.

Yet, faded away or plagued by NINA in a life *with* Tim, she could be happy. Without him, she just wasn't. When she cleared away the mind-clutter, with the way things currently stood, she'd probably max out at worried, but happy. Like Tim, but different, too. She could settle better, if only she knew whether or not Tim still loved her. He admitted still being bitter, but he hadn't mentioned loving her.

A totally legal marriage.

Legal.

What was she supposed to make of that?

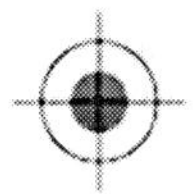

From the sidewalk, Crossroads Crisis Center didn't look like a clinic, not with its warm-colored stones, welcoming entry, and lighted candles in every window.

Inside, other than the receptionist's desk, it seemed more like walking into a welcoming parlor where people gathered and relaxed than a clinic for people in crisis seeking sanctuary. Soft colors and the absence of sharp edges appealed to Mandy, and the whole area smelled of fresh flowers. Not cloying or too sweet, just calm and soothing.

She spotted a large arrangement of irises and carnations, lilies and tulips, on a long, slim table below a portrait of a beautiful blond woman. Pausing, Mandy read the brass placket attached to its ornate frame. *Susan Brandt.*

Calculating the length of her life, Mandy's chest went tight. She'd been close to her age. What a shame Susan Brandt had died so young.

Tim stepped up behind her and whispered, "Susan and Ben Brandt built the center. It was her dream. She passed away a couple years ago, right before it opened.

"She never got to see it finished?" Clearly, she had worked hard to get everything just the way she'd wanted it.

"No, she didn't. But she planned every detail down to the candles in the windows."

"How sad." Mandy glanced back at Tim. "Not that she planned it but that she never got to see it finished, or to see the work that's done here." The center had made a world of difference in people's lives.

"You know about the work?"

Mandy nodded. "Lisa told me a bit about it earlier. Impressive—the people and the place."

"Susan would have loved what's been accomplished. She was all about helping others. They all are. After she died, everyone was worried about Ben. He had a tough couple years." Tim sighed. "Then Kelly came along. Theirs was a rocky start, but they helped each other. Now, they're married and have a new daughter." His voice turned tender. "They named her Susan in this Susan's honor."

"Kelly must be very secure in herself, to name her daughter after Ben's first wife. Most women would feel threatened by that."

"She's been threatened by worse." He looked away. "It's a complicated situation, but Kelly is special." Tim nodded at the portrait. "If you should see her, don't be startled. A lot of people think Susan and Kelly favor, but they're very different women. The longer you know them, the less they look alike. I'm not sure why."

They even look alike? "That must have been really hard for her and Ben."

Tim dropped his voice. "It was beyond hard. NINA was involved then, too."

Surprise shot through Mandy. "NINA came after them?"

He nodded. "Oh, yeah."

"I'm so sorry." Mandy winced. "But I have to say, I'm encouraged, too. If Ben, Kelly and Lisa survived their conflicts with NINA, maybe we can, too. We have reason to hope."

"Everyone wasn't as lucky. There were fatalities. But we do have reason to hope." Tim gave her hand a little squeeze. "I need to tell you. It's safe to speak openly to these people, but don't mention Shadow Watchers. They know—well, a lot of them do, but we don't talk about it."

Each of the Shadow Watchers was free to tell only one person, though what they could say was limited. Tim had told her. The others had their chosen ones, but who they were, only they knew. The people in the center who knew, according to Tim, had discovered the truth about the former team still being connected as consultants due to attempted terrorist attacks in which they had been personally involved as targets or victims. "It's safer not to say anything to anyone." Mandy informed him of her position on his professional life. "You're a private security consultant. That's all I know."

"Wise." He agreed with a nod. "And nothing in that has to be reported."

She'd figured out on her own that military Intel operatives never really retire. They just stop being active. But there's no way to take the knowledge and secrets put into their heads out of their heads, which means they must remain aware of what's going on even if they're not officially active.

She could be off in her reasoning on that, but she didn't believe she was. Tim and the guys had their own private security firm, but they still went up against NINA, and when they did, those had to be active, official missions. Whether the team was officially still active or occasional consultants for one of dozens of agencies tasked with such matters as Tim claimed, she had no idea. She considered asking him once to clarify, but then thought better of it. Some things were better left unsaid, not discussed, and frankly, left unknown. It *was* safer for Tim and for her.

"I've missed you, Mandy."

The quiver in his voice arrowed straight into her heart. She looked up at him, let him see her regret and the tumble of sincere emotions she was feeling. "I've missed you, too. So much I can't begin to describe it."

He waited for Lisa to walk past them to the front desk and get out of earshot. "Before we take this any further, I need to ask something of you."

"What?" He was the man with everything. What could she possibly give him?

"I need your promise," he told her, brushing the line of her jaw with his thumb. "Never again will you keep secrets from me."

She deserved that. She deserved worse. "I promise. Whatever comes, we'll face it together."

He smiled. "Perfect."

"You aren't still bitter?" If he'd done to her what she'd done to him, she couldn't say she wouldn't stay bitter. Even with protective intentions that were good, she'd still be bitter—or she thought she would.

"Honestly? I am. But I'm trying to forgive and forget it. I understand why you did what you did, which is something I haven't been able to do for nine months." He sobered. "I can't say I'm not bitter at you letting me think you were swept off your feet by another man. That hurt."

She could see that it did. Shame washed through her. "I am so sorry. I—I thought you'd be safer. I thought you'd accept that excuse and you'd—"

"I know. Ask no questions." He looked past her shoulder. "I'm working through it."

He hadn't yet. That was plain. "Tim, are we going to be able to get back to where we were?" They'd been so incredibly in love.

"Honestly?" He waited for her nod, then went on. "No, we aren't." He hiked a shoulder. "Time and the things that happened . . . they've changed us. We're not the people we were then. We're the people we've become."

True. Sad but true, and having no idea how to respond or where they would settle in, she wasn't sure what to say, so she said nothing.

"Don't worry. What we build from here will be extraordinary."

He sounded sincere. She let him see her doubt. "Do you really think so?"

"I believe it—and you should, too." He clasped her hands and squeezed. "We are going to have an extraordinary life."

Extraordinary. Surely extraordinary couldn't fit their lives unless he also loved her. How extraordinary would their lives be if that love only went one way? A flicker of hope inside her fanned to a flame.

"Mandy." Lisa came walking up with two women.

The youngest of the two seniors looked too much like Lisa to not be her mother, Annie. The elder was raw-boned and Scots, which meant she had to be the village mother, Nora. "Hi." Mandy nodded a greeting.

Lisa smiled, one arm around each of the women. "This is my mother, Annie Harper and this is my second mother, Nora. She pretty much raised me."

"Very nice to meet you both."

A fourth woman joined them. Short and round, she wore chunky jewelry and her dark hair styled in a classic bob. "And I'm Peggy Crane, Director of the Center."

Mandy smiled. "Nice to meet you all."

"Blast it, bud." Sam's voice carried over from the far side of the room.

Peggy stiffened. "Excuse me a second. I'll meet you all in the conference room."

"Oh-oh." Annie clicked her tongue to the roof of her mouth. "Things are not looking good for Sam this morning."

"Sooner or later my boy's going to remember to mind his tongue. Until then, I ain't sparing him." Nora grunted. "Peggy ain't having none of that kind of talk—and he knows it. I told him myself at least a dozen times in the last three days. Even made him tamales to help him remember." She looked from Sam to Mandy. "He's fond of my tamales."

Tim looked down at Mandy, his warm eyes twinkling. "He'll be griping for a week about getting jalapeno pepper juice in his tea."

Poor Sam. "Who does that to him?" Mandy asked.

"Peggy." Nora said, and then sniffed. "Or me." She dropped her voice. "Or Lisa, Kelly, Roxy, or . . . well, just about anybody in the village but Annie. She can't bring herself to it—even if it is for the boy's own good."

Annie's mutinous defiance had Mandy biting a smile from her lips. "I see."

Nora mumbled. "My boy knows if he's loose-lipped, it's coming. Apparently, he likes the stuff or he'd button it up."

Mandy smiled at Tim. She liked these people. You knew right where you stood with them, and exactly what to expect.

Annie looped Mandy's arm. "Nora and I will be planning your wedding. Of course, you've thought about exactly what you want."

She really hadn't. She'd thought a lot about being married to Tim, but not much about the actual wedding. "I expect it'll be coming soon, so that limits—"

"Day after tomorrow," Nora said. "Ain't that right, Tim?"

"Yes, ma'am."

That decision must have been made after she'd drifted off on Mark's sofa.

"Will your folks be here, Tim?" Annie asked.

"I'm afraid not. They're in Switzerland and won't be back in the States until spring."

Had he even told them? Mandy wondered, but didn't ask.

"I see." Annie swerved her gaze to Mandy. "And what about your father, Mandy?"

"I—I—"

"We know about the issue, dear. But he is your father. Wouldn't you at least like to offer him the opportunity to attend?"

Annie Harper sounded so reasonable and rational and not at all judgmental. Mandy looked at Tim.

"Ask him," Tim suggested. "All he can say is no."

"For pity's sake." Nora elbowed Tim. "She's still miffed that the man didn't come to her mother's funeral—I'm with you on that, Mandy. Unacceptable, no matter what." Nora drew a quick breath then set her chin. "I'd ask him for that reason alone."

"Nora, keep your stubborn streak to yourself." Annie

admonished her. "Mandy doesn't want to poke at him."

"Of course, she does. The woman needs to know whether he'll *ever* be there for her. If he won't for a funeral or a wedding, well, that pretty much tells her she can't depend on him for a spitting thing. That's information she needs to know."

Everyone hushed and just stared at Mandy, waiting for her to make the call. A nagging uneasiness settled over her and stayed put. Did she want Charles Travest to come or not? Should she want him with her? Walking her down the aisle? The war between what she should feel and what she did feel raged. Down deep, she knew she had to forgive him. If not for him, for her.

Carrying around all the anger and disappointment in him took a heavy toll, and frankly it was a burden she was tired of carrying. Wasn't it bad enough that things hadn't been totally at ease between her and her mother? Now, that could never be fixed. She had to live with it. She didn't want to live with that kind of thing with her father, too. "I'll ask him, but I wouldn't count on him showing up." Day after tomorrow—her wedding day—was Monday not Tuesday. That pretty well cut the odds of his attending to near zero.

"What colors do you favor?" Nora asked.

"Purple. I love purple." Mandy felt a little thrill. "And simple. Nothing fussy."

"Write that down in your book, Annie." Nora lifted a finger. "Purple and not fussy it is."

Annie wrote in a neat hand: *Purple. Simple, understated and elegant.*

A stir at the front entryway snagged Mandy's attention. A man in a suit and tie shook hands with nearly everyone he encountered.

"Ah, that's Jeff Meyer," Tim told Mandy.

"Who is he?" Everyone greeted him warmly. They all knew each other well, and from appearances got along well. Even Sam took being chastised by Peggy like a dutiful son. How lucky they were to not be outsiders, to have each other, helping them through life. Celebrating and mourning together through the ups and downs . . . She could only imagine.

"Jeff's a detective with the Seagrove police," Tim said.

More authorities involved. "Why is he here?"

"We have to assume NINA is active again. He's gone up against them with us before—I'm sure I mentioned that—and he's done well." Tim nudged her arm. "We'd better get to the conference room."

More questions. Mandy staved off a sigh and moved with Tim down the hallway.

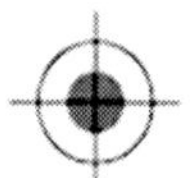

Forty-five minutes later, Jeff Meyer had revisited all the old ground that she and the guys had covered overnight. He'd taken copious notes in a little brown leather notebook that rested on the gleaming tabletop. It looked like chicken scratch to her, from across the table, but no doubt he interpreted just fine, based on him reviewing her comments then asking for clarifications.

"So," he paused to look up at her, seated across the conference table. "You know nothing about Jackal, nothing about NINA, and nothing more on the Jackal connection to Tim than your mother telling you not to marry him to protect him or Jackal would kill all the guys and their families."

"And my mother and me. That's right." Succinct summation. Mandy nodded to add weight to her claim. "She intended to tell me more that night. That's why I was going to her house for dinner. But when I arrived, she was already dead."

"You don't ever go to her house for dinner otherwise?" Jeff asked.

"Actually, no. I phoned to check on her, and occasionally went over when she needed something, but we haven't been as close as we used to be for a while now." She'd hoped not to have to reveal that. *Couldn't she have any luck at all?*

"How long a while?" Jeff pushed.

"Since I was seventeen." The others would put the puzzle pieces on that together quickly.

Jeff tilted his head. "Why? What happened?"

"Her mother and father weren't married, Jeff," Tim said. "He has a wife and two children. Mandy learned that when she was seventeen and everything changed. That's that."

"I'm sorry." Jeff scribbled notes into his book. "So when you got to your mother's and learned she was dead, did you call your father?"

"Not until the next morning, when he was at work."

"Because you didn't want to risk getting his wife on the phone."

"Because he forbid me to ever call him for anything—and I didn't want risk getting his wife or his children on the phone."

"You couldn't call him even to inform him of your mother's death?"

She shrugged. "Ingrained habits are . . . ingrained. It didn't occur to me to do anything different. It never crossed my mind."

Jeff nodded, clearly having a strong grip on her home life and situation. "It must have been really hard for you to walk away from Tim."

"Yes." She'd believed they'd spend their lives together. He loved her. Really loved her—or he had. Whether or not he did now, she couldn't begin to guess. *Bitter.* "It was hard." Shunning the only person in her life who'd ever been totally honest with her. Loved her without condition. Oh, yes, it had been beyond hard to walk away from him.

"I don't have any more questions right now," Jeff told the guys seated around the table.

"Great." Mark flattened his hands atop the table. "You all know what to do. We reconvene here in two hours."

People began filing out of the conference room. Mandy couldn't yet make herself move. She'd been through the mill, and then had been through it again. Jeff Meyer was every bit as detail-centric as the guys had been, leaving no stone unturned or secret concealed.

"You okay?" Tim asked, keeping his voice soft and low.

"I'm fine." Humiliated. Ashamed. Quivering inside. But then who could air all their dirty laundry to this group of principled people devoted to helping others and keeping people safe and *not* feel those things?

Would Mandy ever fit in here? Find her own place among them? Or would she always feel like an outsider?

Tim leaned closer. "You want to do lunch or talk wedding with Annie and Nora?"

"I cut Annie and Nora loose on the wedding."

"But it's your wedding, Mandy."

"I know, but the circumstances are . . . unusual, and there isn't much time. They're experienced, and I don't want to make anything harder for them."

He nodded, turned quiet and thoughtful. "Lunch it is, then. We can run over to Ruby's Diner and get a roast beef on rye."

Her stomach growled. "With onion rings?" Whether he was disappointed or relieved about her lack of involvement in their wedding, she couldn't tell. Maybe he was a bit of both. Maybe she should be, too. Heaven knew she was terrified of what might happen there. *NINA bait.* But as fearful as she was of that, she feared something else even more.

Her mother didn't interact with anyone but her and, on Tuesdays, Charles Travest. She was murdered on a Thursday.

Despite Jackal's threats, Mandy had believed Detective Walton's conclusion based on the evidence that the murder had been the result of a random break-in. But then Tim and the guys had made the NINA connection through Jackal. Now, she had these horrific suspicions. Was Charles Travest somehow involved? Could he be the murderer?

Surely not. He did love her mother.

He didn't come to her funeral.

It wasn't on a Tuesday.

You're burying your head in the sand.

I'm not. He has a sterling reputation and, except for when it came to my mother and me, by all accounts he's a man of character. A high-profile attorney and pillar in the community. She'd checked him out herself—him, his wife, and their children. They all had sterling reputations. How could she not dig into their backgrounds or be curious about them?

Outsider . . . Appearances can be so deceptive. You know it, too. You lived it.

She had. But her father? A murderer? Connected to NINA? Surely that was impossible.

It had to be her resentment that made her even consider the possibility. Her resentment and anger demanded she consider it, but of course those same things skewed her deductions. Nothing colors assessments more than emotions. He couldn't be involved in anything so sleazy that hurt so many.

Of course, he could.

No. No, he couldn't. It's impossible.

Is it really?

"Mandy? Are you okay? You've gotten so pale."

"I'm fine. Just hungry." She answered by rote and riveted her attention to Tim. A snippet of conversation had gone right over her head. "Sorry. What did you say?"

"You asked about the onion rings at Ruby's. I said, they're great."

"We'll have to try them, then."

"Absolutely." He smiled. "They're your favorite."

He remembered. Moved, she swallowed a knot in her throat. With Tim, she never felt like an outsider. She always felt like the center of his world. Amazing how much comfort she found in that—being at the center of someone special's world. For the first time in nine months, Mandy smiled from the heart out.

"Let me just tell Mark where we're going, in case he needs anything."

She nodded and watched the others, all busy with various tasks. Nora, lecturing Sam on his language. *It's the sign of a weak mind, I'm saying . . .*

Annie, on the phone with someone she knew well, talking about the wedding, and shooing Lisa, who kept interrupting with calls for a chocolate groom's cake at the reception. Lisa insisting, *But, Mom, it's got to be Double Dutch chocolate. It's Tim's favorite.*

It was Tim's favorite, and he loved it. Smiling inside, Mandy let her gaze drift past Peggy Crane to Mark and Tim, who had stepped away from everyone else and whispered in low tones. Tim's smile faded and worry replaced it. *Why?*

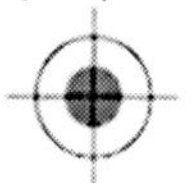

"She's definitely holding something back." Tim cringed at revealing that much to Mark. Voicing doubts about Mandy had guilt tugging at him, him feeling the sting of betraying her, though he knew for a fact he wasn't and he was doing the right thing.

"What do you think it is?"

"I don't know. If I did, I'd be less concerned." Tim swiped a hand through his hair. "She's always been present in the moment, you know?" He loved that about her. "But again just a minute ago, she retreated to somewhere inside her head in the middle of a conversation about onion rings."

"In all fairness," Mark shrugged, "onion rings isn't exactly a riveting topic. After all that's gone down, no one could fault you for being a little skittish, but she was up being grilled most of the night and Jeff put her through it all again this morning. The woman's grieving and worn out. Are you sure you aren't putting too much weight on this?"

"Maybe, I am." Tim conceded. "I don't know. But onion rings are her favorite food. She's into food—and she doesn't usually drift like that. I could be wrong—I am touchy—but her retreating like that got my attention. It's not normal for her."

"Must have been significant, then." Mark paused to think a second, then added, "What's your gut saying about it?"

Tim forced himself to look Mark in the eye. "She's holding out on us."

"The woman sacrificed her heart for us, Tim. For you. She loves you, no doubt about it. It's in her eyes every time she sees you. But she gave you up to keep us all safe," Mark said. "She told us all about that and about her mother and father. If she'd tell us about them, feeling as she does about it, why would she hold back anything else? I mean, can you get closer to the bone than your parents betraying you your whole life?"

"You never get over that," Joe said, joining them.

"Ah, the voice of experience." Mark hooked a thumb at Joe. "He'd know."

He would. *Thugs, thieves and outlaws. His thugs, thieves and outlaws.*

Joe cocked his head, reluctantly spoke to Tim. "Not to change the topic, and I don't want to rattle you, but I've got to say it, bro."

"What?"

"Mandy's holding out on us."

"See?" Tim flipped a hand toward Mark. "I told you." Tim turned to Joe. "I just told Mark that." Something burned hot in Tim's stomach, crawled up his neck and stung his eyes. *Bitterness. She'd promised, no secrets.* "What do you think it is?"

"Been thinking about it." Joe stuffed a hand into his jeans' pocket. "It's got to be about her mother's death. She says only she and Travest interacted with her. Mandy didn't kill her mother, so maybe she's worried Travest did."

"That's logical," Mark said. "And I can certainly see her not wanting to go there in her own head, much less be eager to plant the thought in ours."

"She wouldn't want to go there. She'd hate it." Tim agreed, thoughtful. "Mandy's always been the outsider. Not that she said so, but that kind of thing shows up in a lot of ways."

"It does," Joe said. "In the conference room when we were hassling Sam, she got this hungry look in her eye. It wasn't about Sam. It was about the way we are with each other."

"Like I said, she's always alone and an outsider. She accepted it because it was the way it'd always been. To her, that was normal. But when she sees us, she knows what she's been missing."

"Her normal isn't the normal she wants anymore." Joe let out a staggered breath.

Tim resented her having to deal with that, too. Something fierce. She should feel loved and cherished. Every child should grow up knowing someone is on their side and putting them first. Mandy's mother had been good to her, but she'd never put Mandy first. Well, not until she'd warned her off marrying him.

"Tim," Mark said. "She's got to suspect her father is Jackal. That's got to be what's going on with her. She's hurting from losing her mom and things not being right between them because of him. But he is her father. Suspecting him of killing her mother couldn't be easy to wrap her mind around, you know?"

"It would eat at her. She'd hate it." The woman had a lot to hate in her life. Tim resented that, too.

"She seems to hate him." Mark said.

St. Augustine spun through Tim's mind. "I think she loves him more than we could imagine. Otherwise, he wouldn't have the power to hurt her as much as he does."

"That's true. What he thought or said or did—or didn't do—wouldn't matter." Joe conceded that point. "Yet we also know there's a razor-thin line between love and hate."

Mark rubbed at his jaw. "Lisa says girls have serious hero-worship for their dads."

"He's the first man they love," Joe said. "Sure they go through hero-worship, and every man in their lives after him has to measure up to him in their eyes."

"Mandy never got to really experience that—hero worship—if you know what I mean," Mark said. "I'm thinking that'd make it even harder for her to stomach doubts about him toward her mother."

"Definitely." Tim sighed. "She begrudges what he did to her and her mother, but don't doubt she loves the man, because I'm telling you, she does. I think she'd give her eyeteeth for him to be a doting father to her just one time."

"Sam and Nick are checking him out," Mark told Tim. "Joe, hit your contacts and see what you can scrounge up."

Revealing as much about himself and his family life as his opinions, Joe nodded. "Well, we can't be her father, but we can be doting big brothers—except for you, Tim." Joe walked across the room to the hallway and then disappeared down it.

"What do you want me to do?" Tim asked Mark.

His gaze turned steely. "Reconsider marrying this woman."

"What?"

"Seriously. You can't start a marriage without trust, Tim."

"I trust her, and I understand why she's holding back on sharing her suspicions. She just lost her mother and Travest isn't much of a father, but he's all she's got. She's been angry at him a long time and she doesn't want to falsely accuse the man."

"He's not all she's got," Mark said softly. "She's got you—and us."

"She doesn't know that yet." Tim countered. "Well, she knows about me, but she's not sure if marrying me is good or crazy and she's worried she's going to get us all killed."

"You believe in her."

"Of course, I believe in her." Tim rolled his gaze. "Would I get engaged and want to marry her if I didn't believe in her?"

Mark let out a little hmmm . . . "One question."

"What?"

"Did you pray on it?"

Tim knew the importance of his answer. He prayed on everything he deemed important in life. "I've prayed on it," he said, and then confessed. "And I've prayed for her every day since the minute I decided I wanted her to be with me for the rest of my life."

"Even during the past nine months?"

"Especially during the past nine months." He couldn't be sure she would be all right and have a good life. He was sure that no other man would love her like he loved her. Of course, he'd prayed for her.

"That's that, then." Mark clasped Tim's shoulder. "Take her to lunch and make her believe she's not alone anymore. She's got all of us. That reassurance should get her to open up."

"Sounds reasonable, provided it's true."

"It's true," Mark assured him. "So long as she isn't Jackal."

Not at all surprised Mark had picked up on his unstated worry, Tim clamped his jaw, let his gaze slide down from Mark's face to his neck and on to his throat. "She isn't Jackal."

"Why?"

"Not ruthless enough."

"I'm down with that. But we can't think, we have to know," Mark reminded Tim. "We've been wrong before, and we've paid a steep price for it. We have to be certain."

Mark's point hit home. They had paid a steep price for being wrong. Worse, others had paid a steep price, too. "Right."

Being wrong on some things was just an annoyance. No big deal. Others created little messes that were a pain to clean up but they could be cleaned up. But when NINA was involved? It changed everything.

Any error then carried high odds of ending up deadly.

CHAPTER 8

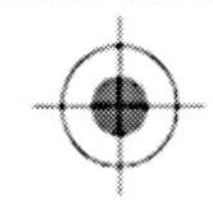

Mandy dropped into a conference room chair and covered her tummy with her hand.

"I told you not to overeat." Tim sat down beside her. "You need a 7-Up or something?"

"I'm fine." She was miserable, stuffed to her eyeballs. "I should have stopped a long time before I did."

Peggy Crane frowned at Mandy. "Stopped what? What's wrong with you?"

"Eating." Mandy stifled a groan. "Onion rings at Ruby's. They're the best I've had in my life."

Tim grinned. "Mandy's a connoisseur of onion rings, Peg."

"Been there, done that myself, more than once." She sent Mandy a sympathy-laced smile. "Just a friendly warning. The fried green tomatoes are even better. Best avoid them. No sense hurting yourself on them, too—and you will. I do at least once a week."

Mandy smiled. She loved this group. They were so quick to

poke at themselves and so slow to poke at anyone else. That was rare in Mandy's life, and joyfully entertaining to watch.

"Well," Lisa chimed in. "You'd better knock-out the sweet potato fries, too, then. Because I really believe Ruby puts something addictive in them. I don't know what, but something."

"Lisa has said that—every time she's placed a second order." Mark shared a toothy grin.

"Watch it, you." Lisa wagged a finger at him.

"Are we late?" Sam plopped into his seat.

"I told you we were." Nick sat down beside him. "Would you listen to me? Uh, no."

"Cut me some slack, bud." Sam lifted his beefy arms. "I was running a lead."

Mark nixed the nonsense with an authoritative, "Let's get started."

Silence fell and Mark looked to Nick.

He picked up his cue. "I've run both Olivia and Charles Travest. Mandy's right. She's been a recluse for at least the last ten years. People know of her but don't know a thing about her. No complaints but no insights, either. Apparently, she's a good listener but doesn't say much. More than one seemed shocked to realize that."

Mandy had seen it happen time and again. "I agree and confirm."

Nick went on. "Detective Walton said none of the neighbors had seen anyone other than Mandy come to her house. He knew nothing about Charles Travest, and not one neighbor had mentioned ever seeing him or any other man there."

Mandy stilled. "That strikes me as odd."

Tim looked over at her. "He came on Tuesday nights and parked in the garage, right?"

She nodded.

"Never went out into the yard. Never went on outings with

you two, right?"

She nodded again, her stomach souring. "He was a ghost and didn't exist to anyone else. I never picked up on that."

"Kids learn what they live. It was just the way things were." Joe shrugged. "The first time my dad showed up at school—my brother got into some trouble and my mom was in the hospital—no one believed he was really our dad. They'd never seen him before and figured we'd called in a ringer to stay out of trouble with Mom. Her, they knew well." He grinned. "Too well. One of us was always in the office for something."

Why hearing that made Mandy feel better, she had no idea. But it did. She smiled at Joe. "Kindred spirits."

"Do I need to be jealous?" Tim asked, lifting an eyebrow at her.

"No, but I might claim Joe as a brother," Mandy said. "I've always wanted one."

"I'd be honored." Joe dipped his head in a mock salute.

Mark snagged control. "Sam, what about financials?"

"Travest is set for life—a couple of lives, actually. The bulk of the money comes from an inheritance—his wife's. He has a successful law practice. No red flags there. Everything on paper looks clear and straight. The guy looks clean."

Mandy let out a breath she hadn't realized she'd held.

"What about Olivia?" Mark asked about Mandy's mom.

Sam, not Nick, answered. "A little something odd going on there."

"What do you mean?" Mandy asked.

Sam swerved his gaze to her. "She paid cash for everything."

"Travest gave her cash. It's all she had. She didn't have a career of her own."

"Did she inherit money, or what?" Sam said, clearly puzzled.

"No. Her parents died before she even started school. She was raised by an aunt—Beatrice, I think. No, it was Bertha. After college, my mother moved out on her own."

"What about the aunt?" he asked. "Where's she?"

"Long since passed. I never met her. She lived in Arizona somewhere, I think. I don't even know her last name."

"Did your mother inherit from her?"

"Maybe some debt. I don't think there was anything else."

Sam looked more perplexed. "Have you met anyone from your mother's family? Ever?"

"Actually, no. I haven't. There was just Mom and Bertha. Her mother's sister, I think. Those weren't easy times and Mom didn't like to talk about them." Mandy cocked her head. "What point are you trying to make, Sam?"

"No point," he said. "Just trying to understand. Your mother had an impressive portfolio. I can't find a credible source for it."

"How impressive?" Mandy asked. "It couldn't have been much."

Sam's gaze locked with Tim's. "Thirty million in liquid assets."

Shock streaked through Mandy. "Thirty—*what*?"

"Do I need to repeat it, really?"

"I don't believe it." Mandy looked from Sam to Tim. "She wasn't worried about money but we didn't live some lavish lifestyle. Where would she get that kind of money?"

"I don't know." Tim glanced at Mark. "But we have to find out."

Sam stuck the tip of his pen through his curly hair, under the edge of a red-and-white bandana circling his head. "I can tell you it didn't come from Travest. He doesn't have that kind of money."

"Mandy?" Tim placed his hand over hers atop the table. "Is there anyone in your past—even from when you were little—you can link to this money?"

Mandy sat stunned and at a total loss. "No. It's always just been Mom and me and Charles Travest on Tuesdays. That's it."

"Did your mom's sister maybe come into money and leave it to your mom?"

Mandy clawed through the cobwebs in her mind, back to the rare occasions when her mother had mentioned her sister. "I don't think so, Joe. I think they struggled to keep up with regular bills. She mentioned the power being cut-off once. Like I said, I don't think Mom had many happy memories, and she preferred not to think about them much less talk about them."

Mark turned to Sam. "Keep digging."

Sam nodded.

They had to be thinking exactly what Mandy was thinking. *NINA money*. But for what? Was that even possible?

A thought plunged into her mind and took hold. She gasped.

"What is it?" Tim asked. "Remember something?"

"No." She made herself look at him. "Tim, do you think my mother could have been Jackal?"

"Your mother?" He shrugged, weighed the possibility. "I don't know. Raven was a woman—a honcho in the NINA organization we brought down. I guess it's possible. Raven didn't seem a likely candidate, either, but . . ."

Mandy didn't want to ask. Didn't want to, but she had to if she ever again wanted to meet her own eyes in the mirror. "What about my father?"

"What about him?"

Mark had spoken, so Mandy reluctantly swung her gaze to him. "Could my father be Jackal?"

Mark smiled.

Mandy bristled. "Why does that amuse you, Mark?"

He ignored her and focused on Tim. "Good job at lunch."

What did that mean? She looked at Tim. "Care to explain?"

"Later." He promised. "I think right now we have to consider that either of them could have been Jackal—or he could be someone entirely different. Though, you need to prepare yourself. With all this money and no known source for it, a third party is looking less and less likely.

"She could have been holding it for Travest," Nick said.

"Possible," Mark said. "Or it could be hers."

Mandy groaned. "I hope not." She sought Tim's hand for comfort and reassurance. "I've dealt with a lot from those two. But being in a terrorist organization? I'm not sure I can take that, too."

Tim gave her hand a gentle squeeze, but it was Mark who first responded. "You can, Mandy. We'll help."

"Dang right."

"Sam!" Peggy admonished him.

Nick shrugged. "Dead from the neck up but, in this case, he's right."

Tim squeezed her hand. "When you can't, we can and will, Mandy."

"You're one of us now." Joe winked at her. "For better or worse."

"Really?" Even she heard the hope in her tone. The hope and the uncertainty. The fear of believing.

"You bet."

"Absolutely."

"Naturally."

"Of course."

Overwhelmed, she wasn't clear on who had said what, but they all had agreed. Beside herself, she felt her heart swell and her eyes fill with tears. They were bringing her into their fold. She'd belong. No longer be an outsider. Overwhelmed, she couldn't stop the tears from falling.

Gracious as they were, every single one of them pretended not to notice.

Tim slipped her a tissue under the table. "That okay with you?"

She dabbed at her eyes. "It's better than okay. Better than better." She glanced to Tim, saw that his eyes shone overly bright. He knew how much this meant to her, and why.

Just as he knew she'd protect every one of these people with everything in her. They'd taken her in, made her belong, and unlike others who took that for granted, she knew the value of it—a rare and treasured gift.

Mark cleared his throat. "Time to shift gears. Mandy, did you invite your father to the wedding?"

"Not yet."

"Call him."

"Now? Here?"

"Why not?" Sam asked. "Save you from repeating it all to us anyway."

He had a point. "I don't have—"

Four phones stretched toward her from around the table. She grabbed Tim's. "I don't have the number."

"His office or home?"

"Office." She told Nick. "Definitely."

Nick reeled off the number, and she dialed. Her hands turned clammy.

"She's turning green." Sam looked to Lisa. "You see it?"

"I think now's a good time for that 7-Up," Peg said. "Sooner the better."

Lisa rushed out to the center's kitchen and returned with a can. She popped the top. It fizzed out and Lisa put the can on the table before Mandy. "It's okay. You're not alone anymore. No matter what he says, he can only hurt you as much as you let him."

Mandy looked up at her, gratitude and misery at war inside, making mush of her stomach. "Unless he's Jackal. Then he can hurt us all."

"Whatever comes, we'll deal with it," Lisa promised. "Listen, he can be bad, but he can't be any worse than Dutch Hauk."

"Who's he?"

"My step-father. He sold me into slavery—twice." Lisa

leveled a flat look on Mandy. "Collectively, we've seen and been through a lot. You're not going to surprise anyone here with anything. We've seen it before and probably will again. But no matter what comes, we deal with it together and we get through it."

"Dang righ—"

"Sam!"

Peggy, Mark, Nick and Joe all said simultaneously.

He held up both hands. "Sorry. Sorry. Okay, already. I'm sorry."

Nick frowned. "Like I said. Dead from the neck up."

Mandy keyed the number into the phone. Seconds later, it rang, then a woman answered. "Travest and Hudson. How may I direct your call?"

The law firm was staffed even on weekends. "I need to speak to Mr. Travest, please."

"May I tell him who is calling?"

His daughter. "Mandy Dixon."

"And may I ask what this is in reference to?"

"No, you may not."

A slight static crackled through the phone, but the woman didn't miss a beat. "One moment, please. I'll see if he's in."

Tim shot her a thumb's up.

She shoved his arm down. "I was rude," she whispered. "But if I'd told her the truth . . ."

"I'm sure she gets that a lot," he said. "People want to keep private matters private. Attorney/client privilege and all that."

"Ridiculous notion." Mandy grunted. "Secretaries and assistants know everything."

"She's right," Joe said. "They're great sources."

Tim rolled his eyes back in his head. "Joe charms them."

"He likes them, and they know it," Mandy said.

"True."

A little click sounded, and then she heard his voice. "This is Charles Travest." His tone was brisk, all business.

"This is Mandy."

"My assistant shared that information with me. What can I do for you, Miss Dixon?"

Someone was with him, in his office. "I'm getting married in Seagrove Village tomorrow afternoon at two o'clock. Seaside Church on Highway 98. I realize it isn't Tuesday so you probably can't come, but if you could manage, you are invited." She tried not to choke on the words. He might have killed her mother. But if he was Jackal, she needed to get him here, if possible. To entice him, she added, "It would mean a lot to me for you to walk me down the aisle."

He hesitated a long second. "I understand, Miss Dixon."

That was more than she expected. "I'm marrying Tim."

"Of course, you are."

How did he know about Tim? "I'm assuming my mother told you about him and our engagement and breakup."

"Yes." He paused, longer this time. "Anything else?"

"No. Nothing else."

"I'll see what I can do."

She opened her mouth to say thank you and heard the disconnect. He'd ended the call. Slowly, giving herself a second to stop shaking inside, she moved the phone from her ear and powered off the phone then passed it to Tim.

"Well? Is he coming?"

"I have no idea." Admitting that bit her hard. "He said he'd see what he could do."

Lisa lifted a hand. "Well, he didn't say no."

He hadn't. "We'll see. If he didn't show up for my mother's funeral, I doubt he'll show up for my wedding."

"If he isn't Jackal, how does he know about me?" Tim frowned. "I heard you ask, which means you didn't mention me to him. What did he say?"

"Yes," she told Tim. "That's it, just yes."

"So do you believe him?"

"I have no idea what to believe, and that's the truth, Tim."

"I'm sorry." The look in his eyes proved he meant it.

"If he shows up, fine," Joe said. "If not, I'll stand in for him."

Mandy looked at Joe.

He gave her a lazy smile. "Least I can do, being your big bro."

Touched at his thoughtfulness, Mandy smiled back. Had he known she'd dreaded walking down the aisle alone? "Thank you, Joe."

"My privilege and pleasure."

"I was going to do that, Joe. I should do it. I'm older." Nick shot Joe a dark frown.

"What about me? I can walk down a dan—dangerously long aisle as good as either of you, and I'm better looking." Sam challenged them, pleased with himself for recovering from another near-slip.

Mark hiked his chin. "We could all walk her down the aisle."

"No, we can't. It's too narrow." Joe lifted his hands. "Sam, you'd have to wear a tux. You look miserable in a tux because you can't stand ties, remember? And Nick, you won't smile. You guys want lousy pictures of the wedding? Mandy and Tim looking like a million bucks, and you looking strangled and gloomy. No. It's not happening. I called it first, and I get to walk the walk—if his majesty deigns not to show up." Joe looked at Mandy. "You good with that?"

She nodded, dazzled by them.

"That's it, then." Joe slapped his hands down on the table. "It's settled."

Dazed, Mandy glanced over at Tim.

He smiled. "You'll get used to it," he promised her. "They grow on you."

"Yes, they do," she said, glancing man to man around the table, feeling amazingly blessed.

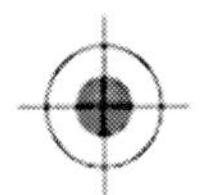

"Time's up, boys." Nora walked into the conference room with Annie trailing in her wake. "We got a wedding tomorrow and we've still got a few details to iron out."

The Shadow Watchers all stood up. "We were just leaving."

Nora brushed past Sam. "Get on with the going then. Tim and Mandy ain't gonna have no half-baked wedding. I won't have everyone in the village saying I didn't do right by one of my boys."

Tim brushed a kiss to Nora's cheek. "Thank you, Nora."

"Be gone, I said."

He smiled. "Yes, ma'am." With a wink at Mandy, he and the other guys filed out of the room.

Sam stuck his head back in the door. "Nora, one thing."

"What?"

"Are you making some of those crab cakes like you did when Ben and Kelly got married?"

"Wasn't planning on it. It's October. They ain't in season."

His face fell. "Oh. Okay, then."

As soon as he cleared the doorway, Nora turned to Annie and wagged her finger. "Get your book and put crab cakes on your list."

"But you just said crabs aren't in season."

"One of my boys wants crab cakes, he's getting crab cakes, Annie Harper. Now are you gonna write it down in your little book, or do I have to do it myself?"

"I'm writing. I'm writing." Annie cracked open her book and scribbled it down, right beneath the Double Dutch chocolate groom's cake.

"Make this quick, okay?" Lisa said. "I have plans."

"Oh?" Annie's interest perked.

"So do you. We all do, and Kelly and Roxy—that's Dr.

Harvey Talbot's wife. Ex-FBI—" Lisa reminded Mandy.

"We all have plans?"

Mandy looked from Nora and Annie to Peggy and then to Lisa. The guys might have taken her into the fold but not yet so with the women . . .

"We do," Lisa said. "We're having a bridal shower for Mandy."

A bridal shower? For *her*? "Oh, you don't have to do that, Lisa. It's too much. The wedding and a reception and now this? There's no time for all this."

"There most definitely is time. Kelly and Roxy are handling it. That's why they're not here."

Nora tapped Mandy's hand. "Let them do it, dearie. They want to be part of this, too. Tim's been so sad without you, and now you two are back together and everyone wants to celebrate."

"I don't know what to say." Mandy truly didn't. "I'm . . . overwhelmed."

"Marrying into this bunch," Peggy warned, "you'd better get used to it. You'll stay overwhelmed most of the time, and we're a package deal."

They wanted her in their fold, too. A solid knot parked dead center in Mandy's chest. "I'm not seeing that as an issue, Peg." Mandy readily confessed. "This group is great. All my life, Mom aside, I've been alone with no one. Well, until Tim."

"Hold that 'great' thought, hon." She patted Mandy's hand. "You're going to need it now and then."

"Isn't that the truth?" Lisa giggled.

Mandy couldn't help herself. She smiled. "Oh, wait. What about Tim? I doubt with everything going on the guys . . ."

"Ben Brandt is taking care of Tim and the guys. The bachelor's party is the reason he hasn't been here today, though Mark's kept him posted on developments by phone."

Ben and his wife Kelly owned Crossroads. "Well, thank you. All this . . . It's lovely and generous of you."

Lisa softened her tone. "We've been where you are, and we understand how you're feeling. We're with you, Mandy. We always will be."

Tears again welled in her eyes. "Sorry. My emotions are all over the place."

"You're getting married tomorrow, you darling girl." Annie put down her pen. "Of course, your emotions are all over the place. You know, being happy can be just as stressful as being unhappy."

"Maybe, but I'm beside myself. Losing Mom . . . I'll never forget standing at her funeral all by myself. I felt so lost and empty. Then Tim came and now all of you . . ." Tim *and* this amazing group of people in her life—she could scarcely believe it.

Reaching down, she pinched herself on the thigh. It stung. Bad.

"Hurts, huh?" Lisa whispered.

"Yeah, but only in the best possible way."

"I know just what you mean."

Mandy looked at her and realized Lisa did know. Exactly. That had her torn. Wishing Lisa had been spared and bonding with her because she hadn't. "Thank you, Lisa."

"Thank you. If I had to see Tim heartbroken one more time, I think I'd be sick inside forever."

"I'm so sorry about that."

Nora guffawed. "Get over it, dearie. You did what you had to do to protect the man you love and the rest of my boys. We've all had our share of hard choices in tough times. Shameful ones, too, like Annie and Lisa with that awful Dutch Hauk, may his black soul rest in peace." She crossed herself.

Mandy cocked her head. "Are you Catholic, Nora?"

"No, why?"

"You crossed yourself. I've only seen Catholics do that."

"I went to Catholic schools most of my life."

"So true about hard choices." Annie moaned. "Me with

Dutch and Lisa, and you with your sister."

"Ain't that the truth?" Nora laced her hands atop the table. "A body can't get worse than my fickle sister. Humiliated me to no end, but she did worse to herself. I was sure the entire village would shun me. But it didn't."

"Shun you? Don't be absurd, Nora. You *are* this village." Annie assured her. "You've loved us all through everything."

Curiosity got the better of Mandy and she asked. "Who's your sister?"

"Raven." From Nora's expression, just saying the name put a bad taste in her mouth. "She was a honcho for NINA—likely still is. Those people have a way of doing bad things, even when they're locked up in prison. That's where Raven is now. In Leavenworth, which is right where she belongs for the duration." Nora sniffed, clearly taking strong exception. "She's mean as a snake, that one."

"It's over, Nora, and there's no need for you to be touchy about it. She committed the crimes. You didn't."

"She tried to kill me and my boys, Annie Harper. I ain't touchy, I'm miffed."

Mandy looked at Lisa. "Her boys?"

The Shadow Watcher team you're marrying into—and Jeff Meyer." Lisa shrugged. "Don't worry. We all know about the Shadow Watchers, we just don't talk about it with anyone from the outside."

Mandy wasn't touching that statement with a twenty-foot pole. "I really don't have any more secrets. You guys have heard them all."

Annie gave Mandy a frank look. "Nora was ashamed. Lisa was terrified. I was—so many things—all bad. And you . . . Your mother and father deceiving you like that had to hurt badly."

"It did. It still does." No sense in denying the obvious. "But we endure what we must, and we survive."

"Amen, sister." That, from Lisa.

"Dang right." Nora realized what she said and clapped a hand over her mouth, stunned. Annie, Peggy, and Lisa stared at her gape-jawed. "First one mentions that little slip outside of this room will regret it the rest of their days—especially if Sam gets wind of it."

Smiling, Lisa zippered her mouth with her fingers.

Peggy did, too, though her frown remained evident. "See why we have to stay on him? I can't believe it's rubbing off on you, Nora."

Annie exaggerated a sigh. "Peggy, I do believe you've slipped a time or two—we all have. So let's just not mention it again, mmm?"

"Thank you, Annie." Nora looked to Mandy. "Do you even know your half-brother or sister?"

"We've never met. I know of them, though."

"She did background on them after finding out they existed," Lisa said, filling in the blanks.

"I did." Her face burned at being outted. "I was curious."

"And shocked, I'd guess." Peggy took a sip from her teacup.

"That, too." Mandy leaned forward. "They seem like good people. Bright and active in all kinds of things. They have no idea I exist, of course."

"Your dad never told them."

"He never told anyone. I think if he could forget himself, he would have."

"I'm sorry." Lisa let out a longing sigh. "I adored my father. He was a doctor, too. I loved going to the office with him and pretending I was the doctor."

"You wore out a couple stethoscopes before you turned ten." Annie smiled indulgently.

Lisa propped an arm on the table. "Sometimes when he'd look at me, he'd seem so amused. Like I was the heartbeat of his universe, and I hung every star all by myself. He made me feel as if I could do anything."

"You were, and you did, in your father's eyes," Annie said.

"He adored you."

Lisa nodded. "He adored you, too, Mom."

"He did."

"I always wanted a dad like that, but I never got one." Mandy confessed.

"I'm sure he loved you."

"He loved his other two kids. I saw it in his face when he looked at them. And I thought he loved my mother. Now, I don't know. But me?" She shook her head. "When I'm not furious with him, which isn't often, I think he was too afraid of getting caught and ruining his picture-book life to risk caring about me. When I'm not feeling that generous, which is most of the time, I accept that I was never anything more than an inconvenience to him."

"I'm so sorry." Annie said and meant it; it showed in every line in her face.

"Sorry?" Nora grumped. "I'd say it's more for the best. Look what it's gotten you."

"What do you mean?" Mandy looked at the list of tasks done—flowers, food, drinks, booked the church, the reception ballroom, the minister. These two were marvels! "He took care of us."

Nora pursed her lips. "Ain't you figured this out yet, dearie?" When Mandy remained quiet, Nora went on. "If you ain't NINA, and your mom wasn't NINA, then Charles Travest has gotta be NINA. It's only common sense."

Mandy rubbed at her temple. "He could be, which is what has my stomach in knots about this wedding. He could be, and he could come here." Her stomach twisted tighter. "He probably won't, but he could. Oh, man. With everything going on, I'm so scattered. I've wondered if he was one of them, but I'm not sure I mentioned it. If he is one of them, there could be trouble. I—I have to warn Tim." She started to rise.

"Keep your seat, dearie." Nora looked down the bridge of her nose at her. "He knows it."

"You told him," Lisa assured her. "You told all of them."

"I don't remember doing it."

"I heard it," Lisa said. "You've been under a lot of stress. It's normal to get things jumbled up then. Nothing to worry about."

Whenever someone said don't worry, Mandy worried. She started shaking. "What if Charles Travest is Jackal? Surely he won't do anything here. Surely he wouldn't dare."

"He might," Lisa said. "Sorry, Mom. Frown if you must, but we can't let Mandy be blindsided."

"You're right, of course," Annie agreed. "I just want her to have a happy wedding."

"She will," Nora said. "Either he won't show up, or he will. If he doesn't, fine. Joe will walk Mandy down the aisle—I heard he won the honor. If the man does show up, he'll either pull some stunt, or he won't." Nora stilled. "Either way, my boys will be ready for him."

They would be ready. "Oh, no." Mandy grabbed her stomach. "Murder on my wedding day? Blood shed at our wedding?" She pushed her chair back. "What was I thinking? I—I can't do this. I can't." She rose and ran for the restroom down the hall, hoping she made it before losing her lunch.

"Nora!" Annie admonished her. "Look what you've done."

"Don't you start with me, Annie Harper. It was necessary."

"Necessary?" Annie grumbled. "It was not necessary."

"It was, I'm saying." Nora sighed. "Mandy can face facts now and be sick in private, or face 'em tomorrow and ruin her wedding. I figure, she'd rather do it now. Either way, she's got to face facts, Annie. If Charles Travest is NINA, blood's likely to be shed. If he's not, it's likely Jackal will show up and blood will still be shed. Either way, she's likely to see blood. Best she's prepared for it."

"No. No blood on her wedding day. I will not tolerate it. She deserves better, and for once, she's going to get it." Annie stood up. "Lisa, you go see about Mandy."

"Where are you going?" Nora called out.

"To warn Peggy." Annie looked back at her. "Your boys will be ready for a fight. The rest of us need to do all we can to make sure there isn't one, and be ready to keep the peace."

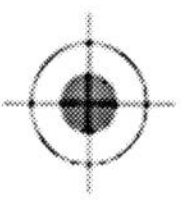

Mandy splashed her face with cold water. As stark and blunt as Nora had delivered the truth, Mandy couldn't disagree with a word of it. Where had her mother gotten all that money? She hoped Sam would find some explanation besides NINA, but what if there wasn't one? What if her mother or her father was Jackal? Was up to their necks in NINA and its criminal activities? Mandy heaved again. Tim was already bitter. How in the world would he take that kind of news? How would he feel about marrying her then?

Maybe that's why he hasn't said he still loves you.

She groaned and heaved yet again.

It wasn't just him. It was all of them. How would these people who'd brought her into their fold feel about her then?

Jackal. Who had tried to kill them, threatened to kill them all. NINA. Terrorists.

They hadn't shunned Nora, but they all had already loved her. They didn't love Mandy. She'd be shown the door and left alone again. Her empty stomach hollowed, threatened to again rebel, and the urge to weep slammed into her.

After a taste of what belonging felt like, she didn't want to go back to being alone. When it is all you know, well, that's one thing. But when you get a glimpse of what it's like to be surrounded by people who take you in, when you belong . . . That changes everything. Getting that glimpse and then being kicked to the curb—she couldn't handle it. She really couldn't handle it.

Wasn't it enough to not know if her legal wedding would

be real and produce a real marriage? After their lunch today, after Tim telling her this morning that he wanted her to be happy, she thought they had a good chance of him getting past his bitterness and everything being real, but he still hadn't told her he loved her, and her parents' connection to NINA could be why.

They couldn't have a real marriage if only one of them loved the other. Marriage was hard enough when both partners loved each other.

Did she dare to hope? *Really?* With Jackal looming and NINA on the fringe?

Oh, I don't want to go back. I don't want to go back.

It'd be just her luck to find a place she belonged with the man she loved and for fate to snatch it all away.

Fear that it would swelled inside her, opened a dark, empty place that threatened to suck her in.

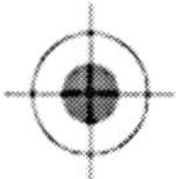

On the grounds of the crisis center, the men congregated at a picnic table with benches positioned under a canopy of craggy old oak limbs, certain they wouldn't be overheard. None of them sat down.

Sam hiked a sneakered foot and planted it on the end of the closest bench. "So what's the plan, Mark?"

Tim, Joe, and Nick waited to hear his answer.

"I'd rather lose my tongue than say this," Mark looked at Tim, "but we all know Mandy's mother or father could be Jackal. Even she suspects them."

"My money's on him," Tim said. "From what Mandy said, her mother was devastated at telling her to break our engagement."

"NINA operatives are good actors, buddy. That's worth remembering."

"They are, and it is, Sam. But there's the mother/daughter

thing going on there, too."

"Tim's right, bro." Joe added his opinion, crunched a crisp leaf between his forefinger and thumb. "Liv was terrified, Mandy said. If she was Jackal, she might fake being scared, but Mandy knows her well. She'd sense the difference and know it wasn't real."

"She would." Tim watched two kids on their bikes make their way down the sidewalk. "Mandy's perceptive, and they were really close. At odds over Travest, but still really close."

"I'm with Tim." Sam kept one eye on the kids. "I can tell when my mom is ticked and just faking it." He sucked in air between his teeth. "I vote Travest."

Mark looked to Joe. "Travest."

"Definitely Travest," Nick said, tapping at his glasses.

"I think he's Jackal, too," Mark said. "But her money worries me. He's too rigid to risk putting thirty million in Olivia's name—it was in her name, right, Sam?"

"Yep, sure was—actually, is. It's still there."

"Does it go to Mandy now?" Nick asked.

"It's a Swiss account," Sam said. "I'm waiting to hear who else's name is on it, if anyone's. But I'm doubtful it's Mandy. She had no idea the money existed. Anyone could see that by her reaction to hearing it."

"Shocked."

"Totally." Joe agreed with Nick.

"We can't yet rule out third parties," Tim said. "When will you know about the account, Sam?"

"Omega One is working it now." He cited a good friend of the team, and especially of Mark. Before being gunned down on a mission, the little sister of Mark's heart had been an active operative. Omega One had been her partner. "He's been slowed down by Homeland Security. Can't say why."

Nick crossed his arms. "So will we know before or after Tim's wedding?"

"Before, I hope," Sam said.

"It doesn't matter." Tim put them all on notice. "I'm marrying Mandy."

"We know you are, Tim." Mark nodded.

Nick frowned. "You started out marrying her for the mission."

"I'm marrying her because I love her."

"Got it. But I have to ask . . . Are you sure it's what you really want? NINA? Jackal? In-laws who want you dead and can make it happen? Think about it long-term, Tim."

He hardened his voice to match his resolve. "I said, I'm marrying Mandy."

"Got it." Nick held up a staying hand, looked to Mark. "So what's the plan?"

"Standard pre-op. Security checks at the church and resort, get Jeff and a local team on alert. Pre-position whatever we might need in the way of weapons." Mark stuck a toothpick between his teeth and held it into place with his lips. "If Travest shows up, we'll see if he tries anything at his own daughter's wedding."

"She doesn't believe he'll show up," Tim told them.

"Easy to see why," Joe added, parking a hip on the edge of the picnic table. "Jerk's never acknowledged to anyone other than her and Olivia that she's his daughter. Never recognized her, acted like he'd never seen her before in his life on the street, and she was just a kid—"

"While he was with his *family,*" Nick interjected. "She can't even call him to let him know her mom's dead. Oh, yeah. He's a peach, all right."

"She'll never need him again." Seething, Tim vowed, claimed control, then changed the subject. "If he is Jackal, he'll expect a trap."

"I'd like to snare him in one," Sam said.

"Unfortunately, we don't know enough about him to snare him." Mark watched a black Lincoln edge down the street. When it moved out of sight, he looked back at the guys.

"What do you think?"

"It's radical." Tim answered.

"Tell us anyway," Joe said.

Tim looked from Mark to Joe then back again. "We let Travest come to his daughter's wedding . . . and we let him leave after it."

"What?" Sam looked shocked, and ready to spit nails. "You crack your head or something, bud?"

"No. Just listen," Tim went on. "We let him come and go and we keep him on our radar."

"On Omega One's radar." Mark nodded. "That could reveal Phoenix."

"Exactly." Tim lifted his hands. "It's not perfect, but it'll have to do until we gather irrefutable evidence one way or the other. I'd hate to accuse the man of being Jackal if he isn't, and, if he is, then I'd like to expose him and Phoenix. This gives us a shot."

"Good point. Falsely accusing him would make for poor in-law relations—even with him." Nick grunted. "More importantly, Mandy should have a nice wedding."

"She should," Tim said. That she'd forfeited something she treasured so much to protect him and the team . . . It got to him every time it crossed his mind. "Travest could be Jackal. After Raven, we know NINA is capable of using anyone. Even Olivia. I'm praying hard *she* isn't Jackal. I think that would break what's left of Mandy's heart. But, either way, I'm not certain her mother is innocent. Thirty million in liquid assets without a traceable source creates a lot of doubt."

"I hate to agree, bro, but I do."

Nick groused. "Either way, Mandy's heart gets broken again."

"What're you saying?" Sam asked.

Tim lifted his left hand. "Her mother's Jackal." He lifted the other. "Her father's Jackal—and her mother knows it." He shrugged. "Either way, Mandy's heart's broken. Again."

Sam let out a whistling breath. "She ain't thought that far yet. But she will."

"Oh, yeah." Joe said.

"Unfortunately, there's nothing we can do about it." Mark took a long swallow from a canned soda. "Though I agree she deserves a nice wedding." He let his gaze drift. "I put myself in her place and I don't know if I'd be able to walk away from Lisa like that. I like to think I would—if I didn't and she died, I'd never forgive myself—but . . . I just don't know if I could do it."

"She's a strong woman." Tim knew it, but he hadn't known how strong. Now that he did, he wished she'd had no reason to be.

Sam tugged his cap down over his eyes. "That jerk of a father messes this up for her, and he's going to regret it."

"If at all possible, we shed no blood on her wedding day, Sam." Tim held up his fingers signaling *eyes-on*: he was watching. "That'd really upset her."

Joe pursed his lips. "She could figure it's a bad omen."

"Sure about that?" Nick cocked his head. "She might think the jerk deserves to hurt a little. He sure has hurt her and her mom for a long, long time."

"Revenge isn't her style," Tim said. He'd love to vent a little righteous indignation on Travest's head but it would offend Mandy's spiritual sensibilities.

"There is one thing we can do," Tim said. "About her getting heartbroken, I mean."

All gazes swerved to him, including Nick's. "What?"

"Given the circumstances, we do all we can to see to it she has a wedding with happy memories." More and more Tim had come to understand Mandy hadn't had many happy events in her life. He hated that, and he resented it. "If we're given a choice."

"Sounds good to me, buddy." Sam shoved back his cap.

"Definitely." Joe popped a fresh piece of gum into his

mouth.

Mark lifted his can in mock salute. "That's it, then. Priority one. If possible, we do everything humanly possible to make it a good-memory day."

Grateful for their support, Tim dared to hope they wouldn't be forced into fighting a war at the wedding. He tapped his soda can to Mark's. "To Mandy."

CHAPTER 9

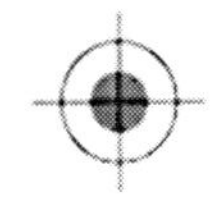

Charles Travest spent Saturday tying up loose ends.

Freedom away from his *family* couldn't come soon enough. He'd thought about making this break from them for years—and from NINA. But only in the last year had he gone from dreaming and thinking about it to planning his escape. Being careful wasn't enough. NINA tolerated no mistakes and it rewarded those who cut-and-run the same way it rewarded disloyalty: death.

He wasn't ready to die. Not now that he finally had a chance to live!

Driving down the lonely, dark stretch of highway, he adjusted the radio to play softly in the silent car. Soothing music that would help settle his jangled nerves. He'd gotten enough cash to last him a lifetime, cut a deal with a former unsavory but talented client to get him a new identity, and he'd completed the requirements for that new identity to practice family law throughout the Pacific island chain. The attorney general couldn't touch him. His wife couldn't touch him, even if she should somehow find him. And his investments were protected. All set, and excited; eager for his new beginning. More than eager to leave this old life behind and shake its dust from his shoes.

A wistful feeling slid through him. He'd planned the new beginning with Liv, but she'd made that impossible. He wished she hadn't, but if she had to betray him, better that she did it before the break rather than after.

He double-checked his rearview to be sure he wasn't being followed. Nothing but darkness behind him. He blew out a cleansing breath, let himself calm down. Traffic didn't exist on the back road, at least not at the moment, leaving him feeling isolated and alone. *Content. Finally, content.*

And yet the green dash lights cast an eerie glow that whispered a warning. It sent a chill up his back. His skin crawled in the same way it had when Mandy had phoned him at the office.

His stomach clenched. He was there a total of fifteen minutes and that would be exactly when she called. He hadn't planned on going in when anyone else was around, but with the unexpected developments at home, he'd had to be flexible and drop in to buy himself a little more time and to clean out his office safe before his wife got around to locking it down legally, too. She'd already jerked the noose on everything else. Fortunately, she didn't yet realize she was too late.

Mandy phoning at just that time, and his dumb luck of being there to receive her call, had seemed like a bad omen. He feared it had been, but it couldn't be. He refused to accept that; he'd been methodical, cautious, implemented backup plans to his backup plans. Of course, it wasn't a bad omen. Everything was going to work out fine.

The internal alarm niggled at him again.

Maybe she had thrown a wrench into his clean getaway. Okay, but if so, how? In what area? She didn't know anything about anything. Had Liv left her something? He hadn't seen anything at the house, but he hadn't gone through every sheet of paper or every file folder in her cabinet, either. She might have mailed something to Mandy. Liv was malleable, but when she made her mind up, she found a way to accomplish what she wanted.

That Mandy might have something that could interfere with his plans infuriated him. *Crazy woman would use it. She'd been nothing but trouble since St. Augustine. A constant bone of contention between him and Liv—and she'd always been a thorn in his side. Daring to phone him at the office on a Saturday, no less. Idiot. What if NINA . . .?*

No. No. Don't go off the deep end. NINA had no way to connect Jackal to Charles Travest, and no way to connect Charles Travest to anything or anyone. He'd been meticulous.

So Mandy had called. At least, she'd had the sense to refuse to give his staff any information. Oh, he'd bet his eyeteeth that she'd wanted to; she had to be totally ticked-off about him not showing up for Liv's funeral. But Mandy had restrained herself. Good thing, too. No doubt the result of her mother's warnings about consequences. "You taught her well, Liv."

A little empty hollow seized in his chest. He missed Liv. She had made his life bearable. If he hadn't had her to escape to on Tuesdays, he could never have lasted all these years with his blackmailing wife and ungrateful kids. He couldn't have successfully faked being happy. It was amazing really, how much one person could influence your whole life.

Now she's gone.

And it's your fault.

She was gone, and part of the fault was his, and he'd take responsibility for it, but he wouldn't accept all of it. Liv herself was partly to blame, too. She'd gone too far, backed him into a corner. From the start, he'd been clear. If their relationship ever came down to the point of *it's-you-or-me*, you—whoever you happened to be—was going to lose. She knew that and pushed him anyway, and she'd lost.

Yet he had lost, too.

And so had Mandy.

Mandy. This was all her fault really—with Liv and him. She was the reason Liv had pushed him too far. If after St. Augustine Mandy had been civil and not gone crazy about him being married, and if she hadn't hooked up with that Shadow Watcher in the first place, things would have been fine. But, no. She wouldn't or couldn't just take the news in stride. *Stubborn, selfish woman.* She had been full of outrage and indignation, and created all the problems for them.

Yes, every bit of the problems. She had berated Liv about his wife and kids and then she had brought Tim and his team—NINA's nemesis, for pity's sake—right to Liv's door. *Stupid, stupid stubborn woman.*

Oh, yeah. Mandy had created all their problems. She'd wrecked his life and caused her mother's death. It was her fault. Every bit of it.

Anger swelled inside him and churned. How he hated that girl. Who did she think she was to dare to judge him?

Before St. Augustine, she'd been like a puppy, willing to do anything to get his attention, panting for a single kind word from him or any sign of approval. But after that day on the street, and the subsequent blowout between her and her mother, Mandy had avoided both of them. She'd been in the same house with Liv, but never again shared what was on her mind or any emotion with either of them. Polite but distant. Civil but detached. She built her life on her own, away from them in both mind and heart.

That suited him fine. But Liv? Liv had been crushed and never had been the same. And after Mandy had ended the engagement and severed from that Shadow Watcher . . . Well, that's what really had sealed Liv's fate. Why couldn't that stubborn idiot just have gotten over the guy, put him behind her, and gone on with her life?

No, instead she had to ruin *all* their lives. *Selfish twit.*

Stop it Charles. Stop it—now. This is no way to start a new life. They're all out of your way now. Forget it. Build something new. Something that's all yours. Something . . . good.

Determined to do just that, he turned up the radio to block out the internal dialogue in his head then took the next exit and headed down the clover toward the little southern Alabama town of Pineville.

When he reached it, he smiled. Barely nine o'clock on a Saturday night, and the town slept as if it were two in the morning. The islands, he imagined, would be a lot like that. Quiet. Peaceful. Remote. The perfect place for a man who wanted to get lost to actually do it and stay lost.

He looked around. Thickets of hurricane-twisted pines, some magnolias, and a ton of scrub brush. A light here and there, set back off the road in the distance. Homes were at least a football field from the roadway. He rode on into town. Pineville wasn't much good for anything but losing yourself. A couple traffic lights and stores, a spatter of houses here and there, and not much else. Unlike the islands, it lacked the laid-back allure and the promise of any sophistication. That was essential to him.

Another half-mile up ahead, a yellow neon sign flashed *Open 24/7*. He closed in on it and saw the thick metal poles holding the sign up out in front of a two-pump gas station with an attached café. A cup of coffee sounded good.

He pulled into the parking lot. Gravel crunched under his tires and his stomach rumbled. Maybe he'd grab some dessert, too.

After that miserable meal at home, he needed to cleanse his palate and clear his head of bad thoughts. About Mandy and Liv, and definitely about his son and daughter and that manipulative tyrant of a woman he had the misfortune to call his wife. Never in his life had he met anyone so evil—and between his criminal law practice and his extracurricular NINA ventures, he'd routinely interacted with a lot of raunchy people.

But even their worst didn't come close to the low-down things that occurred under his own roof. His family won the prize hands-down for scraping the bottom of the barrel.

His former family.

Yes. The excitement returned. In his new life, he had no family. He liked that, and he intended to keep it that way.

Now, he could finally choose. The persistent heaviness on his chest lightened. In a couple weeks, after he settled it, that too would become a distant memory.

Earlier tonight, he'd choked down their last lousy meal together and then he'd cited needing to work and left. His wife hadn't bothered to ask where he was going . . . and he hadn't bothered to tell her.

That rebellion, after years of toeing her lines in the proverbial sand, had felt good. Really good.

That was all over now. From this point forward, *he* controlled his life.

Finally!

He swung into an open parking slot next to a rusted out pickup, got out, locked the door, and then headed across the parking lot to the little brick building. His legs felt half numb. Guess he needed to move around a little more than he needed coffee and dessert.

A sleepy guy sat on a stool behind the register. Charles nodded and walked on, through the store to the back café. Three other people sat in two of its six booths. He walked to the far end away from them and sat down in the worn-out booth with his back to them, discouraging conversation. The cracked green vinyl stabbed into the backs of his legs.

A waitress in her sixties, wearing too much makeup and too short a skirt for a woman her age, set a clear plastic glass of water on the table. "Hey. What can I get you?"

Should he risk eating here? He was a little hungry.

Why not? You're already living dangerously, right?

He looked at the waitress. "How about a pastrami on rye and a large coffee. Black."

"Coming right up." She walked away, crackling her chewing gum.

He stretched and sipped at the water. To make the flight out of New Orleans to Tokyo, he'd have to drive the rest of the night. The coffee would help keep him awake. From Tokyo, he took a two-hour hop. He could sleep then.

"Jackal."

The whisper from behind him caught him off-guard. An icy chill streaked up his spine. Charles didn't turn around—didn't have to turn around to recognize that voice. NINA had found him. Already. *How?*

Paul Johnson walked to the opposite side of the booth and then sat down, his suit impeccable, his shirt crisp. How he managed that, Charles had no idea.

The geriatric waitress bounded over. "What can I get you, hon?"

"Coffee, please."

"Anything to eat? Your companion's having pastrami on rye . . ." she said, attempting to entice him.

"No, thank you." Johnson glanced her way. "Just the coffee."

When she'd gone, Johnson focused on Charles, his face expressionless. He didn't utter a sound, just waited for Charles to explain himself.

His throat dry, he did his best not to shake. Johnson *shouldn't* know him. "And you are . . .?"

His eyes turned stony. "Don't even go there. You know who I am, and why I'm here."

He definitely knew. *NINA definitely knew.* How Phoenix had discovered the truth, Charles didn't know. From the very beginning, he'd been so careful . . .

The waitress must have picked up on the tension at the table. She placed their orders before them without a word, then quickly left.

Charles glanced down at the sandwich. *His last meal.* His stomach curled then coiled into fist-sized knots. "How long have you known?"

"Your real identity?" Johnson sighed, sipped over the steam in his white mug. "We've always known."

The coils clenched tighter. Total failure. "So Liv died for nothing."

"Actually, she died because we needed her to die." Johnson sipped from his steaming cup. "Mmm, decent coffee for a hole in the wall."

"Why?" Charles asked. "She didn't even know you existed."

Johnson laughed. "For a smart man, you're incredibly dense." Johnson set down his mug. "Her daughter was engaged to a Shadow Watcher, and you actually think everyone on either side hasn't turned over every rock to find out all there is to know about both of you?"

The truth smacked Charles between the eyes. "You set me up to kill her."

"You did fine on that front without any help from us. But your sacrificing her to save yourself was entirely predictable." Johnson pulled a paper napkin from the dispenser and folded it into a neat square. " You've always done it—with her and your daughter."

Something in Johnson's body language alerted Charles. He'd seen it too often in clients, witnesses, and jurors to miss it. "Are you telling me I didn't kill Liv?"

Johnson nailed him with a level look. "You shot her."

He had, but there was something . . . They expected he would shoot her. Had they prepared her? "Is Liv dead?" Charles didn't know what to think. Not now, not about anything.

Johnson's narrowed eyes gleamed. "Officially, yes. She is dead."

Afraid to assume, Charles pushed, mindful that to get the

right answers, he had to ask the right questions. "So what you're saying is, unofficially she isn't dead." Was that possible? He'd fired the shot, seen her blood stain her blouse, pool on the floor where she'd fallen. His mind raced. *Liv alive? Was that remotely possible?* He shoved at his plate. It scraped across the table. "I don't believe you. I watched her die."

"Did you?" Johnson took another sip of coffee.

Charles thought he had. She'd looked dead, though he hadn't checked her pulse for fear of leaving evidence on the body. He would have sworn, but now, looking at Johnson, Charles wasn't sure. Wait . . . Wait. *Mind games.* Phoenix, or someone with NINA, knew he was running, and now they were playing mind games with him to torment him. Johnson was notorious for torment. He thrived on it. "She's dead," he told Johnson. "Mandy was at the scene. She saw Liv's body. So did Detective Walton and the M.E. and half the Maddsen police force."

Johnson paused a long second, retained his icy calm, and his face didn't twitch. That *tell* of his warned when he was emotional, and it was nowhere to be found. "Mandy never went inside the house. Can't contaminate an active crime scene."

"What about the others? Cops were all over the place in there."

"Cops, you say?" Johnson paused. "Hmm, were they now?"

"I saw them." He'd been in the side yard across the street with binoculars. He'd seen everything.

"Really? Are you positive?" Johnson twisted his mouth, leaned forward and laced his hands on the tabletop. His cufflink winked in the weak florescent light. "Or did you see what we wanted you to see?"

Beyond scared, Charles grew angry. "To pull off what you're suggesting, Walton, the M.E., and every cop out there would've had to have been NINA affiliates. Do you expect me to believe Phoenix—NINA—arranged that and staged the whole thing?"

"Not being involved, I wouldn't know." Johnson held up his cup, signaling the waitress for a refill. "You do know well, however, that NINA and Phoenix compartmentalize, revealing operational details on a need-to-know basis."

True. No one conducting any aspect of a mission knew the entire mission, only that part for which he or she was responsible. It was safer for everyone that way—and it added additional layers of protection and distance for the honchos. One can't disclose what one doesn't know.

The waitress carried over the coffeepot and then poured.

"Thank you." Johnson looked up at her and smiled.

It chilled Charles to the bone. Phoenix, or someone above him, must have staged everything except him pulling the trigger. Yet he'd shot Liv in the chest. He'd seen the blood . . .

Maybe he hadn't. Had he seen anything a vest and fake blood couldn't produce? He scanned his memory.

"Ah, reality finally bites."

It could have been staged. Charles frowned at Johnson.

"Another fact to consider, should you be suffering lingering doubts or delusions," Johnson said, straightening his forefinger from where it'd been curled around his mug. "In your experience, how many new homicide investigations have gone from being opened to cold-cased—unofficially, of course—in under seventy-two hours?" Johnson hiked a shoulder. "In my experience, which admittedly isn't as extensive as yours, that's way too fast."

He'd been duped.

The truth revealing itself to him so slowly did bite Charles. Hard. "Is Olivia still alive?" He tried to keep the hope that she was out of his voice but wasn't sure he'd succeeded.

"I'm afraid only Phoenix can answer that question. You can ask him yourself, of course."

She had to be working with NINA. Why else would it engage her on this? It wouldn't. Had she betrayed him, too?

Betrayed him, or been a forced participant? It could have come down either way. "Why did Phoenix want her dead?"

"I told you once. Weren't you listening?" Johnson seemed irritated. "Her daughter was engaged to a Shadow—"

"No. I'm not buying that." She'd broken off with Tim and stayed away from him with no contact whatsoever. "There's more." Charles thought a second, spun scenarios and landed on one that made sense. "The Shadow Watchers made a connection between Liv and NINA—or it feared they would." NINA would definitely want her dead before that could happen.

"Maybe you're not totally dense," Johnson said. "Though it wasn't the Shadow Watchers."

"Then who was it?"

"A special team of active-duty operatives. One of them is particularly troublesome. He goes by Omega One. We had to have Homeland Security intervene to, shall we say, protect our interests." Johnson sat back. "But that's no longer relevant to you. Neither, for that matter, is Olivia."

Because you betrayed NINA. You're a dead man.

Charles read between those lines to the unstated but obvious just fine. 'So what happens now? You kill me here, in the parking lot, or what?" Resignation inched into his tone. He couldn't run or hide. If NINA wanted him dead, he would be dead. He couldn't survive against their will any more than anyone else had been able to do it, and both Johnson and he knew it.

"Actually, for now NINA wants you alive. It has plans for you."

That surprised Charles. "Plans?" They weren't going to kill him? How . . . odd. "What plans?"

Johnson nodded. "You're going to go to your daughter's wedding tomorrow and walk her down the aisle."

"I—I *what*?" Johnson couldn't have said anything that could have set Charles further back on his heels. *What was*

Phoenix up to now?

"You heard me correctly. Phoenix has decided to give you an opportunity to redeem yourself. We're the only two in NINA currently aware of your attempted unauthorized exodus, by the way." He rolled his shoulder. "If that were not the case, this . . . reprieve would not be possible."

His heart beat hard and fast. "Why does Phoenix want me at Mandy's wedding?"

Johnson circled the rim of his coffee mug with his thumb. "Unfortunately—well, fortunately for you—you happen to be known as the father of the bride. That gives you a unique advantage we can't substitute on such short notice. So you get to live."

"For . . .?" Did he die after the wedding? Just how long a reprieve was this?

"For the purpose of observing and learning as much as you can about the Shadow Watchers and their methods," Johnson said, answering a different but equally important question. "They've cost our organization a great deal of time and money and sidelined a number of key personnel. We'd like to inhibit their future efforts by any and all possible means. You're going to help us do that." Johnson watched a brawny man walk by and on to the restroom. "Phoenix thinks your daughter being married to one of them gives you the best access. If you want to live, which you clearly do to have made all your future plans, you'll use that access for us."

"You don't understand. This won't work." Charles frowned, unsure if disclosing this was a benefit or would earn him a bullet now. "They've surely made the connection and suspect I'm Jackal."

"I do understand, and you're correct, at least in part," Johnson said. "They currently suspect both you and Olivia as Jackal."

"But she's dead, so they're focused on me."

"You're assuming again, Charles. Surely you're beyond that

same mistake."

On this, he wasn't mistaken. With her dead, they had to have their sights focused squarely on him. "So you're sending me into the lion's den to be slaughtered."

"Slaughtered? At your daughter's wedding?" Johnson pulled his lips back from his teeth. "I don't think so. Remember who you're dealing with, Charles. We'd make the wedding a bloodbath. They won't."

Johnson didn't make sense. Charles hated having to ask for clarification, but he hated stumbling around in the dark more. "What?"

"We're ruthless. They're not. It's their flaw, and we exploit it with monotonous regularity."

"They're not stupid. They won't tell me anything," he insisted. "And, even with the wedding, they'll never let me walk out alive."

"You're going, Charles." Johnson stripped the veneer from his tone. "Either to your daughter's wedding or straight to the cemetery. It's your call. I'm up for either."

That was blunt enough to hit home. "I didn't say I wouldn't do it. I said, they'll kill me on sight."

"On any other day, they might. But not on Mandy's wedding day. Not to spare you, of course. To spare her."

"Spare her? From what?"

"You have no idea who they are, do you?" Paul let his impatience and disdain show. "Hard to believe you made the cut. NINA's typically far more discerning. You really should do your research."

"Would you just tell me your point?"

"I already have. Lazy *and* inattentive. It's amazing that you've survived as long as you have with us. You really should pay closer attention." Johnson frowned. "These men are nothing like us."

Everything in him wanted to object to Johnson's aspersions, but being on borrowed time, he didn't dare. Visions of his new life faded. He tugged them back, held on tight. He'd find a way. There had to be one. He wasn't nearly so dense as Johnson claimed. Hopefully, he'd be gone before Johnson or Phoenix came to understand that. "Meaning?"

"We do whatever, whenever, wherever to whomever. They don't."

"You told me this. We're ruthless and they're not."

"They're principled." Johnson grunted. "They'll want a decent wedding for your daughter. It's sad, really."

"Why is it sad for them to want a decent wedding for her?"

Johnson leveled him with a cold stare. "It isn't. It's sad that they care, and you do not. You're her father and you couldn't care less. That's not only sad, it's pathetic—even by our standards, or lack of them." Johnson cleared his throat. "But relax. If they'd made the connection between you and NINA, you'd already be arrested or dead."

Charles took the hit about Mandy because he deserved it. He didn't care. About Liv, however, he cared very much. He had to find out if she was alive, which meant he had to talk with Phoenix. "Statistically, I agree with you. But not enough time has elapsed since Mandy first contacted Tim for them to get the required clearances." This was a small comfort.

Johnson's expression turned icy. "They're Shadow Watchers, Travest. They don't need clearances. You should know that, too."

"*Former* Shadow Watchers," he said. "Small but distinct—"

"Do you *really* think that makes a difference?" Johnson's disgust etched into every line on his face. "If so, you're even more incompetent than I thought."

Did it really make a difference? Charles had assumed it would, but now he accepted the flaw in his thinking. "No, not really."

"Phoenix will be at the wedding. If you get into trouble and you're lucky, perhaps you'll have backup. Frankly, that could go either way. It depends on whether or not he sees you'll be of future value."

Hopefully, Charles could buy himself enough time to revise his plans and stay alive. "We've never met, just talked on the phone. How will I know Phoenix?"

Paul smiled. "Don't worry about that. Phoenix, and everyone else there, knows you. If they choose to reveal themselves, they will."

Charles was afraid to ask, but he had to know. "What about after this wedding? What am I supposed to do then?"

"Go home to your family, of course. Keep living your life the way you have been, and await further orders."

Everything in Charles rebelled. "I can't go back to that woman, Johnson. Or to those spiteful kids. You don't understand. They know about Liv and Mandy. I don't have a home with them anymore." And once his wife discovered he had raided their accounts, he wouldn't have a life anywhere else, either.

"You don't have a choice."

Johnson seemed pretty cocky for a man who'd tangled with the Shadow Watchers twice before and lost both times. He'd landed in prison and had been forced by NINA to confess to the murder of his brother, Edward. After a while, the organization had bought him out—at a steep price. NINA owned Johnson for life.

That's what being on the losing end of a tangle with the Shadow Watchers could do to a man.

In a similar spot now, Charles wondered what Johnson thought. Had his brother or he gotten the best deal? Death? Or a life with NINA calling every shot?

A sinking feeling overwhelmed Charles, and a fear that ran so deep it made his life with the dragon lady and their two ungrateful offspring seem tame and uneventful. Almost pleasant.

He needed time to think. Time to figure out if Liv was dead or alive. If she'd been a party to setting him up . . . Of course, she had. NINA couldn't fake her death without her knowing it. But, in that case, she wouldn't have been given a choice about it. NINA issued orders, not suggestions or recommendations. If it said die, you die or it kills you.

That possibility, that Liv had been an unwilling participant, raised a whole different set of questions. If NINA hadn't killed Liv, why hadn't it? Who was she that it would keep her alive?

She might have loved Charles once. Maybe even for a long time. But he had shot her, and a woman wasn't likely to willingly overlook that.

So he had to return home, and his situation was not better but worse. Not only did he have the dragon lady and her fire-breathing offspring to contend with, he had NINA watching his every move and calling his every move, and, if Liv was alive, she would be gunning for him, too.

A cold certainty seeped down into the marrow of his bones. His future would be even more bleak than his past.

Death looked better all the time.

Tim hung up a secure line and crossed the makeshift ops center set up in Mark's media room. "Where's Mandy?" he asked, standing between Nick and Sam, who were both seated at their computers.

"Wedding stuff with Nora and Annie." Joe passed through, carrying a mason jar of iced-tea. The cubes clinked against its sides.

Mark rushed in. "Tim, I need that authorization now."

"She's not here. I've got to locate her."

"Call her and get the okay. Omega One is on site, waiting to execute."

"What's going on, buddy?" Sam asked Tim.

"The thirty million got Omega One's attention. They've been tracking the money. A transaction took place on the account twenty-four hours *after* Olivia's murder. The film of it came in an hour ago."

Sam sobered. "Olivia made the transaction."

Tim nodded. "It looked like her, anyway. Omega One wants to confirm the corpse's DNA and compare it to some they picked up at the bank."

Nick frowned. "Better call her now. Mandy's the only one who can give the okay outside of a judge."

"We can exhume without it, but she'd never forgive me." Tim dialed her secure phone. It rang twice, then a third time. Finally, she answered.

"Hi, there."

She sounded happy. He stifled a groan, hating to ruin that for her. "Mandy, I'm in a hurry. Sorry, in advance, but I have to be brief."

"What is it?"

"Someone made a withdrawal on your mother's account after she died. We need to exhume the body to get a DNA sample."

"Can't you use mine?"

"We could, but we need hers to rule out any doubt."

"About what?"

"Anything." He hedged, and then called the question. "You okay with that?"

"If you need it, you need it. Do what you need to do."

"Thanks." He hung up, told Mark. "Go."

Mark rushed out of the room and back into the white-noise protected secure area they called the vault to pass on the authorization to Omega One.

Nick stared at Tim. "She didn't ask any more questions."

"No." Tim both loved and hated that.

"She trusts him." Sam lifted a hand. "Don't be shocked by that Nick, but some people actually do trust other people."

Nick frowned. "She's got her head in wedding stuff. When she thinks about it a minute, she'll ask."

Tim agreed with Nick, though her questions wouldn't be rooted in a lack of trust. She was naturally curious. "I just hope she waits until after tomorrow. She sounded . . . "

"What?" Sam asked.

"Happy." Rarely had Mandy sounded the way she had on the phone. "Carefree and really happy."

"Wasn't she really happy before your breakup?" Nick asked.

Tim paused. "Yeah, but not like this. It's different."

"How?" Nick asked.

"I don't know," Tim said. "Just different."

"That's good, bud," Sam said. "Sorry to have to say it, but she ain't had a whole lot of chances to practice being either."

Sam was right. Resolve swept through Tim. "I'm going to change that."

"I hope you do." Sam looked at Nick, half-expecting an acidic comeback.

"Counting on it," Nick said, surprising them and, from his expression, also himself.

Mark came back into the media room. "Omega One says, if Homeland Security doesn't sideline us, he'll have what he needs by tomorrow morning."

"Why so long?" Tim asked.

"Night cover going in—in case NINA has the cemetery under observation."

"I can't see where it matters," Tim told Mark. "If Olivia's with NINA, they already know she's still alive. If she's not, they have no reason to watch her gravesite."

Mark snagged a handful of pretzels from Sam's bowl. "Safer for our guys, and not our call."

"I'm betting she's NINA." Nick looked from the computer screen to the guys. "That's the only way her having $30 million makes sense."

Hard point to knock down. Tim wished he could knock

it down, but logic wouldn't let him. "What's going on with DHS? Why are they sidelining Omega One."

"He has no idea, but the orders came down from up the chain."

"Interesting." Tim didn't like the sounds of this.

"Ain't it though?" Mark bit down on a crunchy pretzel. "What about Travest?"

"He has to be NINA," Sam said. "I've been waiting for you to wrap up in the vault to tell you."

"Tell us what?" Mark asked.

"After Travest talked to Mandy, he left his office. He drove home, had dinner with his family—and a whale of an argument. We had visual but no audio, so I can't tell you the nature of the dispute, only that there was one, and it was three to one against him."

"What else?" Mark asked, withholding comment.

"He left right after dinner," Sam said. "Bugged out, I mean. Gone for good."

"Where'd he go?"

"He bought gas and food in Pineville, Alabama." Sam hooked a thumb north. "I've got a call into the waitress who was on duty last night. Her name is Sherry Harness. She's due back in to work in a couple hours. No phone, and we don't have anyone close enough to drop in sooner unless you want to bring in local law enforcement."

"No, don't do that."

"Didn't think so." Sam sniffed.

"Where is Travest now?"

"We don't know. No assets picked him up in real time." Sam's computer pinged. He checked the screen. "Whoa. Nix that. He's surfaced."

"Where?" Tim bent low and checked Sam's screen.

"Here." Sam met Tim's gaze. "He just checked into the Five Palms Resort."

Their wedding reception was going to be held at Five

Palms Resort. Tim grimaced.

"Guess he's going to make the wedding." Nick grumbled.

Tim didn't know whether to be happy or upset. Worse, he didn't know how Mandy would feel about her father showing up.

"I'd better let Omega One know," Mark said, but he didn't move. Instead, he watched Tim, waiting for a cue on how he was taking the news.

Tim ended the wait. "Travest wrecks this wedding for Mandy and all bets are off."

"Think steel," Mark said, then headed toward the vault.

"Yeah." Tim grimaced. Thinking steel had gotten everyone on the team through tough, impossible times. And if marrying a woman who had NINA operatives for both mother and father didn't qualify as tough, nothing did.

Nick took off his glasses. "I hate to say it, Tim, but a peaceful wedding or marriage doesn't appear to be in your future."

With these people for in-laws? It didn't seem probable or even possible. "Or in Mandy's."

"Yeah, and you get to tell her. Lucky you."

Tim frowned at Sam. "Suggestions on how I should go about doing that?"

"Straight out." Nick motioned with his hand.

"You've got a mean streak a mile wide, Nick." Sam pushed back his cap. "At least, soften it up for her as much as you can. Having one parent as a crook is bad, but both? It'll knock her to her knees, bud."

Joe shook his head, grunted at Tim. "I know you're not seeking advice about a woman from these two dead stumps."

Tim shrugged. "Course I am. I'll take it from wherever I can get it."

"Please." Joe crossed his chest with the palm of his hand.

"In my situation, you would, too. No groom is eager to devastate his bride on the night before their wedding, Joe."

He lifted a finger. "On her wedding day, bro."

"Oh, no. I'm not waiting to tell her this on our wedding day."

"Unfortunately, you have no choice. She's otherwise occupied, and you're not messing that up with this kind of news."

"She's going over last minute details with Nora and Annie," Tim countered. "I can talk to her and not mess up anything."

"No, you can't. I just got off the phone with Beth. They wrapped that all up and left for a shower Roxy and Kelly put together."

A bridal shower. No, Tim couldn't mess that up. Or maybe he should. Mandy would want to know.

"I know that look. Don't do it, Tim. Don't even think it." Nick parked his glasses back on the tip of his nose. "If Travest shows up tomorrow, and he could since he's at the resort, anything could happen. We've got planning to do to be ready for him. Let Mandy at least have her bridal shower. She needs it, and you guys have plenty trauma and drama to overcome."

"Yeah, Nick's right, bud. Women need some good memories for when we drive them nuts." Sam offered his two-cents, rocking back in his seat. "We shed blood at her wedding and you're gonna need all the good will you can get just to stay in the dog house."

"We do what we have to do. That's the point of this, right? No choice on the matter."

"We'll carve that into your headstone." Nick groused. "Wait, we'll be dead with you."

Tim hiked a questioning shoulder.

Nick frowned. "If Mandy doesn't take us out, Nora will."

She would. Tim again thought of calling her, but Sam's warning replayed in his mind. *Good will.* The redneck had a point. So did Nick about Nora. She'd take serious exception, not that it mattered when push came to shove. They'd do what they had to do, and that was the bottom line.

"Hanging with you guys, I probably will need a mountain of help to stay in her good graces." Tim would wait to call. "I guess there's no harm in getting the DNA results or a positive ID on the woman who made the bank transaction before talking with Mandy."

"No harm at all." Nick folded his arms. "A little delay's definitely in order."

Tim looked to Joe. He was the best authority on women.

"For once, the dead stumps are right. "No man ever deliberately messes up a good mood on anything where there's no re-do option and prospers."

Three to one settled it. Tim stuck with the decision to wait, hoping he wouldn't live to regret it.

CHAPTER 10

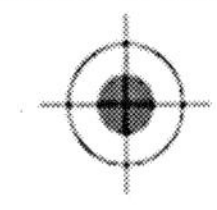

Monday, October 27th

The unflappable Nora stood just beyond the church's front door and gave Tim the news. "Wendy Colter—the organist—just cancelled. She has the flu."

"Oh, no." Tim groaned, looked to Mark. "What now?"

"Sorry. I don't do musical instruments. Nick can do something technical . . ."

"The music isn't a problem." Nora frowned, clearly miffed that they thought it would be. "She's sending a substitute named Viviana Hayes. I figure, you boys might want to check her out so we don't have no surprises here today. I ain't having no wedding for one of my boys waylaid by unexpected shenanigans."

"Thanks, Nora." Relieved, Tim turned to Nick.

"Already on it," he said, punching her name into the system on a secure phone.

Sam dropped his voice, spoke into a tactical throat mic. "Groom Walker One, report." A long ten seconds later, Sam relayed to Tim. "Jeff 's team hasn't spotted Travest here yet. He left the resort about ten minutes ago and headed this way, so he won't be long."

Tim's throat went dust-dry. "I need to talk to Mandy. She should know before the wedding what's going on."

"You can't do that to her." Nick propped a hand in his slacks' pocket.

"No way." Sam fidgeted with his tie. "Man, I hate these things. I've had less aggravating torture."

Nora wagged a finger at him. "Mess up this day for Mandy, and I'll strangle you with that tie, boy."

She made the empty threat and sounded as if she meant it, which warned Tim she'd taken Mandy under her wing. Grateful for that, he winked at her. Thank you, Nora."

"For what?"

"Everything. You and Annie, pulling all this together for us. It's wonderful. Mandy will love it." The church looked pretty with big bunches of flowers at the ends of the pews bound with purple ribbons, and a long stretch of purple carpet up the aisle to the altar.

Nora beamed but grunted and used her gruffest tone. "Our biggest accomplishment was getting Sam into a tux."

Tim laughed but he didn't dispute her. Left to his own devices, Sam would have worn jeans and a sawed-off sleeved shirt. "I'm amazed by that."

"Threats were involved," she confessed.

"Groom Walker, you copy?"

Tim heard the transmission and excused himself, then tapped his throat mic. "Go ahead One."

"Package has arrived."

Travest. "We'll intercept." Tim nodded to Sam. "Got it?"

Sam nodded, then relayed to the others.

The outer door cracked open and a tiny, frail-looking woman walked in and said to no one in particular, "Hello. I'm Viviana Hay—"

Nora stepped forward. "Wendy's organist. Wonderful. Come with me, dearie."

"Just a second, Nora." Tim approached Viviana with his iPhone. "You have to be scanned. Security purposes."

"No problem." She shoved her purse at Nora. "Go ahead and check it, too. Can't be too careful these days."

Nora opened the purse, and Tim activated the scanning app. *Clean. She wasn't armed.* "Nora?"

"It's fine." She passed the purse back to Viviana Hayes.

The organist smiled, then she and Nora walked into the Sanctuary.

Before that door fully closed behind them, the outer front door swung wide and Charles Travest walked in wearing a dark blue suit and a pale gray tie. Tim studied him. A large man, probably a ballplayer. Raw-boned, ruddy complexion, an imposing air, and clearly uncomfortable about being here. He and Mandy didn't favor at all. Tim stepped forward to greet him. "You must be Mandy's father." Tim extended his hand. "I'm her fiancé, Tim Branson."

That reception clearly hadn't been expected and it ratcheted down the tension in Travest. He clasped Tim's hand, firmly shook it. "Have our special circumstances been explained to you?"

Worried about himself, before even a hello? "Yes, they have." Tim swallowed his distaste. Nora assured him, as did Lisa, that Mandy would be thrilled if her father walked her down the aisle. "I guess you want to see your daughter before the ceremony." Maybe the man would explain skipping her mother's funeral. Mandy needed to hear that. Tim wouldn't mind hearing a decent explanation himself.

"Um, yeah. Yeah, I suppose I should have a word with her." He pointed left and then right. "Which way?"

"I'll take you." Lisa stepped in, her purple gown swishing with her steps. "I'm Lisa, Mandy's friend. She'll be happy to see you, I think."

And Tim was happy to see Lisa. If Travest pulled anything, dressed to the nines or not, she'd use her black-belt skills to clean his clock, providing Mandy didn't beat her to it. Twenty-eight years of resentment against a black belt, he'd put his money on resentment any time.

Tim watched them go.

"Don't worry," Mark said softly. "Lisa's wired. Nick's watching the whole thing."

That relieved some pressure but, honestly, Tim wouldn't stop worrying until this was over.

"Groom Walker?"

Tim tapped his mic. "Go ahead." It was Nick.

"Viviana Hayes checks out. Nothing on her. Not even a traffic ticket."

"Thanks." Tim stiffened his shoulders. A couple more hours. The security checks had all been done. The perimeter stood secured, and everyone inside it was known or cleared. Well, except for Charles Travest.

If anyone had told Tim a week ago he'd be marrying Mandy today, he'd have considered them loony. Yet here he was, about to marry the woman of his dreams.

He just hoped that her parents' NINA connections wouldn't turn those dreams into nightmares.

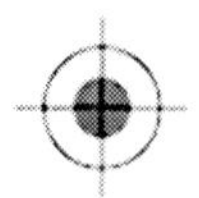

A tap sounded at the door. Mandy turned toward it. "Come in."

Lisa entered, closed the door behind her, and smiled. "You look stunning, Mandy."

"Thanks." She laughed. "I look in the mirror and I still can't believe it's me." The dress was her fantasy dress, delicate, flowing and frothy. "Nora and Annie actually found *my* dress."

"You gave them good hints at what you wanted. What

those two can do when they put their heads together makes the rest of us feel like slugs." Lisa laughed, then stilled. "I have something to tell you."

Mandy frowned. "Is it bad news? I—I really don't want bad news today."

"I wish I knew. I'm going to have to leave it to you to decide, but either way, you need to know this."

That had Mandy's attention. "Okay."

"First, don't get mad at the guys. They talked Tim out of telling you right away." She slid Mandy a knowing look. "They're protecting you so you have a wedding with good memories. Even Nora said they should wait to tell you."

"So why aren't you waiting?"

"Because we suspect NINA is here or coming, and you should know it."

"That was the objective, Lisa, so I do know it." Mandy frowned. "Is there more?"

"There is, yes, but I can't tell you everything because I don't know it all. I do know that you, better than anyone else, will pick up on anything odd or strange."

"Seriously?" Mandy shuddered. "It's all odd and strange."

"You know what I mean." Lisa licked at her lips. "Look, I love most of the people in this building, and you will, too, in time. I think you're on your way to it already." When Mandy nodded, Lisa added, "There's danger and we all need to be aware and to know to expect it. Make sure you're aware and your internal radar is engaged. Trust it."

"I understand all that, and I will. So what's happened? What exactly are the guys protecting me from?"

"I only know two things you don't yet know," Lisa said. "After your mom died, someone withdrew some of her thirty million from the bank."

"Tim already mentioned that when he wanted permission to exhume her body. Do you know who went to the bank?"

Lisa looked her right in the eye. "She looked like your

mother, but no one is sure who she really was yet. They're still working on it."

That stunned Mandy. "Lisa, are you saying there's a chance it could have been her? That—that my mother could be alive?"

"I don't know. NINA has substituted doubles before, so probably not, but there's an outside chance. You didn't see the body, but the detective there—"

"Walton, yes."

"He says she's passed and so does the medical examiner. And there were a lot of cops at the crime scene. That says it wasn't her at the bank, but . . ." Lisa lifted her hands. "All I know is, whenever NINA's involved, things are seldom what they seem. And they're here. I can't prove it, but I feel it. So I wanted you to know and be on your toes. That's all."

"I trust your instincts, and I appreciate your telling me." Mandy reasoned through this input. A puzzle piece that didn't fit slid into place. "Tim isn't sure she's dead. That's why he needed her DNA and not mine."

"Like I said, with NINA, little is ever what it seems. The dead show up alive. Some appear to be one person but they're actually someone else—they pulled that on Nora, for pity's sake. You never know who is who or what they're up to until they strike."

"Which is why you're so afraid."

Lisa nodded. "I've tangled with them before. I know what they're capable of doing. That's why I'm so afraid."

Mandy swallowed hard. "You think my mother is with NINA."

"I think that's a logical deduction, considering all the money. But no logical deduction is proof it's the truth. I truly don't know." Lisa frowned. "Where else would your mother get that kind of money?"

Thirty million dollars? Mandy frowned. "She wouldn't. There's nowhere I know of that could explain it."

"I'm so sorry, Mandy. Having questions about her like this

. . . It has to be incredibly hard for you."

"It is, and I'm so sorry."

"You haven't done anything." Lisa sent her a stern look. "Everyone is responsible for their own actions. No more."

"And no less," Mandy countered. "How could they both be involved in something so evil and I not know it?"

"They worked hard to keep it from you." Lisa clasped Mandy's arm. "I've been down this road, and I'm telling you. They're very good at deception and diversion. Don't beat yourself up for what you didn't know or do. You knew what you knew, and did all you could. Be at peace with that."

"Thank you, Lisa. I just hate feeling stupid. That they could do these things right under my nose makes me feel really thick."

"You're not. Like I said, if they're both NINA, they're motivated to keep you in the dark. Nora's twin got past her. If she didn't pick up on her twin sister—everyone knows she rarely misses anything—the rest of us missing signs is a given."

They weren't going to ostracize her. Relieved, Mandy took in a deep breath that filled her lungs and then slowly expelled it. "I've been standing here wondering about her and NINA and still wishing she were here for the wedding. Isn't that crazy?"

"Not at all. Regardless of what else she might be, she's your mother."

"Then I remember if she were here, she'd be warning me not to marry Tim, and she'd be in a lot of trouble—deservedly so, if she is with NINA." Mandy glanced away to a place far beyond the wall. "I just can't imagine that she is—was—but that's the only way any of this with Jackal makes sense, isn't it?" Lisa withheld her opinion, and Mandy continued, "Oh, how I wish I had an explanation that was . . . different."

"Of course, you do. Who wouldn't?" Lisa asked. "Listen, your heart is torn about her and your father. That's normal and you couldn't be any other way and still be honest. You might not like them or what they've done, but you love them because they're your parents. I get it."

"I do." Mandy nodded. Stilled. Her mother being gone made it possible for her and Tim . . . That was insane. She'd been murdered. "How can you love and hate someone at the same time?"

Lisa's expression turned tender. "You love them in spite of their actions, and you hate their actions. Not them." Lisa clasped Mandy's hand, gently squeezed. "All normal. Not fun, not easy, but completely normal."

"Just once, it'd be nice, if something could be easy and straightforward."

"Something is." Lisa smiled. "The way you and Tim feel about each other is easy and straightforward—no matter how hard others try to complicate it."

"True." Mandy smiled, but it was admittedly shaky. She still loved him, but did he still love her? She wasn't sure. Yet, loving him was easy and straightforward. It was just whether or not he loved her back that had gotten a little muddy.

"Anyway, keep your eyes and ears open. You see or hear anything, press this." She pressed a pearl near the neckline of Mandy's dress.

"Press a pearl?" What good would that do?

"It's a panic button." Lisa's smile faded and regret pierced her eyes. "Don't be afraid to use it. Anything at all looks out of line, you push the button."

"Okay."

"And speaking of panic, I'm afraid I have one more thing to tell you."

"What could possibly be left?"

"Your father is out in the hallway. Mark's with him, so it's okay. He'd like a word with you—before the ceremony."

Her father? Here? Shock pumped through her body. It took a long minute to recover. "He came?"

"He did. Are you okay with that? Because if you're not, just say so, and the guys will boot him out the door."

"I'm fine with it." Scared to death, but fine. "It's what we wanted, remember? I—I just didn't expect him to actually show up." Mandy leaned against a chair, half afraid her knees would give out. Did she embrace him in gratitude, or slap him for his lack of respect to her mother? Not showing up for her funeral. How could he do that? And not for the first time, Mandy wondered if he hadn't felt threatened by someone or something and shot her mother to protect himself. Mandy hated even thinking it, but if it came down to him or her, or him and anyone else, he'd choose himself every time. Of that, she had no doubt.

If only she knew for fact what had happened that day, she'd know what to do. But she didn't know . . . yet.

"Shall I let him in, then?"

Mandy nodded. "But, Lisa, stay close. I don't know that he shot my mother, but if he did, he could shoot me, too, to keep me from telling anyone about him."

"I will. But, for the record, if he had that in mind, he never would have come here. You've got more security than the president right now, and long before he came inside, he'd been scanned, presented identification, and been questioned, so he would know it." She gave Mandy's shoulder a reassuring pat. "Besides, I know for a fact he's not armed."

"He could have stashed something somewhere. You can't be sure he doesn't have a weapon."

"Yes, I can." Lisa nodded. "I stumbled into him on the way back here to double-check. He's clean."

"So talented." Mandy smiled. "I have such gifted friends here."

"You do. And life's going to keep getting better. You'll see. You just remember that, okay? We're all with you."

A rush of emotion washed through her. She wasn't alone anymore. Mandy nodded, wanting desperately to believe it.

Lisa opened the door. "You can come in now, Mr. Travest."

He stepped inside. Lisa stepped out and closed the door.

When it clicked shut, he nodded. "Hello, Mandy."

She nodded back. "I'm surprised you came."

"Frankly, so am I. But here I am."

He looked nervous. Uncertain. She'd never seen him like this. "Are you going to kill me to keep your secrets?" Might as well get the question out on the table and see what he said.

He hadn't expected her to baldly ask. His tone took on a reprimanding edge, and his expression tightened. "You're my daughter. I'm going to walk you down the aisle to marry the man you love."

She reminded herself that he was a lawyer. A good one. Great with words. Not so great with actions, especially positive ones toward her. "Did you kill my mother?"

"I loved your mother."

"You didn't answer my question."

"No." He looked her in the eye. "Did you?"

Anger rippled through her. "How dare you ask me that?"

"How dare I do to you exactly what you just did to me?"

He had a point. She shifted on her feet, held tight to the back of the wing chair. "You didn't come to her funeral."

"I couldn't."

"Because someone might tell your wife or your children?"

"Because I was in court on a three million dollar case and the judge refused to give me a continuance. I asked, but the request was denied."

"You didn't tell him it was for a funeral."

"No, I didn't."

Inside, Mandy again felt torn. Part of her wanted him to be innocent and good, and part of her wanted to strike out and hurt him for hurting her all of her life. Lisa was right about loving and hating the actions of a person. Not the person. But if he was Jackal and he had shot her mother . . .

A knock came at the door.

"Yes?" Mandy called out.

"It's time." Mark's voice carried to her, not Lisa's.

Mandy looked at her father. "It's time."

He crooked his arm. "You make a beautiful bride, Mandy."

The kind words shot straight to her starved heart. Had that been honest or intentional manipulation? "Thank you."

His eyes took on a dreamy quality. "You look so like your mother."

The bubble of joy popped and, inside, she seethed. He wasn't here for her. Once again, he looked at her and saw only her mother.

Maybe he wasn't here for her or her mother. Maybe he was here for NINA. They could have sent him. But it didn't matter. Not really. Not anymore. Whatever motivated him to come, it wasn't her. He wasn't here for his daughter. She was an end to some means only clear to him in his own mind.

And Nora was right. Mandy couldn't count on him for anything. Not funerals or weddings. Nothing. As much as that hurt, she did know it for certain now, and having realistic expectations settled doubts and distanced guilty feelings for lacking faith in him.

Still, the truth hurt. But like on so many other things, it had to faced, addressed, and accepted.

"Wait." With an outstretched hand pressed against the wood, Mandy stopped him from opening the door. "I want no trouble here today. You know what I mean, so don't insult either of us by pretending you don't." She looked him in the eye. "Beware."

"Of what?"

Her tone turned deadpan flat. "You're unarmed, but I'm not."

His eyebrows shot up on his forehead. "You're going to shoot me?"

"Am I going to have to shoot you?"

He didn't answer.

"For once, let's be honest and totally candid," she said.

"You say you didn't kill my mother but, frankly, I don't believe you. So *could* I shoot you? Oh, yes, for that, I could. But I'd rather not. Recalling that on every wedding anniversary from now on would be awful. So here's what I want—and it's not negotiable. You're going to walk me down the aisle, cause no trouble during the wedding, then after it, you make your excuses and leave."

"I should stay for the reception, Mandy."

"No." She lifted her chin. "I don't want you there."

"But—"

"Don't push me. Not today." She let him hear her resolve. "You walk out of this church and get in your car, and go. Stay away from me and mine—and for the record, everyone here is mine."

"Unbelievable."

"Believe it."

"I put everything on the line to be here today, and this is how you thank me?"

"I loved you and look what you did to thank me." Anger shook her voice. "Something you've never understood is that I am not my mother. You can't use or manipulate me like you did her. At one time, you had that power. But you don't anymore."

"I'm your father, Mandy. I'll always be your father."

"Yes, I guess you are. But all I ever wanted was a dad, and that's something you've never been. At least, not to me." She looked at him from under her lashes. "You might or might not know it, but there's a big difference between a father and a dad." She drew in a staggered breath. "I'm offering you détente. Accept it, and leave us all alone."

"Or?"

"I'll do whatever I have to do to take you down—and believe it or not, I have a lifetime of ammo with which to do it."

"Blackmail?"

"If you insist. I considered this a truce but, like you, I'll go to any lengths to protect what's mine."

"I've always suspected you were ruthless."

"If I have to be to protect mine, I will be. Don't doubt it."

He seemed appalled and pleased by that. "We're more alike than you know."

"We're nothing alike," she countered. "I would never do to another human being what you've done to me or to my mother."

"Yet you'd shoot me."

"Would I?"

He stared at her a long moment. "Yes, I believe you would."

"Then I wouldn't provoke me, or force me to choose."

He lifted his jaw. "So they know I'm Jackal."

"Jackal?" She gave him a puzzled look. "You're a vulture, that much I know for sure." She clasped the doorknob. "Like I said, beware. You're not armed but I am. I've given you fair warning. I suggest you remember it."

He stared at her a long moment, took stock in what he saw, then backed up a step. "Very well. Détente, it is then. I wouldn't want you to splatter my blood on your wedding dress."

"That would not make me happy," she said honestly. "But, a woman does what a woman has to do."

Clearly he believed her, and just as clearly being afraid of her annoyed him. He grimaced. "I'll leave right after the ceremony."

"Great. Make your polite excuses to me, and then go."

"Fine."

They walked out of the bridal chamber and into position at the doors to the Sanctuary.

Lisa intercepted them. "Excuse us, Mr. Travest. I need a quick second."

"Of course." He stepped away, just out of earshot.

Lisa fluffed her dress, whispered. "Are you okay?"

"I'm fine." Mandy smiled. Inside, she shook like a leaf.

"I had to ask. You just threatened to shoot your father."

"I didn't."

"I heard you, Mandy." Lisa tapped the fabric near the special pearl on Mandy's dress.

The transmitter. "I forgot about that." Caught red-handed, Mandy sighed. "Don't worry. I wasn't really going to shoot him."

"You convinced me you were, and obviously you convinced him."

"I meant to convince him, but I couldn't have shot him. Well, not right this second, anyway."

"Why not?"

"I don't have a gun."

Lisa took in a sharp breath. "You're lucky he didn't put you to the test."

"Maybe. But after all the years of him and his lies, treating us like . . . Let's just say I have a formidable amount of pent up anger at him to vent."

"Maybe he *was* the lucky one."

Mandy gasped then groaned. "Tim couldn't hear all that, could he?"

Lisa studied her a long moment, let her gaze drop. "I'm not sure."

"Oh, no." Mandy seemed totally distressed. "He heard it all."

"Don't you dare cry and make your mascara run. Even if he did hear it, what's the problem? All you did was defend everyone you love. He wouldn't think a thing of it. You didn't do anything the guys haven't done a million times."

"But I threatened to shoot my own father." Why had she let her temper get the better of her? She'd meant it, but she should have been more diplomatic. She should have had more discipline and control and appealed to his higher angels. Surely he had some.

"Well, yeah, you did," Lisa said. "But you couldn't actually do it because you don't have a gun."

"Right. Right, I don't. Tim would know that. He'd know I was bluffing." Mandy let out a relieved sigh. "Oh, thank you, Lisa."

Knowing an exit line when she heard one, Lisa passed Mandy her bouquet. "You're very welcome." She motioned to Charles Travest to rejoin them. "It's time."

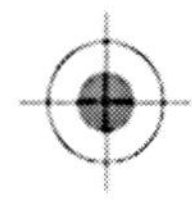

People packed the little church, filling both sides of the aisle.

Tim would appreciate that kindness. He stood near the minister, scanning their guests' faces. Judging by his body language, he recognized most of them. Mark stood to his right, his best man, and he was smiling. Tim appeared serious. *Happy, but worried.*

Mandy's stomach fluttered and tears threatened. The church looked stunning, decorated simply and elegantly, just as she'd hoped. Prisms of sunlight streaked in through the stained glass windows and cast rainbows throughout. Knowing the promise they carried left her breathless.

Tim smiled at her.

The music shifted from a prelude to *The Wedding March.*

Everyone stood up. Charles Travest looped their arms and they began the walk down the aisle.

When Mandy passed her, Annie sniffled.

Nora elbowed her.

Benjamin Brandt and his wife Kelly smiled, Kelly patting their infant daughter gently on the back. She had a purple ribbon in her hair in Mandy's honor. When Mandy had met Kelly at the shower, she'd been amazed at how much she looked like the center's founder, Susan. Tim had warned her to prepare for that. But within hours, Mandy wondered how she'd ever thought they strongly resembled. Kelly was so unique and vibrant.

The music caught Mandy's ear.

Her mother's extra note.

She stumbled.

Her father looked over, silently asking if she was okay.

"I'm fine." She surreptitiously glanced at the organist. Didn't recognize her. Had she really heard that note, or was her mind playing tricks on her? She had been wishing hard her mother could be here for the wedding . . .

Mandy kept moving, kept walking toward Tim. He looked so handsome, so strong and trustworthy and . . . genuinely happy. That beloved twinkle she'd seen in his eyes the first time he'd looked at her greeted her now. How she loved that twinkle. *He had to still love her.* Certainty fueled her steps. Fifty years from now, that twinkle would still be there. That twinkle, and a lifetime of memories.

The chorus came again. She listened intently. Waited. Her stomach in knots, her hands clammy beneath her gloves, her heart pounding.

And she heard the note. Again. *Her mother's note.*

It's my signature note, darling . . .

Mandy didn't dare to glance at the organist. Didn't dare. The woman didn't look remotely like her mother, but she had to be. Had to be. No one else knew that note.

She was alive. Alive and here to see her daughter marry Tim. After Jackal's warning, she had to be terrified, but still she'd come. How had she faked her own death? Why?

Surely she hadn't anticipated all that had happened. The events had to be because of NINA. Something it did or wanted to do. But why her?

Thirty million reasons…

Was her mother one of them? Could that truly be possible?

Her father stopped at the front of the church. "Good luck to you, Mandy."

"And to you." She stepped away from him and clasped

Tim's outstretched hand.

He lifted her veil, and smiled.

Would he love her if he knew about her mother? Would he smile then? Look at her with that beloved twinkle in his eyes?

She had to know—and to give him what neither of her parents had ever given to her. The truth. Dropping her voice to a whisper only he would hear, she offered it to him, praying he didn't hate her for it. "When they open the grave, it's going to be empty."

Confusion burned in his eyes. "What?"

Regrettable, to have to have this conversation at the altar, but they had no choice. She had to be honest with him. She'd promised, no secrets. "My mother's grave. They won't be able to exhume her body. It's empty."

"I know." His confusion didn't clear. "We just heard. But how did you know?"

Don't push. Take a chance on your heart, Mandy. Have faith in him, and in yourself.

"I'll tell you after." She looked up at him. "Right now, we're a little busy."

A resigned expression flitted across his face and then returned and stayed. "You know that the woman who made the transaction on the money appeared to be her."

She nodded.

"You also know NINA is here."

Boy, did she. "Jackal?" Oh, how she hoped only her father was a NINA insider.

"And Phoenix."

"Who's Phoenix?" Her heart thudded, seemingly dropped into her stomach and dumped acid.

"Jackal's boss," he whispered. "We're not sure if it's a man or a woman."

Jackal's *boss?* Mandy stilled. Glanced at the organist. *His boss?*

"Excuse me." The minister interrupted, clearly out of sorts

at their choosing now to have a private conversation. "Are you ready to proceed?"

"Sorry," Tim told him. "I'm ready." He swept his gaze to her. "Are you ready to marry me, Mandy?"

Her mother? Could she be NINA's Phoenix? Charles Travest's boss? Now that was rich. Extremely unlikely, but rich. Her mother was a recluse, not a likely candidate for a covert operative. Some kind of cover? No. No way. She had many abilities and skills, but not those kind of abilities or skills.

Thirty million can buy a lot of skills—and nobody pays thirty million to anyone without a lot of skills and abilities.

Mandy squeezed Tim's hand until he looked at her. "Will you love me, no matter what?"

Tim didn't hesitate. "Until my last breath."

Mandy studied his eyes. If her mother was Phoenix, he'd breathe a lot longer. She'd do everything possible to protect them both from NINA. Rather than not marrying him to keep him safe, now she had to marry him to keep him safe. And to pray he didn't come to hate her. The line between love and hate could be thin. Razor thin.

Either way, she had only one choice. She nodded at the minister. "I'm ready."

"Ah, good." He looked beyond them and his voice rang out loud and clear. "Dearly beloved . . ."

CHAPTER 11

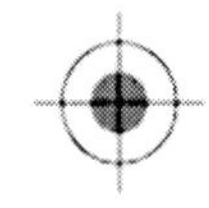

The ceremony went perfectly.

When leaving the Sanctuary arm in arm with Tim, Mandy slowed her steps. Nora looked immensely relieved and Annie Harper stood dabbing at her eyes with a tissue. That they cared so much touched Mandy.

In the Narthex, she paused beside her new husband and accepted well wishes from their guests. The guys seemed sincerely delighted and surprised her, hugging her as enthusiastically as they did Tim. Never in her life had she felt so much a part of a group. They knew her worst, and yet they had accepted her into their circle, their lives, and into their hearts.

A lump rose in her throat and stayed.

"You okay?" Tim whispered close to her ear.

"Moved. These people awe me."

"I know what you mean. They still awe me. It's humbling, isn't it?"

She nodded, spotting her father approaching them.

Something was wrong. Not wrong, but off. Odd. She couldn't pinpoint exactly what, but recalling Lisa's warning to stay on her toes, she couldn't let go of her certainty either, and studied him closely.

"Congratulations," he said to them both, then focused on her. "Mandy, I'm afraid I won't be able to stay for the reception."

His teeth. The hair on the back of her neck lifted. How had she missed that when they'd talked earlier? "I'm so sorry to hear that." It took effort, but she kept her tone steady, cordial yet formal, appropriate for speaking to a stranger. "Thank you for coming."

The veins in his neck swelled, proving he wasn't accustomed to and didn't appreciate being summarily dismissed. Reaching into his inner suit pocket, he pulled out an envelope. "I want you and Tim to have this."

She considered refusing it. She didn't want anything from him. But good sense insisted she take it. It galled her, but she accepted the extended white linen envelope with her gloved hand. "Thank you."

He paused, as if uncertain what else to say, then finally added, "You look so like your mother today."

She braced for the bite those words summoned. Twice, he'd done this—on *her* wedding day. He would never see her for herself. She waited and waited, but for the first time in her life, the bite didn't come. An annoying sting pricked at her. Mildly irritating, but nothing more. Nora had been so right. There was wisdom in truth. Even the truths that hurt empowered.

Yet, another reason his words couldn't cut to her bone surfaced. If not for her father, her mother likely would have been here as herself—*if* this series of events and her marriage had still somehow come about. It was unlikely that it would have. It seemed far more likely that Mandy would have gone on doing what she had done, avoiding Tim to protect him.

Stop it, Mandy. Don't go there. There'll be time for processing all that's happened, but not today. Today, count your blessings. She's alive. This man can't hurt you like in the past. You and Tim are married and together. Celebrate that. Be happy.

She gave herself a mental shake, then lifted her chin and looked him in the eye. "Have a safe trip home."

Accepting that their conversation was over, he nodded then turned and walked out the front door.

As it closed behind him, Mandy breathed easier and noted that the guys had all positioned themselves close to her and Tim. "They're protecting you," she whispered to him, uncertain he'd noticed the touching gesture. "How lucky you are to have them."

"I am. But they're protecting you, not me." Tim mumbled low and deep. "They're determined that you have a perfect wedding with good memories. If he'd done or said anything to wreck it . . ."

Protected. She let the alien feeling spread through her. Liking it, she warmed and smiled. And she regretted her suspicions about her mother. What the explanation for the money was, she had no idea. But there had to be one. Her mother couldn't be a part of NINA. It went against the values and ethics she'd taught Mandy from the cradle. "Is that what you want, too? A perfect day for me, or for us?"

"We are us now." He smiled. "But okay, I'll admit it. Mostly for you, because I know what it cost you to lose what we had. I'm enjoying the day, too. I'll enjoy it more now." The crackle in his tone warned her he'd expected trouble from Charles Travest and Tim was relieved the potential for it had passed with his departure.

Well, he was mostly right about that. She hated to shatter the illusion, but had no choice. "Can you use that throat radio thing to get an evidence bag over here?" She wagged a fingertip in the general direction of his mic.

"What for?"

"This." She held up the envelope, pinched between her forefinger and thumb.

"Why?"

"To run prints on it."

"We have Charles Travest's prints."

Oh, but she hated to ruin their reception and his perfect day. Unfortunately, it was necessary. "I'm afraid that we still need these prints."

He sobered. "Why?"

"Because the man who was here was not Charles Travest."

"How do you know that?"

Sam, Joe and Mark overheard that comment and circled her, Mark mumbling into his mic for Jeff to keep a tail on Travest. "If he sneezes, we need to know it. Priority One."

Mark frowned. "What do you mean, Mandy?"

"It wasn't him." That was as blunt and clear as she could get.

"Who was he?" Sam asked.

"Give her a minute," Joe said, sliding a worried glance at Tim.

His frown matched Mark's. "Spill it, Mandy."

"I don't know who he is. That's why we need to run the prints."

Tim sobered, his full focus shifting from the personal to the professional. "Why do think he wasn't your father?"

"I don't think he wasn't, Tim. I know he wasn't." Her neck warmed and her face heated. "In the bridal chamber earlier, we spoke. I told him to leave right after the ceremony and not to start anything with any of you. That he wasn't armed, but I was." Her face grew hotter.

Tim's eyes stretched wide. "You threatened him?"

Well, great. He hadn't known it, but he did now. "Not exactly. Well, I guess I did, but the point is that the real Charles Travest would have taken exception. He would have stayed for the reception just to show me he could."

Joe shrugged. "Maybe he didn't want to ruin your wedding day."

"Unlikely," she countered. "He's been perfectly content ruining my life."

"I can't believe no one told me you had to threaten him." Tim looked from man to man, clearly seeking an explanation.

Sam grunted. "Seemed appropriate to me. Natural, too."

Mark and Joe mumbled their agreement.

"What's the problem, buddy?" Sam shrugged. "The woman needed *some* privacy. She didn't tell Travest a thing we all ain't been thinking."

Tim accepted an evidence bag from Sam, held it open, then motioned for Mandy to drop the envelope into it. "What alerted you that he wasn't your father? His eyes? Voice? What specifically gave him away?"

"You know me so well." She smiled, loving the comfort she felt in that. "His teeth." She pointed to her lower front teeth. "No gap between them. My father's have a gap."

Tim's eyes gleamed. "Observant."

"I didn't trust him not to come here and try to kill you." She frowned. "Definitely observant. Working hard at it, but I should have caught it in the chamber before the wedding and I didn't. I only noticed the missing gap in his teeth when he was walking toward us here and he smiled at Nora."

"Maybe he's your father's brother or something?" Mark speculated.

"No brother. A mask." She cocked her head, saw Lisa motioning to Mark to join her. "A very good mask."

"So what do you think he's doing?" Mark held up a finger for Lisa to wait a second.

"My guess is he expected trouble. He either suspects or knows we're aware of his other identity." She avoided saying Jackal out in the open for anyone outside their circle to overhear.

"He said we knew it, in the bridal chamber when they

talked," Joe told Tim.

"What did you say to that?" Tim asked Mandy.

"Something about him being a vulture. I played stupid about . . . you know. Like I'd never heard it before."

"She came across great," Mark said. "Like a pro."

"My father wanted to do what he's always done. Keep himself safe." She brushed a fingertip to Tim's jaw. "He sent in a sub, but I bet he's close, watching everything here like he did at my mother's funeral."

Tim frowned. "You told me he wasn't there."

"He wasn't. But he was close by. Maybe across the cemetery, on the other side of the lake, or in the woods that abut it. I don't know exactly where he was, but he was close. Slinking around like some slug instead of paying proper respects to my mother. I'll never forgive him for that."

Still puzzled, Tim prodded. "You obviously didn't see him, so how do you know he was close?"

"I told you. I felt him there, hiding in the shadows, protecting himself, ignoring his responsibilities to us yet again. A decent man would have stood with his daughter at her mother's grave. But he didn't. He couldn't risk being seen by anyone, so he stayed in the shadows and hid like a coward."

Tim repeated her. "You felt him there."

"Yes." She countered his skeptical look. "It's like when you walk into your house and you know it's empty. Or you sense someone following you. Don't tell me you don't get instinctive nudges. Not in your job. I won't believe you."

"I get them." Tim motioned to Sam. "Run these prints and get someone to tag Travest."

"Already tailing . . . whoever the guy is." Sam took the evidence bag. "So he's definitely not Travest." Sam looked to Tim.

"No."

Mandy didn't much care for Sam questioning her judgment, but she let it slide. This was too significant and too high-risk for ego to get into anyone's way.

Joe rubbed at his neck. "Could be Phoenix posing as Travest."

"No," Mark countered. "My gut says Mandy's nailed it. Whoever he is, Travest hired him to cover his sixes. He expected trouble here."

Nora came over, lifted a staying hand. "Enough business, boys. No blood shed in my church and everyone lived, so let's be grateful and get moving. Tim, your limo is out front. You and Mandy need to get on over to the reception before my food's ruined." She turned to go.

"Nora, wait." Mandy touched Nora's arm. When she paused, Mandy impulsively hugged her. "Thank you for everything. You and Annie awe me. This wedding has been perfect."

Nora grinned. Her bright red lipstick smeared on her front teeth. "It ain't the wedding that's perfect, dearie. It's the love."

Mandy's stomach quivered. "I'm counting on that."

Seeing the organist in the hallway near the bridal chamber, Mandy told Tim, "I'll meet you right here in five minutes."

"Where are you going?"

"Ladies room." She headed down the hallway, then pushed open the door . . . and saw the organist, Viviana Hayes, standing inside, waiting for her. Caution swelled in Mandy. "Thank you for stepping in last minute."

"It's a hard time of year to get the flu. Comes on so quickly, you know?"

"Mmm." Mandy looked right into her eyes. "Your playing is . . . unique."

The woman smiled.

The eyes. The voice. The smile. Definitely her mother. Mandy moved from stall to stall. "Alone?" She mouthed the word.

Her mother nodded. "I knew you'd recognize the note. I saw the moment you did. Your step faltered."

"It did." Mandy held her breath, afraid she'd sob. She

covered the pearl to mute their voices so whoever was listening wouldn't hear. When the rush of relief that her mother was alive passed, she added, "I'm so glad you aren't dead."

"I'm so sorry you had to think I was and to grieve. I hated hurting you like that, but I promise you, I had no choice. Your reactions had to be totally honest or all of this would have been for nothing."

"Exactly what is all of this?" she asked. "You are going to explain, right?"

"What I can, yes. But we have little time." She clasped Mandy's arm. "The bottom line is that I thought you'd get over Tim, but you didn't. I couldn't bear you not being happy, Mandy. It became clear to me that you never would be happy without him, so—"

The explanation rang shallow, struck her as hollow, like tin to the ear. Maybe it wasn't a lie but it wasn't the whole truth. "Don't be dishonest with me, Mom. Please, don't. I deserve better."

She blushed. "My intent isn't to deceive. I'm trying to protect you."

"I don't want to be protected."

"Yes, you do—and you should." She sobered. "The less I tell you, the better for you and Tim—all of them."

The team. "Tell me something, Mother. Something honest that makes sense."

At one of three sinks, her mother turned on the water, rinsed her hands, and left the water running, adding an additional layer of noise. Still, she stepped close and dropped her voice even lower. "They were going to kill you. They knew you'd eventually reunite with him, and that they could not risk."

"Why?"

"Let's just say NINA appreciates distance between opposing sides."

"Are you with NINA?"

She ignored the question. "Simply put, one of us had to die. You or me. I chose me."

Did Mandy thank her for that? This woman before her was her mother. Mandy had grown up with her, had been with her her entire life, and yet she had no idea who her mother really was. She now knew who she wasn't. Charles Travest's reclusive mistress. "Are you Phoenix?"

"Who's Phoenix?" She looked baffled and sounded sincere.

But it was an act. Her mother had obviously lied to her many times, and only she knew her reasons. Were her motives pure or diabolical? NINA had a horrific reputation, and from all Mandy had learned about the organization, they'd earned it. What was she supposed to think about these developments? Her mother maybe being a part of something so twisted and awful?

"I see your confusion, and I'm sorry. I'm a good person, Mandy. I promise. Remember that, okay? Remember everything I taught you. That was all real."

"It was? Little else has been."

"It was." She didn't argue, just stiffened her tone and her resolve. "I wish I could give you the answers you want and even need, but I'm sorry, honey, I can't. Innocent people could be hurt. Every thing I disclose creates challenges and puts you in more danger."

"You've lied to me most of my life. I want the truth."

"I can't give it to you."

"You can!" Mandy frowned at her.

"I can but you'll die for it, so I won't."

"Where did you get thirty million dollars?"

"Wise investments. Truly." She glanced at the door. "I have to go now."

"I don't believe you."

"I know. I wish things could be different, but they aren't." Clasping both of Mandy's hands in hers, she gently squeezed. "It was incredibly risky coming here but, even dead, I couldn't miss your wedding." Her eyes shone overly bright. "You made a beautiful bride."

A sense of finality flooded Mandy. Left her bittersweet and aching. "You said that when I played bride and wore the scarf draped over the lampshade, too."

Her mother smiled, pressed a kiss to her cheek. "It was true then and it's true now." She moved to leave. "Be happy, darling."

She couldn't be certain she would, but she dared to hope. Still, her mother seemed to need her assurance, so Mandy gave it to her in a nod. "It means a lot to me that you came." That sense of finality grew stronger and dread dragged at her stomach. Mandy hugged her mother hard. "Will I ever see you again?" she asked, hungry for reassurance of her own.

"I think not." Her mother pulled away. Regret burned in her eyes with a sadness that ran soul-deep. "That's hard, I know. It will be hard for both of us. But you're married to a Shadow Watcher now and that makes us seeing each other impossible."

A cold chill rippled through Mandy. "Then you are with NINA."

"Assumptions are dangerous, darling." She lifted a hand. "My position is complicated and unimportant, truly. Just know that, while I haven't always been forthcoming with you, I have always loved you, Mandy. More than anything in the world."

"The thought of never seeing you again . . ." Mandy choked.

"I'll be watching. If you need me, I'll know."

Tears threatened. She blinked hard. "I love you, Mom."

"I love you, too." She blew Mandy a kiss then left through the door.

She did love Mandy. Enough to die for her—figuratively.

Absorbing that and all she had said, Mandy took a long moment and worked at regaining her composure.

Settling for as good as it was going to get, she left the

restroom.

Tim stood waiting for her near the front door. "Ready?"

Mandy nodded, and they walked outside, seated themselves in the limo. Sam sat behind the wheel. He pulled away from the church, then headed toward Five Palms Resort, where the reception was being held.

Blinking back tears, Mandy warned herself to get a grip on her emotions. Yes, working through everything would take a lot longer than the ride, but she had to be alert, aware, on her toes. She had to tell Tim about her mother.

How did she explain being elated at marrying him and devastated at saying goodbye to her very-much-alive mother forever at the same time?

Who was her mother? Clearly, not the recluse she'd known. *A good person?* Was she really? *NINA?* That didn't feel right. *All that money?* Wise investments? Blood money? Mandy was so confused. So conflicted, she didn't know what to think or what to make of their conversation.

Minutes later, Tim brushed her arm. "Everything okay?"

She nodded. "It's been an emotional day."

"Yes, it has." He pressed a kiss to her temple. "But I'm so happy to be married to you."

She looked into his eyes, saw the telltale twinkle. "Me, too." Guilt trickled in then gushed, pooling inside her and filling every crevice. *You promised. No secrets.* "Tim, I have to tell you something."

"Just a second, babe." He pressed his throat mic. "Go ahead, Nick."

Whatever Nick was telling Tim couldn't be good; his expression turned mercurial.

"We'll be there in ten." Tim released the mic, looked past Mandy to Sam. "You get that?"

"I got it." Sam stomped the accelerator.

Clearly this wasn't the right time to tell him about her mother. Mandy grabbed the arm rest and held on. "What is it?" Were they after her mother? Panic set in. "What's wrong?"

"The prints on the envelope," Tim said. "We got a match."

Her breath hitched. "Who was he?"

"Not Charles Travest."

Mandy frowned at him. "I told you that."

"Nick's waiting for us to get there to share the details."

That response coupled with Tim's delivery and Sam's wild driving told her all she needed to know. Whoever the man was, he was connected. Connected and dangerous.

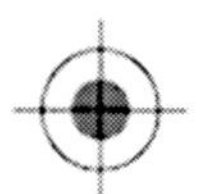

Mandy and Tim entered the resort's ballroom.

Intent on getting to Nick, she couldn't help but pause to scan the ballroom. *Their wedding reception.*

She wanted to remember it forever. Polished marble floors, ornate high ceilings, columned walls draped in soft purple satin that flowed from ceiling to floor. Tables dressed in crisp, white linen and set with fine china rimmed in purple and sparkling crystal that reflected candlelight from the delicate centerpieces that stretched down the centers from one end to the other.

Beyond the tables, near the far wall, a trio of musicians stood before an alabaster statue positioned under a white-lattice archway. Diaphanous sheer fabric ballooned from it, held by bunches of purple and white irises and streaming ribbons. In front of them, a raised dance floor filled the space, softly lit and inviting.

The feel was elegant and simple—perfect.

Annie greeted them. "Well, what do you think?"

Mandy couldn't have dreamed all this. And Nora and Annie had planned and executed their plans in a scant forty-eight hours? Most spent a year or more pulling these events together. "I'm breathless."

"It's beautiful, Annie," Tim said.

"Stunning," Mandy found her voice. "Perfect."

"I'm so glad you like it." Annie beamed.

Nora signaled and the musicians began playing.

Detective Jeff Meyer joined the musicians and announced their arrival. "Guests, please welcome our bride and groom."

Applause filled the large room.

"Oh, no. We have to talk to Nick and we've been announced," Mandy told Tim.

Annie bent toward them. "Slight change in plans. There's been a development. Nick says he's waiting for more information. When it comes in, he'll summon the troops. Until then, enjoy yourselves."

Tim nodded. "Where is he?"

Annie shot Tim a level look. "In a secure area. And, yes, the guys ran in-depth security checks here. Jeff Meyer handled them personally—inside and out."

Satisfied, Tim nodded. "After what happened at Harvey and Roxy Talbot's wedding, I'm glad to hear it—and not at all surprised Jeff handled it personally."

Jeff Meyer. The detective who'd questioned Mandy at the crisis center. Harvey Talbot was a doctor there—Lisa's boss. And his wife, Roxy, was an ex-FBI agent. At the bridal shower, she had told Mandy all about her divorcing Harvey to keep NINA from targeting him, without telling Harvey that was the reason, of course. Still, Mandy remained lost and unable follow this snippet of discussion. Roxy hadn't said a thing about their second wedding. "What happened at their wedding?"

"A chemical attack," Tim said, clearly not having fond memories of the occasion. "Jeff was a few minutes late. He walked in for the ceremony and found everyone passed out."

Mandy gasped.

"No more of that talk, Tim." Annie shot him a stern glance. "That wedding is why this reception is here at the resort instead of at the club." She glanced at Mandy. "The facility there is gorgeous, but we didn't want memories of that wedding to intrude on this one." She sniffed a reprimand at Tim. "The boys," she said, adopting Nora's term for the Shadow Watchers, "all insisted repeatedly that yours must be a perfect wedding full of good memories."

Because NINA had made her a marked bride? Or because she'd tried to protect the former Shadow Watchers—if they were indeed former?

Unsure and having increased doubts about that, she opted not to ask the reason or the team's status. And, especially today, she wanted to believe they trusted her because she'd put them before her own happiness. "That was thoughtful of them," Mandy said. Tim stepped away, probably to check with Nick, and Mandy added, "I hope they didn't put too many demands on you."

"They were determined, but don't worry. Nora handles them well. They'll do just about anything for her," Annie whispered. "I'm a pushover. How can I not be when they saved my daughter's life and mine? If the boys want it, and I can make it happen, they're getting it."

"I see your point." Mandy smiled. "I'm a pushover for them, too—but don't tell them."

"Honey, they know you gave up what you most wanted to protect them. For most of them, that's been a novelty their whole lives. You have no idea what that means to them." She frowned. "The way some of them have been treated just breaks my heart. Nora's, too, which is why no one messes with her boys. I have to say, I wouldn't take kindly to it, either."

Fascinated, Mandy whispered. "How do they do that to us?"

"Do what?"

"Create such fierce love for them in us all?"

"Look at them, darling. They're gorgeous." Annie winked. "When someone who doesn't have to lift a finger risks everything, even their lives, to protect you, it inspires and endears. Of course, you love them and want them to have everything in the world you can give them, including your heart. Nothing is stronger than love, Mandy." Annie nodded. "Naturally, you know that."

"I do."

"Dang it." Sam's voice rang out.

"Oh-oh." Annie rolled her eyes. "I have to warn you, Sam might singlehandedly mess up your perfect day."

Threatening her father who wasn't her father? Saying goodbye to her mother? Not a perfect day, but, bless them, they'd tried to give her perfect. All of them. "Sam?"

Annie sent him a warning glare, then looked back at Mandy. "If Nora hears that boy slip and curse one more time today, I think he might be eating jalapeño peppers as well as drinking the juice in his tea for the rest of his days."

That *boy* was the size of a mountain—and currently being scolded by Lisa, Joe, and Beth, a petite brunette, computer whiz from the bridal shower that Joe adored. Such a pretty woman. Vibrant and not at all intimidated at having to crank her neck back to her shoulders to see more than the underside of Sam's chin to fuss at him.

Reading his body language, he truly was sorry for the slip. Mandy giggled. "He's being reminded." At least three of the others had warned him to mind his tongue this morning—that she'd heard. Could have been more, she hadn't. "Maybe I should go rescue him . . ."

"Don't you dare. Better Beth blisters his ears than Nora. She'll filet him like a fish and have him thanking her for doing it." Annie blew out a *whew*. "We don't want to go there." She patted Mandy's arm. "I've got the Prayer Warriors on it, too. He's a good boy truly, but to break that habit, he clearly needs divine intervention."

Tim stepped back into their circle then cleared his throat. "I'm sorry for bringing up that other wedding. I hope it didn't ruin your perfect day." He swerved to focus on Annie. "Sorry to you, too."

"We're not that fragile." Mandy cupped his jaw, let him see her joy in her eyes, hear it in her voice. "Besides, it's you that makes this day perfect for me."

Tim smiled. Not with his lips but with his eyes. Love burned in their depths. Love and joy and a peace she hadn't seen in him since she'd broken their engagement. Grateful it was there now, she dared to believe everything would work out for them. They'd find the love and joy they'd had and their relationship would be even better and stronger for all they'd been through.

Annie wrinkled her nose. "Just what I love to see. A couple with their priorities in order."

Jeff called them to dance, and the music shifted. Soon, strains of *I Will Always Love You* filled the air and, in her mind, Mandy heard Whitney Houston's rendition of the now-classic lyrics. From the first time she'd heard it, she'd loved it and wanted it for their first dance. She hadn't told Annie or Nora. Tim. Tim remembered . . .

"Our song." Tim led her to the center of the dance floor.

Spotlights high above bathed them in soft light. He opened his arms to her. She stepped into them and and they closed around her in seemingly slow-motion, every move and nuance captured and committed to memory forever. Then, together, they danced their first dance as husband and wife.

Her emotions tumbled into full riot. All she'd thought never to experience, never to know. She'd forfeited all this. But fate hadn't yet had its say, and it had brought them together again. Fate and her mother. Mandy's throat tightened. To lose everything and have it all restored overwhelmed her. To lose her mother for it to happen . . . no, it wasn't that simple.

Her mother had chosen her path for reasons undisclosed. She'd made the choice between herself and her daughter. That made it all the more important that this marriage and this life be not just good but great. And it would be. It would be.

"Sometimes life is so . . . Is something wrong?" Tim

whispered close to her ear, clearly picking up on her tension. His breath warmed her face.

"No. Nothing." Mandy sniffed. "Nothing at all."

"Whenever you say nothing, it's always something." He pulled back to look at her more closely. "What is it—and don't say nothing. You have no secrets, remember? And there are tears in your eyes."

Vulnerable and inexplicably shy about it, she had one secret but couldn't tell him about that in a room full of people. When they talked with Nick. She'd tell him then. She bobbed her shoulder. "I'm happy."

"What?"

"I'm happy." She wet her dry lip with her tongue. "For such a long time, I thought I'd lost you forever. I didn't dare dream we'd reunite much less marry. I wanted to be your wife more than anything, Tim, and I thought you were lost to me forever."

"Not more than anything." He corrected her. "Well, more than anything except to protect me and the team."

She nodded. "Now I am your wife, and I'm having trouble believing it without constantly pinching myself."

His expression turned tender, indulgent, and empathetic. "I know what you mean. Losing you . . . I had about decided my heart would be broken forever."

"I'm so sorry I hurt you."

"I'm sorry we both were hurt. I can't say I totally understand why you didn't just tell me. I would have done everything possible to protect us—"

"I didn't doubt you could, Tim. I didn't think I'd live long enough to tell you that you needed to protect us and yourself and the team and their families."

"I know. And I know you were doing everything you could do to keep us all safe." Tim brushed a kiss to her temple. "But carrying the load alone is over now. We're together and we have a brand new beginning—without secrets."

She should tell him now about her mother. But there was no danger in waiting just a little while. After the reception. It wasn't a secret, she just didn't want another upset to encroach on what should be the happiest day of their lives.

Tell him! Be honest. Keep your promise or you're doing just what was done to you. You know how that's played out. Responding to her conscience, she said, "Almost without secrets." She dipped her chin. "I have to tell you something, and then we'll be without secrets."

"Shh." He nuzzled her neck. "I need a minute first."

That surprised her. "A minute?"

"A moment," he amended. "Just to soak it all in." He inhaled deeply, drinking in her scent. "I thought we'd never have this day. I need to feel it."

His admission touched her heart. "I'm that important to you?"

He looked deeply into her eyes, let her see the truth. "You're everything to me."

Her heart tripped, thudded. Everything. She was his everything. Trying to grasp that, to slot it all knowing it, made her feel wanted and accepted, valued and . . . significant, and more. So much more. Alien feelings swirled inside her. She failed to comprehend them all. New and strange feelings. It would take time. Wonderful, sweet time in a life well lived.

"I see it, Mandy," he said softly. "I had trouble at first, but it's clear now."

"What's clear?"

"Our life. It really is going to be extraordinary." He whispered against her neck, then twirled her on the dance floor.

"Absolutely." She drew the promise in deep, embraced it, harbored it in a chamber in her heart, then placed a butterfly kiss to his neck. "I'm grateful for you, Tim. I don't know if I've ever told you that, but I am. I always have been."

"I'm grateful for you, too."

Others joined them on the dance floor.

In Tim's arms, Mandy rested her head on his shoulder and let all their troubles and worries drift away. The risks and dangers they faced melted into distant murky puddles. When they must, they'd address them. But for now, for this moment, they were safe to embrace and enjoy being in love, celebrating their marriage.

This one . . . perfect . . . moment in their new extraordinary life.

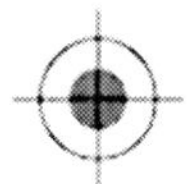

The reception wound down without incident and, per Mark's suggestion, the couple went through the motions of their departure with Sam behind the limo's wheel.

When Jeff Meyer signaled the all-clear, Sam doubled back to the resort, drove around back, and pulled to a stop near where Lisa stood, holding a door open.

Mandy and Tim stepped inside, and Lisa told Sam, "Park and come back in this way. Use a two-three signal so I know it's you."

Mark grunted. "He has a tactical throat mic, honey."

Lisa hiked her chin. "Which anyone from NINA could force him to use." She folded her arms and stood her post next to the door. "If you want in, signal me, Sam."

"Yes, ma'am."

Tim and Mark shared a look. "She had a good point," Tim said.

"She often does," Mark conceded. "We'll wait for Sam," he told Nick.

Seated at a conference table with a laptop unlike any Mandy had ever seen in front of him, Nick nodded to Mark and Mandy asked, "What are all those things connected to your computer?"

"Security," Nick said, keying something in, then blacking out the screen. "I hope you enjoyed the reception."

"It was perfect. All of it was perfect—with one exception. You weren't there and you owe me a dance," Mandy told him. She'd danced with all of the other guys, but Nick never had surfaced from this room. From the half-eaten plate of food on a tray cradled near the door, someone had seen to it he'd at least eaten.

He followed her glance. "Nora."

The village mother. "Of course."

"And I was there. I saw everything. Good to see you happy, Mandy."

This from the wallow on the dark-side Nick? "Thank you. It feels a little alien, but I like it."

"Don't ever let go." Clearly, a warning in that. "It's a long way back."

What had happened to him? Taken him down the dark road. "I'll do my best. That's a promise for us both."

The awaited two-three signal sounded at the door. Lisa opened it and Sam entered, pulling his tie loose. "Man, I hate these things."

He'd worn it in deference to her. "Thanks for enduring it, Sam. I appreciate it. The photos will be great."

"It's a sacrifice." He grunted. "But you're worth it."

Mark steered Lisa to the table. "Seats, folks. Let's get this done. There's a honeymoon waiting to start."

Chairs scraped the tiled floor and everyone sat down. Nick at the foot of the table with his laptop. Mark at the head with Lisa to his left. Mandy sat beside her with Tim beyond her and next to Nick. Sam and Joe sat across the table from Mandy and Tim.

"Go, bro." Joe lifted a hand.

Nick tapped the keys and a screen descended from the ceiling. "As you all know, we struck a match on the prints Mandy collected." He spared her a glance. "Good call."

She nodded but didn't interrupt, watched the screen. An image of a man projected onto it. Blonde, fair, angled features, and somehow oddly familiar. Had she met him? She turned to look at Tim. He stared at her, his mouth slightly agape.

What was wrong? Did he recognize the man? She glanced at the others, and they all stared, their gazes darting from the screen to Mandy then back again. Uneasy, she shifted on her seat. "I don't know him, but he looks a little familiar. I'm not sure why. I know we've never met."

Everyone seemed uneasy and the tension around the table ratcheted up.

"Hand her a mirror and she'll figure it out."

She looked at Joe. "What does that mean?"

"It means no one wants to state the obvious." Without giving her a chance to say more, he turned to Nick. "What's his name?"

"Chase Olsson. He's a Swedish actor."

That didn't help a bit. "So he was hired by my father to pretend to be him at the wedding?"

Nick nodded. "Apparently Charles Travest hired Chase Olsson to pretend to be Travest today."

"And my father is . . . where?"

Nick slid his gaze to Mark, who shot him a subtle negative nod she would have missed if she hadn't been closely watching them both. Again, Nick looked at her.

"Olsson isn't just an actor, is he?" Mandy asked.

Nick hesitated. "No, he isn't."

She skimmed Tim. *Tense.* "Just let Nick talk. I don't want protecting. We tried that. It didn't work."

"Sorry, Tim." Nick grunted. "Olsson's a suspected NINA operative." Nick pressed a key and the slide advanced. "According to Omega One—don't ask any questions about him, Mandy—Charles Travest murdered this man soon after he thought he'd murdered your mother."

Thought he'd murdered her. So they knew she was alive. Mandy's heart thudded. She didn't dare risk looking at Tim.

A bench at a little oceanfront park filled the screen. "This was the scene of Olsson's murder."

"He's not dead, Nick," Mark said. "He was here today."

"Right. Travest hired Olsson to pretend to be him for a meeting with this man." The slide advanced yet again and another man with a familiar face and dark hair appeared on the screen. "This is Paul Johnson, a very well known NINA operative."

Tim rubbed at his neck. "Wait. NINA sends Paul Johnson to meet with Travest and Travest puts Olsson in to sub for him? Why would he do that? Did Travest expect NINA to take him out or something?"

"It's possible, but we aren't certain. Fortunately, DHS—"

"DHS?" Mandy asked.

"Department of Homeland Security. I can't be more specific on exactly who. I wasn't told what agency," Tim said. "DHS intercepted Travest's hired gun and replaced him with with one of its own. Otherwise, Travest's shooter would have killed Olsson *and* a runner he hired to get his money back from Olsson after that shooting."

"He killed a runner, too?" Lisa asked.

"He would have, yes, without DHS's substitution," Nick said, confirming it.

Sam groaned. Joe sighed. "Kind of DHS to keep us in the loop."

"Happens all the time," Mark said. "Need to know basis."

"Dang—and don't even threaten me about saying it." Sam's face burned red with anger, his expression twisted. "We needed to know, Mark. They forget we're on the same side again?"

Nick, not Mark answered. "Getting clearance to bring us in—and Omega One in—took time."

"This has to stop." Tim frowned at Mark.

"I'm all over that," Mark said, his tone level but the look in his eyes scorching.

So DHS had withheld information from Omega One and the Shadow Watchers, which hampered their ability to do what they needed to do and no doubt caused some cross-over complications. Mandy was glad not to be on the receiving end of the anger around this table, but what Nick had revealed . . . it took her breath away.

Her father was capable of murder. She stiffened. Capable of multiple murders.

Shame washed through her. What kind of monster was he? "Do I have this straight?" she asked. "Olsson subs for my father and meets with Johnson. After the meeting, my father pays Olsson. Then he has an assassin he hired shoot Olsson. And then the runner—I'm assuming my father hired him also—retrieves the money from Olsson's supposed corpse and returns it to my father. Afterward, the runner is also shot." She struggled to absorb it all. "Is that right?"

"Yes." Nick confirmed it. "DHS substituted a man for the shooter and warned Olsson and the runner. Neither was killed, but otherwise, yours is a fair recap of what happened." Nick lifted a finger. "Though we'd all feel better if we knew for fact how Travest knew Olsson hadn't been killed then, and how he came to be here today. That puzzle piece is still missing."

"NINA," Mandy said. "If they made my father and Olsson come here, Travest would think they'd spared Olsson at the park." She thought about it. "That's all that makes sense because Charles Travest would not come here to walk me down the aisle and expose to anyone he's my father."

"Possible," Nick said. "Probably was forced. When we pick up Olsson, he'll enlighten us. So far, Travest isn't keen on explaining anything but he had no trouble paying Olsson to step in for him today."

So sometime between then—the shooting incident—and now, her father had learned Olsson was alive. He wouldn't hire him again, not unless forced. Mandy considered keeping her mouth shut, but she couldn't do it. "Do you have any evidence that NINA knew Charles Travest?" Never again would she call or consider him her father. Not after all this. "I mean, did NINA know his real identity?"

Nick perked up. "What's your point?"

"He's militant about protecting himself," she said. "I don't find it odd at all for him to have hired an actor to pretend to be him. That's just more of the same. Conceal his identity, and take himself out of any potential lines of fire. He's all about him. He always has been, Nick. You need to remember that."

Mark frowned. "Could he really work for NINA and them *not* know who he is?"

"No way, buddy." Sam grunted. "NINA's far too thorough to miss something like that."

"Sam's right. But--" Joe lifted a fingertip "—there are benefits to NINA in letting Travest *think* his identity is unknown to them."

Tim nodded. "Added protection for the organization, should he be reluctant to carry out orders and they need to yank his chain."

"Exactly." Joe agreed. "DHS had to know it, though. Otherwise, why would they intercede and sub in one of their own?"

"Mandy, why are you still frowning?" Tim asked.

"If Travest thought he'd killed the actor, he wouldn't hire him again to pretend to be him here unless he learned about the substitution, that Olsson was alive, and Travest was forced to accept him as the sub. I mean who wants to hire someone they tried and failed to kill?"

Tim nodded. "Logical, but there is another possible explanation."

"What?" Mandy said, then waited.

"Travest didn't find out about the substitution or that Olsson was still alive. He thought he'd hired someone else."

"Olson one-upped Travest, took on a new identity and

tricked him." Mandy could see it. "That makes more sense."

She studied Olsson's image on the screen. He looked like . . . her! The truth slammed into her. Travesty wasn't her father. Olson was! Her mind darted through the past, seeking confirmation, replaying Travest's distance from her. He didn't love her because she wasn't his. Olsson. She stared at the man she so resembled. He'd come to walk her down the aisle. In a bizarre way, this helped so much in her life make sense. "Has anyone checked Olsson's financials?" she asked.

"Working on that," Nick said. "Why?"

She swiveled her gaze to him. "Because I think you'll find a link between him and my mother. He could be the source of the thirty million." She looked at Tim, started to tell him she thought this man and not Travest was her real father, but couldn't quite voice her suspicions aloud. Not just yet.

"She's sharp," Nick told Tim.

They already knew.

Nick clicked, and a new image appeared on the screen. This one of yet another man.

"Who is he?" Mark asked.

"He doesn't exist." Nick propped an arm on the table's edge. "This is the park's security tape. Olsson wearing a mask that NINA thought was Travest. Well, that was supposed to be Travest when he met with Paul Johnson."

Sam sniffed, dragged a hand through his curly hair. "Olsson, a runner, a shooter—Travest went to a lot of trouble to keep his identity secret."

"Of course he did." Mandy resented it. Oh, how she resented it. Bitterness seeped into her every pore, and an even more unwelcome thought followed. One that set her chin to quivering. Her mother knew. She knew Charles Travest was Jackal all along.

Tim and Mark shared a look loaded with a *don't do it* warning that confused Mandy. "What?" she asked.

"No real need to speculate," Nick said. "Omega One is all

over it."

"He's arrested Travest?" Tim asked Nick.

"In the process of bringing him in for further interrogation."

Mandy swallowed hard. "What about his family?"

Tim answered her. "They'll bring them in, too. For context, if nothing else."

All those years of secrets and lies . . . and now this. And how did her mother fit into this maze? She had to be NINA. She had to know about Travest. That's the only way all of the puzzle pieces fit into place. Oh, mercy. Her father *and* her mother really were mixed up with NINA?

Tim—none of the guys—would take this news well. Mandy would always be suspect. None of them had treated her as if fearing she wasn't who she seemed or as if she had ulterior motives, and Tim loved her, but how could he not—they not—be suspicious of her now? *Both* parents? They'd have to doubt her. And even if they didn't, Intel honchos would and they'd insist the guys doubt her, too.

Active or not, it didn't matter. Intel couldn't take out what it had put into men's heads and, as a result, it had lots of weird little rules. No one trusted anyone until they'd proven trustworthy. Her having both parents involved with the enemy couldn't bode well for her. And maybe not for Tim.

When first we try to deceive . . .

She cut off the quote running through her mind and substituted her own.

We complicate and destroy others' lives.

And there's nothing they can do about it.

Frustrated, she stared at the screen. Olsson's image returned to it and stayed.

So familiar . . . Oddly so . . .

Hand her a mirror. She'll figure it out.

Joe's words replayed in her mind. *A mirror . . .*

The truth slammed into her. "Oh, sweet mercy." She couldn't stand it another second. "I look just like him."

Tim clasped her hand. "Mandy?"

She looked past him to Nick. "Is he . . . somehow related to me?" That was the best she could manage.

It was enough. "We're waiting for lab results."

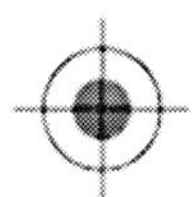

Mark stood up. "Let's break for a minute."

No one moved except Nick. He backed away from the table and walked to the edge of the room.

"I'm sorry, Mandy." Tim clasped her hand. "We wanted to spare you from this today."

"Don't." She let her emotions settle. "Considering the kind of man Travest is, it wouldn't break my heart not to be related to him. I thought I had to be his or he wouldn't have let me believe I was, but Olsson… I'm not Travest's daughter, am I?

"We don't think so. But he might believe you are." Tim glanced again at the screen. "Although how he could look at Olsson and you and not see the strong resemblance, I don't have a clue."

"I didn't see it myself," she reminded Tim. "Not at first." A sinking feeling settled over her like a shroud. "Having one father ignore me wasn't enough. I have to have two?"

"You've never seen Olsson then?"

"Before today, who knows?" She lifted her shoulders. "He has great masks. I'm not sure who I've met and not met. Were those Tuesday visits to my mother really Charles Travest? Or Olsson wearing a Charles Travest mask? Or were they someone different every time masquerading as Travest?" She hated this. Hated the uncertainty and doubt chewing her up inside. Hated the irony that it could have been her real father—Chase Olsson—who'd walked her down the aisle and she hadn't known it. "I don't know much of anything—not when it comes to my parents."

Tim glanced away and thought that through.

Nick returned to the table. "Omega One just reported in. Right after Chase Olsson left the church, he was intercepted. After brief questioning, he made a break and disappeared."

"Another mask," Mandy speculated.

"Appears so," Nick said, confirming it. "They've issued an alert and everyone's watching, but with the way he changes his appearance, confidence of a second interception is low."

"Forget it. He's gone underground," Joe said. "We won't find him until he wants to find him."

"And he's crooked, too." Mandy couldn't keep the disappointment out of her voice. "Figures." Not one but two and her mother. "The whole bunch are bad."

"Yep, Joe's right. Olsson's gone." Sam predicted.

"Why would he run?" Lisa asked. "Mandy gave him no reason to doubt his cover was intact." Lisa lifted a hand. "She even threatened him, which he probably found reassuring that she believed he was Travest."

Inwardly, Mandy groaned. She was going to have to live with having made that threat for a long time.

"He knew we had his prints," Tim said. "He had to at least consider that we might run them."

"So where is Charles Travest?" Mandy asked.

"You were right about him. He was close," Nick said. "Jeff Meyer and his team has had him under constant observation. He left after your first dance and is currently well on his way toward St. Augustine."

"Does this mean we're done with him and his family?" she asked.

Mark not Nick answered. "If he wanted you dead, you'd have been dead a long time ago."

"Would I?" she asked, trusting nothing from any of them anymore. "He thought he'd killed my mother, didn't he?"

"Yes." Tim didn't flinch or insult her by stating he had killed her mother, extending the charade.

"Oh-oh."

Mandy stilled. When a Shadow Watcher says oh-oh, you know it means trouble. She dared to look at Nick.

He frowned. "Travest has dropped off our radar."

Mandy closed her eyes a long second.

Mark hit his throat mic. "You're telling me you lost Travest *and* Olsson." He paused, listened and his face burned red. "And Paul Johnson." The veins in his neck stood out like thumbs.

"Don't worry," Tim told her. "They'll be back. They always come back."

"So what happens now?" Mandy asked.

Mark jammed his phone into his pocket and elevated his voice. "Well, it seems there was a hole in our associate's net and all three fish have escaped. We're done for now."

Done? How could they be done? Mandy looked at the guys. They seemed to accept this news with no fanfare.

"It happens," Lisa told her. "The good guys don't always catch the bad guys. Not right away."

"But—"

"It's hard to stomach, but do it, Mandy. For your own sake."

Mandy let her outrage slow to a simmer. Letting go, when all this hit so close to home, would take a while. But Lisa was right. At least now they knew who Jackal was, and that Chase Olsson, who she believed with all her heart had to be her father, was NINA. The organization had done a double jeopardy type of sting on Charles Travest. Only it knew why.

Tim joined Nick for a private chat.

"It's over. Just like that?" Mandy asked. "I understand but it's so strange."

Lisa stepped over to Mandy. "Get used to strange. NINA's slick and slithery like the snake it is. Unfortunately, it's always strange and it never stays away. But for now, it's gone, and we're safe."

Mandy didn't feel safe. She was a bundle of nerves. "How

do you switch gears like this? I don't understand."

"The serenity prayer helps," Lisa offered her the tip. "Change what you can, accept what you can't. Welcome the wisdom to know the difference. Today, the news is good. You and Tim are married, and we all live to fight another day."

"Except instead of one lousy father, I appear to be the daughter of another lousy father."

"There is that." Lisa sighed. "But he can't be worse than my stepfather. The human trafficking NINA operative, remember?"

"Will the guys ever really trust me, Lisa?"

"They already do or you wouldn't be here."

Mandy wouldn't. She really wouldn't. And she wasn't going to do anything to mess that up. "Tim," she said loudly enough for everyone to hear. "I told you I needed to tell you something and you needed a moment so I had to wait. I can't wait anymore. You—all of you—need to know this now."

They took to their seats and waited.

She began with her walking down the aisle, and hearing the note. Shared why it was significant. Then she told them about her conversation with her mother in the restroom. "I'm not sure, but I fear she might be Phoenix."

Tim started to say something, but Mark signaled him to stand down. Mark told her, "That was quite a shock to you, I'm sure."

"Yes, and not a good one. But I'm glad she's alive."

"Of course." He shifted on his seat. "Why do you think she's Phoenix?"

Mandy couldn't sit another second. She paced the length of the table beside it. "I could give you thirty million reasons why." She stopped. "I have to tell you, I never suspected a thing. She had me totally fooled. I still can't wrap my mind around it."

"Yet you didn't tell me." Tim looked her in the eye.

Her face heated. "I started to tell you in the limo, but you got Nick's message and I had to wait. I had every intention of telling you. Not once did I consider not telling you. When we got to the reception, I—I wanted a moment, Tim. Just a moment that was ours. Then we danced and I tried to tell you then, but you needed a moment."

"She's right. I heard it all through her transmitter."

She spared Nick a "thank you" glance, then focused again on Tim. "When we came in here, I intended to tell you all. And I am telling you all."

"You should have told me right away, Mandy." Tim was hurt.

Well, so was she. "I'm sorry. But nothing lately has been easy, okay? I bury my mother by myself, then at the wedding, I hurt because she's not there. I hear the note and realize she's alive and present but masquerading as someone else. I threaten to shoot my father to keep anyone from getting hurt at the wedding and I realize he's someone else pretending to be my father. And when I come in here to tell you that my mother *and* father are corrupt, I discover that the stranger who walked me down the aisle well may be my real father and Travest no relation to me at all." She paused and drew in a sharp breath.

"The most upsetting part about the men is that neither of them—both of them together—make a patch on a decent man's . . . jeans." She'd almost slipped and gotten herself into jalapeño tea territory. "So, yes. I found out my mother's alive and I didn't tell you immediately. I got interrupted, fell to temptation and stole a moment for us—two, actually. One, I needed. One, you needed. Selfish of me, but I figured because of the money, Mom had to be Phoenix and that could, and probably would, get her killed." Mandy flung her arms upward. "I'm sorry, but I just couldn't take having to bury her again on our wedding day, Tim. I just couldn't do it."

Tim parked a hand in his pocket. "You were worried about my reaction."

"Well of course, I was worried about your reaction. I

still am. My father Jackal, now my mother maybe Phoenix—wouldn't you worry?"

Mark not Tim responded. "Will you see her again?"

"She said no. I'm married to a Shadow Watcher now. NINA likes distance between sides. That comment too makes me think she's Phoenix."

Tim stood up. "Maybe she's not Phoenix. Maybe she's afraid of NINA and running."

"No." Mandy shook her head. "They faked her death. They didn't stage all that for nothing. I know you're trying to spare my feelings, but don't. These people do really bad things. She has to be one of them." Mandy's voice cracked with that painful admission. Her disappointment ran deep, to cellular level.

"Tell her, Mark." Nick urged him. "She's one of us, and she's lost too much already."

"Tell her what?" Tim asked.

Mark worried his lip, debating.

Joe stood up. "If you can shed light, do it, Mark."

"Dang straight." Sam crossed his arms over his chest.

Mark glanced at Lisa, who nodded. "Okay." He let his gaze slide to Mandy. "Your mother is Phoenix, Mandy."

Tears filled her eyes. She fought but failed to prevent them from falling. "I'm so sorry." She swallowed hard, looked at them all. "Really, so sorry."

"Don't be," Mark said. "She's not a threat to us."

Mandy stilled. Sniffed. "What? Have you arrested her, then?"

"No," Mark said. "There's no need for that."

Tim groused, "You're not making much sense, Mark."

"We were just informed," Mark said. "Mandy, your mother hasn't been arrested because she's broken no crime, and she's far too valuable to us in the field."

"I—I don't understand." Mandy thought a second. "You got her to turn against NINA?"

"She's with NINA but she's never been a part of NINA."

Mandy didn't understand. "What?"

Tim touched her arm. "She's one of us. I'm guessing, under DHS or Omega One?" He directed that to Mark, who nodded confirmation.

"So she's on the right side of this." Relief washed through Mandy. "She doesn't work for a criminal terrorist organization." Mandy gasped. "That is what you're saying, right?"

"It is."

Relief, swift and intense, rushed through her. "Oh, thank you." Mandy wept. "Thank you so much for telling me. She told me she was a good person—she promised, but I didn't dare to believe her. I couldn't with all that money."

"She's a good person, Mandy." Mark nodded, serious and thoughtful. "Providing vital services to her country. You can be proud of her—even if you can't tell anyone anything about her."

Her mother had infiltrated NINA. Apparently, a long time ago. "Thank you for trusting me, Mark," Mandy said. "Knowing helps more than I can say."

"No more jolts today," Tim said. "That's it."

"Tim?"

He turned to her. "Yes, Mandy."

"I have a question." When he nodded, she dared to ask. "This is real, right? This marriage? It wasn't just about NINA, I mean."

"It's real for me. Is it real for you?"

"Totally." At the altar, he'd promised to love her to his last breath, but had that been real or mission-essential?

Let it go, fool. Never ask a question when you might not want the answer.

She paused, discovered she did want the answer. Either way, she needed to know the truth. Summoning a courage she didn't feel, she forced herself to be bold. "Why did you marry me?"

"Because I love you. I've always loved you, Mandy." He studied her, then frowned. "Wait. Oh, no. You weren't sure of that, were you?"

"What kind of moron don't tell a woman he loves her after their kind of breakup?" Sam asked, reaching for his baseball cap, which wasn't there.

"Dead from the neck up," Nick muttered.

"What's wrong with you, bro?" Joe stared gape-jawed at Tim. "You didn't tell her you still love her?"

"I—I . . ." Tim looked bewildered. "It never occurred to me she wouldn't know."

Mandy muttered, comforted by the guys' indignation. "I didn't know."

"Wait a second." Tim's expression turned tender. "You didn't know, and you married me anyway."

"I told you, I don't work without you." Tears burned her eyes. The back of her nose. "I didn't know, but I hoped. Oh, how I hoped."

"I'm sorry. I didn't realize." Tim clasped her shoulders. "I've always loved you, Mandy, and I always will. That's a promise."

"I didn't think you'd make vows in church if you didn't." She looked up at him. "But I really needed the words."

Joe let out an exasperated sigh. "You need serious work on this, bro."

"Definitely." Nick guffawed.

"Dang right."

Once again, no one fussed at Sam, though Mandy did see Lisa ease behind him and squirt something into his glass of tea. She must have agreed with the guys because it was just a little squirt.

Tim touched her face. "You'll never doubt it again. That's a promise."

Joy flooded Mandy, washed away any doubt, and she smiled. "Oh, we're definitely going to have an extraordinary life."

He drew her to him. "Definitely."

"A little more work on your dang communication skills wouldn't hurt none."

"Shut up, Sam." Nick and Joe said simultaneously.

Lisa frowned. "That's it. I'm telling Nora."

"Aw, come on, Lisa. She'll never make me hot tamales again." Sam whined. "Man. You know I love her hot tamales."

"Oh, she'll make them, and they'll be hot all right."

"Don't, Lisa."

She crossed her chest with her arms. "Convince me you're going to work hard, too. You've got to clean up your potty mouth, Sam. It's a sign of a weak mind, you know, and your mind is anything but weak."

"You sound just like Nora."

"Great. Knock it off, then."

Smiling Tim bent low and kissed Mandy.

Definitely, an extraordinary life. Mandy had finally found her place, here with Tim in this world they'd shape themselves. Whoever her father turned out to be, Travest or Olsson, it didn't really matter. Both men fell far short of the men in this room. They had valued and protected her, and they always would. No longer did she stand alone. She'd found her family—and her mother would be somewhere watching.

This was a future she believed in. It was honest and good and, like her, flawed to the core and totally human. But faith in herself, in Tim, in the rest of the Shadow Watchers and the women in their lives, melted her fears. She embraced her role as the welcome newcomer. The beloved wife and respected woman who belonged with them in this tight inner circle. Here she'd find peace. A home without secrets and lies and shame. Everything she'd longed for in life now lay before her like a bountiful feast. She had only to embrace it.

In her husband's arms, she mentally stepped into the circle of her husband's world, embraced the feast . . . and shed forever the tarnished image of the marked bride.

AUTHOR'S NOTE

I introduced the Shadow Watcher team in the Crossroad Crisis Center series. Forget Me Not is first story featuring Benjamin Brandt, the owner of the center. Lisa and Mark's story is Deadly Ties. And Joe and Beth's story is Not This Time.

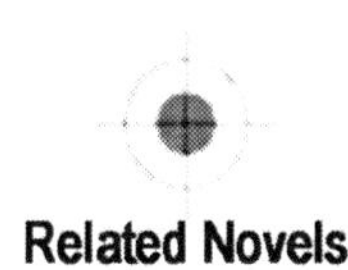

Related Novels

Crossroads Crisis Center

Forget Me Not *(Ben)*
Deadly Ties *(Mark)*
Not This Time *(Joe)*

Shadow Watchers

The Marked Bride *(Tim)*
The Marked Star * *(Nick)*
The Marked Gentlewoman * *(Sam)*

The Shadow Watchers play significant roles in *Not This Time*. Readers requested more of their stories, so I wrote The Marked Bride. I hope you've enjoyed reading more about Tim and Mandy.

There are two more *Shadow Watcher* books planned. I can't leave out Nick or Sam! At the time of this writing, I don't yet have the publication dates on either of those books, but I wanted to invite you to subscribe to my author newsletter so when they're released, you'll be the first to know.

Nick is definitely out of his element when he's asked to help find the grown daughter of a man he's worked with before—the CEO of a weaponry firm. NINA wants the weapons, and they've taken his daughter, a famous singer, hostage. It's an unlikely match, but those are often the most fun. The working title is *The Marked Star.*

Sam has plans to send me on a merry chase in *The Marked Gentlewoman.* Of all the Shadow Watchers, he seems the least likely to hook up with a congresswoman, and yet there's something about the Gentlewoman from Georgia that fascinates him. Together, they fascinate me, and I hope you'll be fascinated by them also.

Thank you for your emails and letters and reviews. Without them, I might not have written these ***Shadow Watcher*** books, and I'm so very glad I've started them. I enjoy the team very much and I can't wait to learn more about Nick and about Sam's stories!

I thought that these three would wind up the Shadow Watcher series, but now I'm not sure it will. The idea of not visiting Seagrove Village again makes me sad—and there is Omega One and his team to consider . . . They've been very much in the shadows and we might just have to bring them into the light and dip into their lives.

I'm game, but before deciding for certain, I'll wait to see what you think, so do share your thoughts. And, as always, thank you for reading!

Blessings,

Vicki

ABOUT THE AUTHOR

Vicki Hinze is a *USA Today* bestselling author who has written over thirty books, fiction and nonfiction, and hundreds of articles, published in as many as 63 countries. She's won a wide array of awards, including novels of the year in multiple genres. All of her novels, general market (secular) or inspirational, include suspense, mystery and romance. The focus determines genre. Her works have been classified in nearly every genre except horror, with the majority being suspense, thriller, mystery and romance.

As well as serving as a Vice President for International Thriller Writers, Vicki has been a consultant to the Board of Directors for Romance Writers of America and several other organizations. She is the former host of radio talk show, *Everyday Woman*, and a current columnist for Social In, a global network.

Vicki was the first RWA PRO Mentor of the Year, and the recipient of the National Service Award. She's also recognized as an author and an educator by *Who's Who in the World.*

ALSO BY VICKI HINZE

Down and Dead in Dixie
Down and Dead in Even
Her Perfect Life
My Imperfect Valentine
Duplicity
Survive the Night
Christmas Countdown
Torn Loyalties
Forget Me Not
Deadly Ties
Not This Time
Mind Reader
Lady Liberty
Lady Justice
Body Double
Double Vision
Double Dare
Smokescreen: Total Recall
Beyond the Misty Shore
Upon a Mystic Tide
Beside a Dreamswept Sea
Legend of the Mist
Maybe This Time
Acts of Honor
All Due Respect

For a complete listing of all Vicki's books, visit the Books page on her website:
http://vickihinze.com/books

Bonus Preview of…

DUPLICITY

Chapter 1

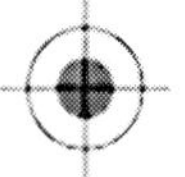

This couldn't be happening to her. Not now.

Again, Colonel Jackson's edict reverberated in her ears. *Keener, I've assigned you to defend Captain Adam Burke.*

Captain Tracy Keener, a Staff Judge Advocate relatively new to Laurel Air Force Base, Mississippi, swallowed a knot of dread from her throat. "Is that a direct order, sir?"

"If necessary, yes, it is, Captain."

She tensed her muscles to keep her boss from seeing how appalling she found the notion. Only a sadist would be elated at hearing they'd been assigned to defend Adam Burke. What attorney in her right mind could be anything but appalled at being ordered to defend him? If the rumors proved true, he'd *deserted* his men. *Abandoned* them to die.

Refusal burned in her throat, turned her tongue bitter. This had to be a bad dream—a nightmare. It couldn't be real.

But from the look on Jackson's face, it was real, and there was no escaping it.

"This won't be an easy case to defend." He passed a file across the desk to her. "On paper, Burke's assigned to Personnel, but he actually works for Colonel Hackett."

"Burke is in Intel?" Could the news get any worse?

Jackson nodded. "And because he is, the prosecutor is going all the way on this one. So far, the charges are conduct unbecoming, disobeying direct orders, cowardice, and treason."

Choking back a groan, she fixed her gaze on an eagle paperweight atop a neat stack of files at the corner of his desk.

Sunlight slanted in through the blinds at his coveted office window. Washed in its stripes of light and shadows, the bird looked arrogant. Sinister.

"It gets worse." Jackson grimaced. "Four counts of murder are coming down the pike."

"Murder?" She really should have seen this assignment coming. Burke's was the last case *any* Staff JAG officer would want to take on. It was a guaranteed career-breaker—which is why, as low man on Laurel's Judge Advocate General's office totem pole, she'd gotten stuck with the unholy honor. "Wasn't this an accident during a local war-readiness exercise?"

"The incident occurred during a local readiness exercise, but it was no accident—at least, not in the way you mean." Jackson rubbed at the bridge of his nose. "The troops were split into two teams, Alpha and Omega. Omega played the enemy. Burke headed Alpha team with orders to infiltrate Area Thirteen—Omega's enemy territory—to jam communications and gather Intel."

"Sounds typical, so far."

"It was," Jackson said. "But the woods are dense in Area Thirteen. Burke got lost and led his men onto an active firing range."

"He got *lost?*"An Intel officer who can't tell directions? That didn't fit.

"According to Hackett, it happens all the time out there. The terrain disorients." Jackson leaned forward. "The worst is that Burke realized he'd messed up and bugged out."

A shiver crept up Tracy's back." He admitted that he deliberately abandoned his men?"

"He's admitted nothing. In fact, he's not talking. But he was the only Alpha team survivor. Four skilled operatives died."

"So why murder charges?"

"Burke threatened two members of his team less than a week before the exercise. Investigators are about to conclude that he carried through on the threat and the other two men were sacrificed."

Could anyone be that cold? "Why did Burke threaten the men?"

"That's classified."

How could she defend him against murder charges when the basis for the murders was classified? Killing and sacrificing men—during an exercise, for pity's sake—and she had to defend him? *Now?*

She had to get out of this assignment. That, or kiss off her career.

Desperately seeking a chink in Colonel Jackson's armor, she studied him. He was a big, imposing man with an intelligent face, pushing fifty and graying gracefully at the temples. In the months she'd been at Laurel, he had earned her respect. More than once during case discussions at the morning staff meetings, compassion had burned in his eyes, and that compassion had come through in his recommendations. According to Tracy's overqualified assistant, Janet Cray, the only thing that sent Jackson through the proverbial ceiling was clutter, and that melded into an odd combination of human characteristics, to Tracy's way of thinking. How could he show a murderer compassion but lack so much as the scent of it for any staff member who tolerated a staple on the carpet near his or her desk?

Yet Tracy had worked for worse. Gutless wonders who'd rather fold than fight were a dime a dozen in the military. Fortunately, so were the dedicated, the proud, and the sincere. Soldiers who took their oaths to serve and protect into their hearts and did their best to live by them.

Jackson fell into the ranks of the latter. Yet no compassion shone in his eyes now, nor did any latitude. There was no chink; his armor unfortunately appeared intact, but he did look...guilty.

Smoothing her uniform's dark blue skirt, Tracy set out to find out why. "You do realize that in taking on this case now

I'd be begging for career disaster, right?"

The veiled empathy flickering in Jackson's eyes snuffed out. He darted his gaze to his office door, as if assuring himself of privacy, and then nodded. "Frankly, yes, I realize the risks."

His tone removed any doubt about his damage-assessment expectations. Enormous risks. Enormous.

Should she feel relieved that he had acknowledged the risks, or despondent that he had realized them and had put her in the direct line of fire anyway?

Before she could decide, he rocked back in his chair. The springs groaned and his stern expression turned grave, dragging down the creases running alongside his mouth, nose to chin. "I'm not going to sugar-coat this situation, Captain," he said. "The Burke case has tempers running hot and hard up the chain of command and the local media is nearly out of control. Between the two of them, they're nailing our backsides to the proverbial wall."

Hope flared in Tracy. If he could see that, then surely he would see reason and assign someone else to the case. "I'm up for major, sir," Tracy interjected. "My promotion board meets in about a month."

"I know." A frown creasing his lined forehead, Jackson doodled with a black pen on the edge of his blotter; a frequent habit, judging by the density of his previous scrawls. "And I know that you're up for Career Status selection."

Oh, man. Tracy hadn't yet even considered Career Status selection. This was her fifth year in the Air Force. Her first and—by new policy adopted three weeks ago—her last shot at selection. If not selected, she'd promptly be issued an invitation to practice law elsewhere, outside of the military.

This was not a pleasing prospect to an officer bent on making the military a career.

Decidedly uneasy, the colonel fidgeted with his gold watch. It winked at her from under his shirtsleeve's cuff. "I understand the personal risks and the potential sacrifices you may have to make, but there's a lot more at stake here than your career. The Air Force Corrections System is on trial, Captain, and all eyes are watching to see if it's up to the test."

He let the weight of that comment settle in and then went on. "Burke is a coward and a disgrace to the uniform. He deserves to die for his crimes—and I have no doubt that he will die. Yet he is entitled to a defense and—"

"I agree, Colonel," she interceded, doing her best to keep her voice calm. "Burke does deserve a defense. But can't an attorney who already has Career Status defend him? If I lose this case—and we both know I will lose this case—then that's a huge strike against me with the boards. Competition is stiff and losses bury you. I'll be passed over for promotion and for Career Status selection. If that happens, my military career abruptly ends."

"I'm aware of these, er, undesirable conditions. Captain." Jackson lowered his gaze to his desk blotter. "But I'm afraid a reassignment is impossible."

The regret in his tone set her teeth on edge. This was another slick political maneuver; she sensed it down to her toenails. Some jerk with more clout, rank, or backing from his superior officers didn't want his rear stuck in a sling, so they were planting her backside in it first. The unfairness of it set a muscle in her cheek to ticking. "May I ask why not?"

"I'd prefer that you didn't."

She just bet he did prefer it. A stern edge crept into her voice. "I mean no disrespect sir, but if I'm going to risk sacrificing my career then I think I'm entitled to know why it can't be avoided."

Unaccustomed to being challenged, even respectfully, Jackson clearly took exception. Red slashes swept across his rawboned cheeks and his tone chilled, nearly frosting the air between them. "Officially, you've developed a reputation as a strong litigator."

Tension crackled in the air and an uneasy feeling that she

had indeed been slated for sacrifice crept up Tracy's backbone and filled her mouth with a bitter taste. "And unofficially?"

Jackson pursed his lips and held his silence for a long beat. "General Nestler specifically requested that you be assigned to defend Burke, and Higher Headquarters agreed."

A by-name request? From Nestler? Oh, great. Just great. No one refused Nestler anything. Within two days at Laurel, while assisting Ted, a fellow attorney, on a contract case, Tracy had learned that. Now she'd learned Nestler's clout ran straight up the chain of command.

She was history. History. Pure and simple. "I wasn't aware General Nestler even knew my name."

Jackson's resigned look faded and the corner of his wide mouth twitched. "Don't be fooled by the actions of some generals, Captain. General Nestler knows everything that goes on with his staff, on the base, and in the community—within *and* outside of the military."

No conflict there with what Tracy had heard and observed. At last month's First Friday gathering at the Officers' Club, Janet privately had referred to Nestler as Laurel's god. *Sees all, knows all.* Since then, others had used that same analogy, and Tracy innately knew she wasn't going to like his rationale for choosing her to defend Burke. "So why me?"

"Why *not* you?" Jackson issued a challenge of his own.

She could think of a dozen personal reasons, but not a single professional one.

Jackson stood up and turned his back to her, then stared out the window at the red brick building next door. Two airmen were washing its windows.

A long minute passed in taut silence, then he stiffened his shoulders, braced a hand in his pants pocket, and faced her. "Frankly, Captain, the general feels your professional acumen, poise, and appearance will be an asset in dealing with the media."

"What?" That response she hadn't expected. She forced

her gaping jaw shut.

"I'm sorry, Tracy," Jackson said, for the first time calling her by her given name. "But it's vital we keep this incident as low-key as possible. That's why we're trying the case locally."

He plopped down in his chair. Air hissed out from the leather cushion, and he leaned forward, lacing his thin hands atop the blotter. "The truth is, the local media's chewing us up and spitting us out on this case. We don't want national-level media jumping in, crawling on our backsides and blowing this out of proportion. The last thing the military needs is another fiasco of the magnitude of Tailhook."

How could she disagree? That scandal, and others since it, had caused a lot of people sleepless nights, agony, embarrassment. Careers and lives had been ruined. And innocents had suffered the shame and fallout as much as the guilty.

"We need every possible advantage. We're fighting deep budget cuts at every turn, base closures that could include Laurel—we escaped the latest short list by the skin of our teeth—and the end of the fiscal year is breathing down our throats. This case has every military member's reputation on the line." Frustration knitted Jackson's heavy brow, making him appear every day of his fifty years. "You're bright and attractive—that surely comes as no surprise to you. You're a media asset, and as unfair as you might deem it, we've chosen to exploit all our assets."

He let his gaze veer to a bronze statue of Lady Justice on the credenza below the window, and then to the flag beside it. His voice softened. "As rotten as it is, we have to exploit every possible asset. We're a war-weary, all-volunteer force with a nation of people depending on us to protect them—not to mention other nations' reliance."

"I'm aware of that, sir." Who in the military could be unaware of that?

"Then you understand the challenge. Burke has complicated

our mission. He's tarnished the image of the entire military in a despicable, unforgivable way, and it's up to us to salvage all we can, any way we can."

She was a means to an end. *He could destroy your career and your life, but, hey, it's nothing personal, Tracy. Suck it up and take one for the team.*

Her stomach churned acid. She stared at the eagle paperweight, at the dark shadows between the glints of light reflecting off it. As much as she hated admitting it, Jackson and Nestler's rationale made sense. As a senior officer in the same situation, she'd use whatever assets she found available to defuse the situation. Could she fault them for doing what in their position she would do herself?

Not honestly. Still, she couldn't stop visualizing her shot at promotion and selection sprouting wings, or imagining her forced exit from the Air Force. Burke was guilty. Everyone knew it. And while she might be media-attractive, she wouldn't get him off. She didn't want to get him off. But even an F. Lee Bailey or OJ's dream team couldn't get Burke off, or come out of this case unscathed.

Yet the man was entitled to the best possible defense. Would any other JAG officer make a genuine attempt to give it to him, knowing personal disaster was all but inevitable?

Probably not—and Tracy couldn't condemn them for it. Given the sliver of a chance, she too would have avoided this case as if it carried plague. But she couldn't avoid it, and that made only one attitude tenable. She had give Burke her best. Not so much for him, but because it was the right thing to do. When this was over, she had to be able to look in the mirror and feel comfortable with what she'd done and the way she'd handled the case and herself. Considering what this would to do her resume, her self-respect is likely all she'd have left.

"We should have word on the murder charges later today," Jackson said.

Tracy nodded. Since she'd lost her husband and daughter

five years ago, she often had imagined herself as an eighty-year-old woman, wearing the same gold locket she wore under her uniform now, looking in the mirror and asking herself where she'd messed up, what she'd done or left undone that she wished she hadn't. In grief counseling, she'd learned that the death of a loved one changes a survivor's perspective, sharpens it, forcing the survivor to focus on what matters most. The one thing she would *not* face the eighty-year-old she'd become with was more regret. She couldn't handle another drop. And that meant she had to do the right thing.

Resigned, she lifted her gaze to Colonel Jackson and accepted responsibility. "I understand, sir. I'll get started on it."

Jackson blinked, then blinked again, clearly expecting her to body-slam him with a sharp-tongued comment. When it occurred to him none would be coming, he gave her a curt nod. "Fine, Captain." He lifted a pen and turned his attention to an open file on his desk. "Dismissed."

Tracy unfolded her legs, hoping her knees had enough substance left in them to get her out of his office before she crumpled. *Dismissed.* And how. From his office and, she feared, from her chosen way of life.

The office grapevine was operating at peak efficiency.

Walking directly from Colonel Jackson's office down the gray-carpeted hallway to her own office, Tracy realized that word of her defending Burke was already out. Sitting in their offices, her coworkers craned their necks and slanted her pitying looks, proving they knew she'd been tagged. The jovial moods of the attorneys behind her confirmed it. Their laughter rang out a pitch too high to be anything but relief that they had escaped the assignment.

All of her training—every single course the Air Force

offered and she was eligible to take: JAG School, Procurement Fraud, Program Managers Attorneys Course, Safety Officer's School, and the Government Contract Law Symposium, a small coup for the junior-grade officer she had been at the time—and a hard-won reputation as a crack litigator—and it could all flush down the tubes because she was bright *and* media-attractive. That combination had gotten her stuck with defending Adam Burke at an extremely critical point in her career.

Once, she might have vented her outrage to a coworker. But after Matthew's death, Tracy had learned not to become emotional. So although she felt the others gawking at her back, she walked wordlessly to her assistant's office, intending to go straight through into her own and privately rage at the walls.

Janet stopped her. Her chin braced on the heel of her hand, she shot Tracy a look of pure empathy. "How about we skate out a little early, go stuff ourselves at El Chico's, and gripe about how life sometimes just isn't fair?"

Drowning her sorrows at Grandsen, Mississippi's sole Mexican restaurant—the only one worth its salt between Jackson and Hattiesburg—sounded like a great place for a good pout, but Tracy rejected it. "Sorry, fiscal year-end budget report is due in today."

"I see." Janet sighed. "I promised myself I was going to keep my mouth shut and just let you dump out all your righteous indignation. But I can't." Tapping the mug's handle, she put a warning in her tone. "Don't do it, Tracy. Burke's case will break you."

If she didn't find a strong legal hook, it definitely would break her. "Thanks for the vote of confidence." Tracy stared at her grapevine-attuned assistant. In her mid-thirties, Janet was about three years Tracy's senior. The lines under her eyes and around her mouth proved Janet's were high-mileage years, not that Tracy's had been easy, and physically, they had little in common. Janet was petite, sleek, and trim; Tracy tall, and curved. While Janet had gleaming black hair and the exotic features of an Asian, Tracy fought with a wild mass of summer-streaked blond hair and, thanks to Scottish paternal ancestors, skin that tanned to the color of a pale rose. Her nose was slightly crooked, her deep blue eyes a little too far apart, and yet tossed together, the package wasn't half bad. Janet's was more perfect—especially her nose. Pert and straight, flawless even now, with her nostrils flaring.

"File thirteen the sarcasm, okay? This doesn't have a thing to do with confidence. We both know you're good at what you do, but Burke's case carries all the signs of becoming Intel-intensive and that's no place for an Intel novice to cut her teeth. For heaven's sake, Tracy. Colonel Hackett, Burke's own boss, is pushing as hard as the rest of the honchos for four counts of murder and the death penalty."

"The death penalty?" That, Colonel Jackson hadn't mentioned. Tracy frowned, upset but also grateful that Janet's former Intel service still netted her the lowdown from on high.

"Intel Rule Number Six. Compromised cover equals death. Figuratively, or literally." Janet shoved her gold bracelet up on her arm. "Refuse the case. Just say no."

Tracy grunted. "I don't even rate an office window yet. I can't 'just say no.'"

"Claim you can't be objective." Janet licked at her lips, warming to her topic. "Everybody knows you're as opinionated as a heart attack on everything—especially Burke's offenses."

"That'll certainly impress my superiors," Tracy retorted, wishing she could say she had an open mind about Burke. But why lie? Janet had made another valid point, too. Tracy wasn't up to defending this case. She met life straightforward and head-on. You play fair, and you deal honestly. If you deserve lumps, then you take them. But in an Intel-intensive case such as Burke's, being straightforward and head-on could jeopardize missions and endanger lives.

Tracy fingered Burke's file. "I'm not surprised they're

pushing for the death penalty." How could she be surprised? Even the compassionate Colonel Jackson thought Burke deserved to die. "But even if I were, I couldn't skate out on this case."

"Now isn't the time to be noble." Janet let out a sigh that ruffled her spiky bangs. "I'm not knocking nobility. I wish we had a little more of it floating around. But don't be stupid, Tracy. This is going to cost you big."

"Probably," Tracy admitted. But she had to do it.

How she'd do it, she had no idea. Not yet. Her sense of justice and trust in the system was at war with her disdain. Burke's crimes were inexcusable. Heinous. Even a saint would be challenged to defend him with conviction. Yet without conviction, she didn't stand a chance.

Somewhere, somehow, she had to latch on to something good. Something she could build conviction on—and her case.

"Tracy, think, okay? Is your nobility worth your life?"

"My life?" Tracy grunted, and shoved a wild tangle of hair back from her face. "This is a case, my career and professional future, but it's hardly my life." Her garden. That was her life. Her garden and her memories.

Janet rolled her eyes back in her head. "We *are* talking about your life. Literally," Janet insisted. "Burke is Intel." She tapped at her temple. "Lots of supersensitive stuff locked inside his head. And lots of creeps out there who'll use anyone—even his attorney—to get it."

Her life. Literally.

Tracy absorbed the gravity in silence. She'd known the risks when she'd joined the Air Force. True, she hadn't expected to actually be called upon to take them, but that wasn't the military's fault. The recruiter had been honest. She'd been in denial—and eager to leave New Orleans, her ex-brother-in-law Paul's domain. Yet Janet jerking Tracy out of denial changed nothing. She still had to do what she had to do. "I have no choice."

"Everyone has a choice," Janet argued. "I'm living proof."

Frowning, Tracy poured herself a cup of coffee from the pot on the corner cabinet. Janet had left active duty and taken the civil service job as Tracy's assistant—though she was overqualified for it—because she'd gotten tired of working Intel. She wanted a more normal life. One free of danger and intrigue. Because she had radically changed her life-style, she firmly believed anyone could choose anything at will. "Hear *and* listen, okay? I have no choice."

Realization dawned and gleamed in Janet's eyes. Bracing her forearms against the edge of the desk, she sucked in a sharp breath and stiffened. "Oh, man. You got tagged to defend him. Word was, you volunteered, but you didn't. You got tagged to defend the jerk." Janet grimaced. "Who did it? Jackson? Higher Headquarters? Who?"

"The baseline is I am going to defend Adam Burke. To do it well, I need Intel expertise and insight and I don't have it. I need your help."

"Oh, no. No way. I'm done with danger, remember?" Janet sputtered a sip of coffee. "Stop looking at me like that. No way."

"You just said my life is at stake. The man's incarcerated and bail is out of the question, so I don't see how I could be in danger, but you obviously do. Doesn't that prove I need you?"

"It proves you should ask for different counsel to be assigned. Make the honchos give the case to someone with the credentials and experience necessary to survive it."

"The honchos have given the case to me," Tracy said, deliberately flattening her tone to let Janet know this point of discussion was closed. "Help me, Janet. Please."

"You're asking me to sign your death warrant. I won't do it—and I can't believe you'd ask me to, knowing how I feel about this, and about Burke. Five minutes alone with him, and I'd fry him myself."

A lot of people, particularly ones in uniform, shared her feelings. "I'm going to defend him with or without your help. My best chance of survival is if you assist."

"Forget trying to put me on a guilt trip. I have no conscience. I'm Intel-trained, remember? Only rules and the drills survived my active-duty days." Janet twisted a scowl from her lips and narrowed her eyes, staring at her long nails. "I've warned you, and that's it for me. You go on from here and get yourself killed, and your blood is on your own hands, not on mine."

"Do you want me to beg?" Tracy rifted a hand, palm upward. "Okay, I will. I'm beg—"

"No!" Janet let out an exasperated groan. "I worked with Burke in Intel. I know how he operates. He's a shrewd, smart operative, and I'm steering clear of anything to do with him. I'm telling you that the fallout is going to be explosive, Tracy. Burke will see to it, and I'm not eager to find myself buried in the rubble."

"But I need a background check on him," Tracy persisted. "One that digs deeper than his manufactured personnel file." Shoring up her courage, she voiced her real need; one that for a truckload of reasons she feared being fulfilled. "I need his Intel file."

"Are you crazy?" Janet screeched.

"I'm desperate. To build a case I can live with building, I've got to find something good about this jerk. I need to know how his mind works. Who he is inside."

"He's a coward. A ruthless, treasonous coward who got four good men killed. Operatives who were my friends."

They had been Intel and, at heart, Janet was still Intel. No one ever walked away and forgot the rules and drills or the camaraderie. They put their lives on the line together, depended on each other to survive, and nothing ever broke those kinds of bonds. Not duty, family, or even death.

"I'm sorry your friends are dead, Janet. Maybe Burke did

get them killed. Maybe he is a coward and in his years of service to this country he hasn't done one thing good or right or made even one small sacrifice for someone else. But maybe he has. And if so, I need to know it."

Janet glared at her desktop, her voice tight and grating. "Intel records aren't accessible."

"Ordinarily, they aren't. But I know you. If you want his records, you can get them."

"*Usually*, I can get access. But I'm not going to do it. Not on this one." Scowling, she focused on Tracy's locket. "The man is guilty as sin. How can you expect me to help him?"

No progress whatsoever. Those Intel bonds were tugging hard. Tracy reached across the desk and touched Janet's hand. "Quit huffing and listen to me. If I fail to handle this case right, we all lose—you, your friends, the legal system, our country, and me. Don't you see? The only way we can win is to do the best job possible for him."

"Don't you see that it won't matter what you do?" Janet stabbed her pen into its holder. "His fate has already been decided. The man's crashed and burned, Tracy. He's going to fry."

Tracy's stomach soured, then filled with resolve. "Maybe. But he's not going to fry before I give him a defense that doesn't get me fried with him."

Janet gasped, stilled then dragged a frustrated hand through her hair. "Your promotion..."

Tracy nodded, her stomach furling. "And I'm up for Career Status selection."

Staring at the mural of a window on the far wall, Janet finally riveted her gaze back to Tracy. "Okay, you can quit rubbing your locket," Janet said. "I'll *try* to run the background check on Burke—for you, not him." She clenched her cup in a white-knuckle grip. "I wouldn't spit on his grave."

"Thanks." Grateful, Tracy let go of her locket, supposing she did rub it when in a crunch. It was her last gift from

Matthew, one that held a cherished photograph.

"That's a pretty romantic habit for a sworn non-romantic," Janet commented. "Rubbing the locket to remember him whenever trouble strikes."

It was anything but romantic. "I wear it to remember losing him, Janet. And so I never forget how much loving someone can cost."

"Good grief." Janet slid her a sour look. "Talk about jaded."

"It's not jaded." Tracy let the pain of losing Matthew and their daughter, Abby, shine in her eyes. "It's realistic."

"No," Janet contradicted. Speculating had her irises flickering golden brown. "It's safe."

"Oh, I hope so." Tracy sipped at her coffee, praying hard that proved true. She had survived all the losses she could stand for one lifetime.

"I'll do what I can on the file—but no promises." Janet flattened her lips to a thin coral line. "After what he's done, there's not a soul in the world eager to help Adam Burke."

The truth in that remark had Tracy frowning and heading toward her office.

"Wait." Janet called out after her. "Randall phoned. You should tell him about the assignment before he hears it somewhere else."

Janet too often fantasized that Tracy's relationship with Dr. Randall Moxley was a heated affair: a ridiculous notion. Randall, a pathologist at the base hospital, was charming and a bit of a rogue, and he did love to playfully hit on Tracy. But if she were to hit back, the man would probably faint. He'd definitely run, which is exactly what allowed them to be friends. "I'll call him when I get home."

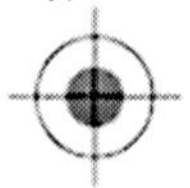

The dreaded call came through from Colonel Jackson's office just before the end of the duty day at 1620—4:20

p.m. Burke had officially been charged with four counts of murder.

The alleged threats remained classified information, and adding that bad news onto the heap had Tracy depressed to the gills. She drove to her suburban home in the Gables subdivision, pulled into the driveway, and stared at the three-bedroom, two-bath cookie-cutter house she called home. The windows were dark, the house empty, and she wondered how long she would live here after she lost Burke's case, failed to get Career Status, and they kicked her out of the military.

Janet thought the house felt cold, and Tracy agreed. It did. But that hadn't been an accident. It was a deliberate warning: *Don't get too comfortable. You're a guest here for a time, and you won't be invited to stay.*

Realizing that warning extended to herself, Tracy harrumphed and tapped the garage-door opener on her visor. Maybe she had become jaded. Morbid, too.

The garage door slid up, and she drove inside. It was at times like this that she missed the perk of having a husband to talk to about her troubles. Before Matthew's death, that's how she'd always found her legal-hooks. She missed feeling close to a man, too, but she'd resolved to move mountains to avoid losing someone who mattered too much again. Even spending Christmas alone, as isolating as that felt and as insignificant to anyone else as it made her feel, didn't make her want to let anyone else matter. Thankfully, those lonesome times were countered by other times, such as when Janet was nursing her weekly broken heart. Then, Tracy felt grateful for the reprieve.

Catching the scent of vanilla potpourri, she locked the kitchen door behind her, then changed into a pair of soft jersey slacks and a baggy T-shirt. Feeling the locket against her skin, she recalled Janet's reaction to it. She clearly considered Tracy an emotional cripple. But Janet couldn't understand. She hadn't lived through loss. Tracy wasn't a cripple, she was a survivor. And for a survivor, she was content. Satisfied. Happy.

Liar.

Bristling at her conscience's tug, she opened her bedroom door. Okay, a survivor wouldn't ignore the holidays as if they didn't exist. But last year, she'd made progress. She still couldn't make herself decorate or put up a big tree, but she'd bought a mini-tree a foot-tall, pre-decorated and put it on the kitchen counter. Okay, she'd set it outside the back door three days before Christmas, but it'd made it into the house for nearly twenty-four hours. That progress proved she was a *nearly* content satisfied, and happy survivor.

At least she had been, until the Burke case was dropped in her lap.

Slipping on the Winnie-the-Pooh slippers she always wore when she needed an attitude, she admitted that sometimes she did feel *slightly* crippled. But only *slightly,* and considering her past, that wasn't bad.

She walked down the short hallway to the kitchen, snagged the phone, then called Randall. Waiting for him to answer, she stared down at the twin Pooh heads on her slippers' toes and again heard her dad's voice: *When the world's kicking your tail, hon, kick back. Just make sure you're wearing steel-toe shoes.*

Randall answered, sounding as if he had a mouth full of toothpaste. "What?"

"Don't you sound chipper?" Glancing through the huge windows to her garden, a sense of calm settled over her. It was her refuge. Her candle in the window. "Most people say hello before biting your head off." Tapping the faucet, she filled the teakettle.

"Mmm, let me guess." His sigh crackled through the line. "She's had a bad day."

"She's had the ultimate bad day." Tracy set the kettle on the stove to heat and then told him she'd be defending Adam Burke.

Ten minutes later, after Randall had given her every reason conceivable to God and man why she shouldn't take Burke's case, Tracy began wishing she hadn't called him. "Would a little sympathy and commiserating be asking for too much?" The teakettle whistled. She filled a mug plastered with Mickey Mouse's smiling face full of hot water. "You're supposed to be my friend."

"You do something crazy and you expect sympathy? What kind of friend does that?" Randall paused, cleared his throat, and tamped down his temper. "Look, I understand you feel obligated to defend the man, but get a grip. You'll be committing career suicide. Claim a conflict of interest. Tell them your personal feelings hinder your ability to defend Burke."

"The promotion board would love that." Her spoon clinked against the edge of the mug, and Tracy grunted. "Their pencils would leave screech marks on my file, adding 'unprofessional' to 'too young and idealistic' in my bio."

"Then lie. Say anything. Say you're in love with the man."

Revulsion coursed through her in shudders. How could *any* woman be in love with Adam Burke? "I won't lie. And I won't say I'm in love with a traitor and murderer. The boards would swear I was either crazy or stupid. Maybe both—and I'd agree with them."

"Do you grasp the severity of this? Your promotion and status selection are on the line."

"My whole career as a Staff JAG is on the line, Randall." Bobbing the tea bag by its string, she grumbled and glanced out the window at her roses. Beautiful—and still in full bloom, though the blazing heat had most gardens sun-scorched and burned. "Giving the board more ammunition against me won't help cinch my promotion."

"Well, you've got to do something to get out of defending this case." His frustration hissed static through the phone line. "My hospital board will go nuts."

About to take a sip, Tracy frowned into her cup. "Excuse me?"

"My board. It'll take a dim view of me being close friends with Burke's attorney, and the members will be very verbal about it. You know how they are about controversy, and you've got to admit, Burke's beyond controversial."

Great. Didn't she have enough to worry about already? But Randall was right. His hospital board was extremely conservative and protective of its image. The members would take a dim view of their friendship. It was the nature of Burke's crimes that would turn everyone against her for defending him. It didn't matter that she'd been assigned: people felt too passionate about treason, murder, and sacrificed men. She stood in Burke's defense, and that would stick in everyone's craw. In situations like this, emotion always buries logic.

Mentally seeing Randall standing front and center before the board members, his blond head bent, his lean shoulders stooped, she barely managed to stave off a sigh.

Regardless of what he said to them, the members *would* come down hard on Randall. "I have no choice." She let him hear her regret. "I didn't volunteer, I was assigned."

"So dream up an excuse and get out of it. My board would be fine with your refusal."

His board? Bristling, she stilled, the tea bag dangling in midair over the sink. What about *her* promotion and selection? *Her* career? All this case could—and probably would—cost *her*.

Irked that her challenges didn't weigh at all in Randall's considerations, Tracy slung the tea bag into the sink. It thumped against the stainless-steel bottom, and steam poured out of it. Any second, she expected an equal amount to pour out of her ears. "Careful, friend," she said in clipped tones. "You're sounding like your convictions only run as deep as you find convenient."

"Image matters." His voice turned cold and distant. "You know my personal goals."

Oh, did she. She snatched up a dishcloth, then mopped at a

tea splash near the faucet. He drove her crazy with his strategy updates, but his attitude on this rated downright selfish and self-serving.

She tossed the cloth onto the counter and cast her slippers a suspicious look. But Pooh wasn't responsible for this attitude. Truth was the culprit. Randall Moxley was a fair-weather friend. And knowing it, Tracy couldn't get off the phone quickly enough. "I think we'd better agree to disagree on this and let it go."

"Fine." He slammed down the phone.

Clenching her teeth, she put the phone down, and resumed searching for her legal hook.

Feeling as she did about Adam Burke, how could she defend him with conviction?

She had until tomorrow morning to figure it out. That's when she was due at the facility, commonly referred to as the brig, to meet Adam Burke.

Just the thought of having to look the coward in the face had her stomach revolting and her head throbbing. She'd bet her bars he would play the innocent victim. He'd blame someone else—*anyone else*—for everything.

It was a safe bet. The guilty assigned blame elsewhere with monotonous regularity. And considering Burke's crimes were positively the worst that could be committed by man, she should expect nothing better from him.

Disgust turned her tea bitter. She dumped the contents from her cup then went out to her moonlit garden, needing to cleanse herself of her distaste for both men.

Dropping to a wicker chair beneath the huge magnolia, she lifted her chin and inhaled its blossoms' sweet scent. Randall—if he appeared genuinely repentant for being a jerk about this—she might forgive, but Adam Burke?

Never.

Duplicity has been released in digital and print and is available at your favorite bookseller.

A portion of all proceeds is donated to the Wounded Warrior Project.